STARWINGS

With his mind, Donalt reached out to the enemy ship and commanded a woman to draw her laser cutter. He directed the weapon at the Swarmer's Con-Web and squeezed her finger around the trigger. Six invaders died before the woman's fire was returned. Donalt did not escape the searing fire that dissolved her abdomen, nor her glimmering recognition that she had been controlled by another human being . . .

STARWINGS

GEO. W. PROCTOR

ACE SCIENCE FICTION BOOKS
NEW YORK

STARWINGS

An Ace Science Fiction Book/published by arrangement with
the author

PRINTING HISTORY
Ace Original / March 1984

ISBN: 0-441-78481-X

Ace Science Fiction Books are published by
The Berkley Publishing Group,
200 Madison Avenue, New York, New York 10016.
PRINTED IN THE UNITED STATES OF AMERICA

This one's for Robert E. Vardeman,
the best of friends.

STARWINGS

◂ONE▸

The warning alarm jarred Lieutenant Adile Kaveri from a light sleep. The high-pitched warble rebounded off curved walls to fold back atop the lone woman harnessed to a Con-Web at the center of the spherical turret. Light flared to life across the consoles encircling Kaveri's control couch. The persistent pulses demanded immediate attention.

Kaveri shifted the couch upright while the fingers of her left hand jabbed a line of glowing yellow buttons. They dimmed, and the alarm died within the turret. The battle alert was now transmitted to the ship's ten other compartments.

Kaveri's right hand flicked a series of seven green switches; an eighth remained undisturbed. The bio-electrical systemry of the Control Web was primed, and a mere nudge of that last switch would send the Kavinite scout ship and its two-person crew into the faster-than-light speeds of tachyon space.

Kaveri left the final toggle untouched. Programming for emergency escape was a trick that she had learned from a sergeant in the Nessa Clump five years ago while on her first tour of active duty.

Any untrained recruit could randomly punch a vessel into tachyon space when the action got too hot, but the risk was high. There was a sixty-five point nine three five percent certainty that the ship and crew making a random jump would be reduced to subatomic particles and scattered across the universe.

Disembodied lieutenants were valueless in war. A lieutenant who lived could fight another day, and Kaveri intended to live. A preprogrammed ship weighed the odds in her favor.

Her left hand activated the Con-Web monitors and her right

found a horizontal red bar sixteen centimeters above the green switches. She twisted the bar to the vertical and shoved down. It locked into place with a metallic *click*. The scout's defensive and offensive ordnances were armed before the lieutenant's eyes rose to the main monitor above the console.

Kaveri's pulse ran berserk.

At the center of the holographic display floated an elongated disc of blue that represented her scout ship. Irregular, gray shapes drifted past—the minor asteroid belt through which the scout now maneuvered. Neatly tucked beside six of the angular gray forms, on all sides of the scout, were six arrowheads of red.

Englobed! Impossible! Six ships simply did not slip from tachyon space in englobement formation amid the flotsam of an asteroid belt. Yet, those *were* ships, and they had not been there moments ago.

The young officer's gaze shifted to a flashing yellow message that filled a display screen below the main monitor:

POSITIVE IDENTIFICATION
LofAl Vessels
Classification: Swarmers
(Individual Personnel Attack Modules)

Kaveri's right hand hovered over the panel that activated the scout's defensive shield. The Con-Web's sensors detected no enemy scanning. The LofAl Swarmers might be unaware of the scout's presence. Single-pilot vessels were designed for close, hit-and-run tactics, not long-range combat. If the Swarmers' sensors were limited, the scout might register as no more than another chunk of debris to the LofAl ships. Raising the energy shield would be a dead giveaway of the Kavinite's position.

Kaveri's gaze rolled up. The six arrowheads moved in perfect unison with the scout. Each maintained an exact sixty-five-kilometer distance from the Kavinite vessel.

Why englobe and not attack? The Swarmers' behavior baffled her. Did they hope to capture the scout?

No. That made less sense. Scanners indicated no harbor vessel within a fifteen-hundred-kilometer radius of the scout's position.

She sucked at her cheeks. The smaller ships might be a

scouting vanguard for a larger force. That *was* why High Command had stationed Loundon and her out here on the edge of nowhere—an advance warning for LofAl incursion into the Arvis system.

A green square of light flashed beside the main monitor, indicating Sergeant Dyre Loundon now sat in the scout's primary control couch. Kaveri tapped on the intercom.

"What are you picking up, Loundon?" Her voice held more of an edge than she wished to reveal.

"Display's quiet up here, Lieutenant." The sergeant's answer crackled from the grille before her. "Why the alarm?"

"Son of a bitch!" Kaveri hammered a fist into the arm of her couch. "More High Command surprises to keep us on our toes!"

Kaveri's fingers darted over the Con-Web keyboard to command the ship's simulator to cancel its present program. The six red arrowheads vanished from the holographic display as the scout slipped free of the asteroid belt.

It had all been a game. Tension eased from Kaveri's muscles. *A goddamn game!*

Anger replacing the adrenaline rush of fear, she punched out a request for an explanation of the simulated attack's initiation. The screen flashed in reprimanding red:

**YOU FELL ASLEEP
ON MONITOR DUTY**

"Fucking wirehead!" Kaveri made no attempt to contain her irritation as she fully derided the lineage of her superiors and their lack of tactical judgment in assigning her to a month-long, useless mission.

A chuckle came from the intercom. Kaveri snorted with disgust at the controls around her to hide a momentary twinge of embarrassment. Loundon had witnessed the exchange between woman and machine on the monitors above.

"Shall I take Con-Web?" Loundon asked. "It's only fifteen minutes to my shift."

"I'll owe you one, Sergeant." Kaveri canceled the program for tachyon transformation by flicking the seven green toggles. "Give me a few minutes. I'm going by way of the galley. Can I bring you something?"

"Breakfast, Lieutenant. I was sleeping when the alarm went

off,'' Loundon said while Kaveri slipped from the Con-Web harness and drifted weightlessly to the bottom of the turret.

Kaveri spread her fingers wide and pressed them flat against a palmlock. The hatch sprang open with a reverberating *clank*. With both hands planted solidly on each side of the entrance, she swung through to the scout's second level.

Rather than using the static strip that ran along the deck of the tunnel-corridor she entered, she push-floated to the galley. She alighted on a static mat before a servo unit. After a brief glance at an eye-level screen displaying the day's bill of fare, she punched in the orders for her dinner and Loundon's breakfast.

Kaveri's gaze moved to the two mess tables on the opposite side of the cramped galley. Like everything else aboard, the tables stood empty and abandoned. She turned back to the servo.

Dwelling on the emptiness did nothing to alleviate the condition. The scout was a converted ten-person surface exploration vessel. Small by normal standards, the ship's lack of full crew gave it the appearance of a deserted behemoth. At the start of the patrol Kaveri had given silent thanks for so much room. Now, she would gladly trade a year's script to see two or three new faces.

Two aluminum trays like foil-coated tongues poked from a slot at the center of the servo. Kaveri took them in one hand and pushed from the deck to drift through an open hatch in the overhead. Within the scout's Level One, she worked twenty meters down another tunnel-corridor to the control bubble.

The bubble was just that, a tear-shaped, transparent blister atop the scout's hull. Stars, fiery glowgems set in pure jet, formed a canopy over Kaveri's head. The bright points of light were widely spaced here at the galaxy's rim, but numerous enough to remind her that the ship was not beyond the normal realms of humankind—or the war that raged between the Kavinite Empire and the Lofgrin Alliance.

Loundon swiveled his couch and waved Kaveri to the empty one beside him.

Behind the stocky man and the ship's curved nose burned Acayib. The red giant of the Arvis system appeared no larger than a soccer ball this far out.

Kaveri cautiously moved into the control bubble's artificial gravity. She silently cursed her superiors for supplying a poorly equipped ship for the mission. Even set at half-gee, the scout's energy system was too limited to provide gravity in the ship's other compartments.

"The first time I lifted off-planet, I thought I'd never seen anything as beautiful as what a man can see from a bubble." Kaveri studied the sergeant's square face while he spoke and wished he were more physically attractive. "Now, I could give a rat's ass if I ever see any of this again."

"Three more days until pickup . . . then four days on-planet leave." Kaveri dipped her spoon into a chalk-white, custard-like substance puddled in a depression at one side of her tray. Its flavor was as noncommittal as its color.

Loundon shrugged and tore the cover from his tray. His gaze scanned the yawning void outside the bubble. "Three days."

"Feel up to chess?" Kaveri edged the conversation away from the forthcoming pickup. She did not want to ponder the three days of monotony left to the mission—seventy-two standard hours filled with the same boredom as the past month.

If the wait were any longer, Kaveri realized, Loundon's physical appearance would not be a consideration. She would offer to bundle with him just to break the tedium.

While he drained a cup of fruit juice, Loundon punched up a holodisplay of a chess board. His fingers tapped the control console keys. The white queen's pawn slid two squares forward.

Kaveri groaned inwardly. The sergeant began with the same stupid move he had made in dozens of games since their arrival in the Arvis system. If he adhered to his usual strategy, she would checkmate him in ten moves.

"Sure you want to do that?"

"Why not?" He glanced at the Con-Web's monitors, then stared at Acayib. "How long since they snatched you off your homeworld and stuck you in the service?"

"I joined the navy five standard years ago—assault force assigned to the Nessa Clump." Kaveri tried a bite of tasteless soya patty. "Received my commission six months ago, after the LofAl push to take the Obram system."

"Joined?" Loundon's head slowly turned to her. "Officers are supposed to be smarter than that."

Kaveri managed to smile around a mouthful of an unidentifiable vegetable. She swallowed hastily. "Every enlisted woman and man knows intelligence isn't a prerequisite for a commission."

"I joined five years ago, too." The sergeant's attention returned to the stars. "Fell for the crap the recruiters spouted. Thought a life in the service would be more exciting than growing soybeans on my father's farm. My old man should've kicked my ass between my ears when I told him I was going to sign up. The trouble was, he believed . . . *still* believes all that shit about the Lofgrin Alliance attempting to subjugate the free people of the Empire. Kavinite to the core."

"And you? You no longer believe in the Empire's purpose for existing?"

"A strong Empire built of free individuals . . . struggling to overcome the chaos of anarchy sown by the maniacs of the Lofgrin Alliance . . ." Loundon paused as though seriously considering the propaganda line. "I guess I still believe. Mostly I believe I'm a soldier. However . . ."

The sergeant's voice trailed off. It was a rarity for a war-hardened veteran to discuss his profession other than to vocalize the constant complaints about officers, food, equipment, and assignment. When one did open up, it was common courtesy to hear him out. Kaveri did just that. "However?"

"It's at times like this, when I'm out here alone, that I get to wondering if any of it makes sense. The galaxy's a big place. . . . Kavinite, Lofgrinist, there's room for both." Loundon scooped a spoonful of opaque, congealed *something* that passed for eggs from his tray.

Kaveri finished her meal and slid the tray into a disposal chute. She did not like to consider the possible futility of the war. Five years of her life had been devoted to destroying the LofAl aggressors. Yet . . .

For the past month, her private reading had centered on histories of humankind's migration through the galaxy—seeking a reason for the twenty-five-year war.

Humankind had been born on a planet destroyed by the Holocaust of 2123 and the brief Global Wars that followed. The survivors cloistered in O'Neill, Lunar, and Martian colonies eventually moved beyond the Sol system to inhabit the star systems they discovered. Two divergent political philosophies polarized on the two hundred colonial worlds: the imperial Kavinites sought to establish a rigid central authority to govern human development, and the Lofgrinists maintained that planetary independence offered the diversity required for continued human existence in the universe.

In 2350 the political rift opened to a yawning chasm—the Century Conflagration, a war between the Empire and the Lofgrin Alliance that left but ten of the two hundred worlds with a semblance of civilization when the Peace Accord of 2450 was finally signed.

For two hundred and seventy-five years, the Kavinite Empire and the LofAl maintained a shaky balance of power and an even less solid peace. Then, twenty-five years ago, something happened in the Reyham Coal Stack, a cloud of cosmic dust and gas near the center of the galaxy.

What actually occurred in this valueless parcel of interplanetary real estate—the exact details of what sparked the confrontation—was camouflaged in a barrage of propaganda from both Kavinites and Lofgrinists. The incident, in which a Kavinite naval cruiser and two alleged LofAl vessels were destroyed, produced an end result all too tangible—war.

Twenty-five years. The figure rolled ponderously in Kaveri's head. She had never known peace in her lifetime, nor was there any indication it would come in the near future.

Five of those twenty-five years she had spent in uniform in the hottest spots in the galaxy—the Nessa Clump, the Amibika system, the Mu Lan Transfer, the Hahnee Sling. If she intended to survive another five years, she needed a four-grade promotion and an assignment to a desk job at some jerkwater outpost.

She sighed softly to herself. How could a person be more isolated than to be stuck patrolling the Arvis system?

"Three days," Loundon repeated. His gaze swept across the Con-Web consoles. "The High Command blew it on this one. The LofAl wouldn't fart in the general direction of the Arvis system. Going to make a move?" Loundon tilted his head toward the chess display.

Another easy win over the sergeant offered no challenge. Kaveri apologetically shook her head. "Guess I'm not in the mood for a game after all. What I really need is several hours of shut-eye."

Loundon flicked off the display while Kaveri pushed from the couch. "Want me to give you a wake-up buzz in a few hours?"

"Make it about eight hours." Kaveri stepped toward the bubble's hatch. "I've still got reports to transmit to . . ."

The warbling wail of the warning alarm drowned the remainder of her sentence. The Con-Web consoles flared alive with panicked pulsings of multicolored lights.

The possibility that this was another simulated attack was dispelled from Kaveri's mind before the thought fully formed.

Outside the bubble, directly before the scout ship's prow, hung a miniature planet that had not been there an instant before.

Kaveri dropped back into her vacated couch.

Loundon's hands flew over the Con-Web. "It slipped from tachyon space. Slow moving, twenty-two kilometers a minute."

Kaveri flicked the seven green switches that programmed the scout for tachyon transformation. Slow or not, the Con-Web located the unexpected invader fifty kilometers out—on a direct collision course with the smaller ship.

"It's *big*. Scans as a sphere five kilometers in diameter. I'm getting a negative lifeform reading."

"What?" Doubt tinged Kaveri's voice. "Something that big *has* to have a crew."

A monitor screen blinked between Kaveri and Loundon:

VESSEL IDENTIFICATION:
Unknown
VESSEL DESIGN:
Unknown
VESSEL ORIGIN:
Unknown

"Maybe High Command was right after all." Loundon's head twisted to Kaveri. "A new LofAl weapon?"

She did not answer. Instead she opened tachyon communications to feed Con-Web's information on the unidentified ship to Fairleigh. Whatever occurred, High Command would have a complete report as it happened.

"Its shields just went up," Loundon reported as he raised the scout's own defensive shields. "Looks like it expects action."

Or intends to serve it up, Kaveri thought. "Let's give it something to think about."

While Loundon armed the ship, Kaveri slapped a white panel near the bottom of the console. A photon screen flared to surround the scout. Simultaneously, two drone decoys were ejected from the ship's underbelly.

The self-contained automatons shot from beneath the scout and winged out in a wide trajectory to each side of the small ship.

Until the invader's sensors identified and pinpointed the decoys, three scout ships would be displayed on the vessel's monitors. A weak charade, Kaveri realized, but it could provide a moment or two of confusion.

"Full plasma barrage, then lay a pattern of stealth floaters," Kaveri ordered. Her hand hovered above the eighth green switch that would punch the scout into tachyon space and beyond the reach of the metallic gargantuan.

Loundon unleashed the plasma barrage.

Two white beams sliced out from the underside of the gigantic orb to home on the drones. The decoy robots exploded in an actinic glare of orange and red.

Kaveri cursed the useless charade. "What in hell are they using?"

"Energy beam of unidentified nature," Loundon answered. "Con-Web can't categorize it."

Outside, twenty blue globes of coalesced plasma energy danced across the rapidly diminishing void that separated the two spacecraft. In perfect synchronization, the plasma globes struck the invader's shield.

Nothing.

Kaveri stared unable to comprehend what had occurred. It made no sense. One moment the barrage was there, the next it was gone. It was as though the plasma bolts had been absorbed into the energy fabric of the vessel's shield.

"Floater impact five seconds." Loundon counted down the flight of the sensor-invisible assault mines. "Contact!"

Again—nothing.

No explosive glare of light washed across the spherical ship's defensive shield. The floaters had no effect whatsoever. As with the plasma barrage, the stealth mines appeared to be absorbed by the shield.

"What the hell is that thing?" Loundon's gaze shifted between the approaching craft and the Con-Web monitors. "What has the LofAl come up with?"

"High Command can decide how to handle this." Kaveri had no time to speculate on the vessel's nature. Analysts on Fairleigh with their planetwide Con-Web could come up with all the answers. She was a soldier who fully intended to live to fight another day. Today was not the day to press prolonged combat with the giant out there. It was time to cut and run. Kaveri's hand dropped toward the final green switch.

Her fingers never reached their destination.

A white beam of energy erupted from the gargantuan's underside and lanced toward the scout ship. Kaveri heard a scream, a human scream. She vaguely recognized the voice of her own agony.

Then there was oblivion.

◄TWO►

The Lofgrin Alliance battle cruiser *Crispus Attucks* slid from the monotonous grays of tachyon space into the star-speckled blackness of normal space. Seconds later, minor trajectory alterations were completed, and the kilometer-long vessel swung into orbit around the planet Chenoa, homebase for cruiser and crew.

Nestled midship on Level Three of the five-level craft, Psi Corps team leader Radman Donalt tried to quell the churning nausea that crept from his stomach into his esophagus. He grimaced as bitter bile seeped into his mouth.

"Son of a bitch," he cursed without thought or meaning—the grumbling common to any man or woman who had lived to see more than six months service. Donalt's career as a Psi Corps mind-merger covered twenty-two of his forty years—twelve of those years in psi teams assigned to various LofAl naval vessels.

To conceal his distress from his two companions within Psi Corps Operations, Donalt swiped a hand over his sharp-featured face—a face that displayed signs of early weathering: deepening lines that inched across his forehead, permanent crow's-feet radiating from the corners of hazel eyes, a gauntness to his cheeks that had not been there five years ago.

He ran the fingers of his right hand—*his* hand, not the flesh-colored, plaskin, bio-mechanical prosthesis that passed for a left hand—through dark brown hair salted with more gray than he preferred to acknowledge.

The gestures were needless. Neither of his teammates noticed his discomfort. They were too occupied with their own nausea.

Michaela Gosheven, the team's receiver-sender, brought her couch upright and pushed herself from the cushioned seat. The diminutive blonde stood and swayed unsteadily for a moment before she collapsed back to the couch. She wrapped her arms about her slim midriff and moaned weakly.

Howin Bickle, one of the finest receivers in the Psi Corps, sat doubled over in a couch beside Michaela. The tall, muscular man—barf funnel clutched in both hands—would have presented a comical picture had Donalt not shared his misery.

Cautiously Donalt drew a long breath and exhaled with equal caution to steady himself. His gaze alighted for an instant on the vacant couch that had been filled for two years by Birgit Keller, the team's prescient, killed a month ago.

The upper portion of the bulkhead opposite Donalt abruptly glowed to life. A holographic image of a turquoise orb, marbled with banks of white clouds, took form. The view of Chenoa came courtesy of the ship's optical sensors.

Donalt touched a button on the arm of his couch. It righted with a pneumatic whisper.

He dreaded planetfall and meeting the new team member who waited on-planet. Under the best of circumstances, the acceptance of a team replacement was rough. A psiotic team was like a single entity with four functioning minds. The loss of any one of the four was traumatic, more devastating than an individual's loss of an arm or a leg.

Donalt knew. He had survived the loss of all three.

Birgit had been good. She had possessed that elusive merging of limitless strength, endurance, and compassion so rare among those forced into the profession of war.

In his long years of naval duty, Donalt had encountered only one other prescient who interpreted the psi currents of alpha level and the symbolic images that bled from the future into the present with such accuracy.

But, Birgit had not been good enough. She had not foreseen the single Kavinite stealth floater that slipped through a momentary rent in the *Crispus Attucks*'s defensive shield during the Tallos–Double Transfer Station offensive. The mine detonation caught Birgit and three crew members in a tunnel-corridor on the cruiser's Level One.

The official casualty report read "instantaneous death." For the psi team's three surviving members, the dying persisted.

Donalt hoped that the time required to erase the scars sustained in two battles from the ship's hull would also heal the open wounds left by Birgit's death.

The month-long stay in Nidori, Chenoa's capital, would also provide Donalt the opportunity to complete the series of surgical operations needed to replace his prosthetic hand and left leg with cloned limbs. The prostheses were souvenirs of another battle ten years ago that had cost him both legs, right arm, left hand—and Evora.

The LofAl surgeons saved his life after that one and patched him together with prostheses guaranteed to function longer than his remaining biological parts. But Evora . . .

A thousand fragmented memories crowded into his head. Memories that refused to be confined.

Donalt balled his left hand into a tight fist, attempting to shove aside the past. The hand and leg served him well. They were indistinguishable from the cloned right arm and leg that Chenoan surgeons had grafted to his body on the two occasions in the past ten years he had been given more than a week's on-planet leave. As efficient as the artifical limbs were, he relished the prospect of standing on two human legs again. Of touching with two hands of flesh and blood.

"I feel just well enough to wish I could die." Michaela's soft, almost child-innocent voice wove into Donalt's thoughts. "I'll trade you a month's pay for your place on the first shuttle down, Rad."

"Two months pay," Howin upped the offer. The receiver glanced at Donalt. His watery coal-black eyes blinked. "I need to feel solid earth beneath my feet once more before I die."

Donalt grinned. He held out his hands, palms open with fingers spread wide as though to fend off an assault. "Rank does have its privileges."

The two younger team members moaned in unison. Howin raised a hand in the current obscene gesture in vogue aboard the *Crispus Attucks*. Donalt had seen at least five come and go.

"Rank?" Michaela rolled her blue eyes in mock disgust. "Starting to take that 'commander' crap the officers shovel out seriously, aren't you? Better watch your step, Grandpa, or we'll report your delusions of grandeur to Psi Corps Headquarters!"

"The corps *does* have seniority. And I *was* pulling cruiser duty before either of you recognized the latent psi potential contained in your infant brains." Donalt chuckled.

"Grandpa" from other than Michaela or Howin would have raised his hackles. From them, the nickname merely acknowledged his knack for survival in a job where psiotic burnout was measured in months rather than years.

"I've never understood why senile old men always manage a place on the first shuttle." Howin stood and slowly stretched. The movement drew his green jumpsuit taut across his pectorals. Donalt thought the fabric would rip.

"Could be this team leader has learned the advantages of common courtesy." Donalt stood. His nondescript white jumpsuit hung loosely on a physique he laboriously maintained by daily workouts in the ship's gym. "Something a certain muscle-bound receiver might do well to emulate."

Michaela edged a stray strand of shoulder-length, corn-silk blond hair from her forehead. She eyed Howin from head to toe. "Muscle-bound? I prefer . . . flesh sculpted to perfection."

Donalt allowed the remark and Howin's answering wink to pass without comment.

The Psi Corps officially frowned on "interpersonal entanglements" among active field agents. The loss of a loved one, even a casual sexual partner, with whom a psi bond has been forged could destroy the delicate mental stability of a psiotic "constantly beset by the stress of battle conditions."

The regulation reflected an understanding of the self-reliance, the individual loneliness needed by a psiotic to function within a universe turned topsy-turvy by a quarter of a century of war. Love, caring, human feeling, only dulled efficiency. Alone, an individual served, died, and was replaced by one of a hundred persons waiting in reserve. Let love take root, Donalt thought, and death might require two replacement parts for the war machine.

Giving, taking, sharing, the things two people found in love brought dependence—a shattering weakness for a psiotic. Loneliness was best; he had learned that with Evora.

Donalt also recognized it was impossible to build barriers between people. Men and women stuck within the confines of a star cruiser, working day after day with one another, touching each other's minds, eventually came to care, to share, to love.

Evora had also taught him that.

"Commander Radman Donalt, report to shuttle bay 1-A immediately," a feminine voice crackled from an intercom inset in the bulkhead beneath the holoscreen. "Commander Radman Donalt, report to shuttle bay 1-A immediately."

"I thought *officers* were the last to leave a ship?" Michaela rose when Donalt started toward the hatch.

"It's a captain who is last to leave a sinking ship. I'm not a captain! And the *Crispus Attucks* isn't sinking."

Donalt slapped a palm against the hatch's pressure plate. He stepped through when it opened, then turned back to his teammates and held out his left hand. "I'm just an aging mind-merger in search of a helping hand . . . and leg."

The two loud groans were appropriately cut short as the hatch hissed closed. Donalt smiled, pleased with the pun's effect. He pivoted on the balls of his feet and hastened down a tunnel-corridor to a nearby dropshaft and stepped in. Seconds later he exited onto the cruiser's fifth level.

The odors of oil, grease, and welding torches mingled in the air filling the immense belly of the *Crispus Attucks*. Mechanics and flight crews huddled beneath the stubby wings of the two blunt-nosed shuttles nestled within the cruiser. Others busied themselves with the maintenance of the twenty single-person assault ships also harbored in the bay.

Meter-high lettering stenciled on the outer bulkhead guided Donalt to bay 1-A. A line of ten white-uniformed officers boarded the waiting shuttle. The psiotic felt a rush of excitement at the prospect of being on-planet after a full year's tour of duty, in spite of the fact that he faced meeting the team's new prescient at Psi Corps Headquarters an hour after touchdown. He reached the bay and took his place at the end of the queue.

"Radman," the familiar voice of Caron Watters, Level Three Mate, called out. "Radman!"

Donalt located the slim brunette at the foot of the shuttle's loading ramp. She waved him to her side. The psiotic did not question the prospect of a shorter wait. He joined her.

"Thanks, I've never cared for lines longer than one person." Donalt smiled appreciatively.

"I'm not just being nice." Caron tucked a hand inside her uniform's coat and withdrew an envelope that she handed to Donalt. "Orders. Read 'em and weep."

As he moved up the ramp, Donalt tore open the envelope and removed the single sheet of yellow paper inside. He

quickly scanned the two lines of print. His head jerked up and
he stared at the young officer. "Naval briefing? What is this?
Psi Corps personnel don't attend official naval briefings."

"You know as much about it as I do. Captain Moven received orders directly from Naval Command when we popped
out of tachyon space. 'The presence of senior officers on all
levels is required,' " Caron quoted. She stopped at the first
two vacant seats and allowed Donalt to sit by the shuttle's
porthole. "Your orders came in about five minutes ago from
Psi Corps Director Thomas Pelsol himself."

Donalt had noted the source of the orders and the additional directive that he proceed to Psi Corps Headquarters
after the briefing. "Any idea what this is all about?"

"Not an inkling." Caron strapped herself in for planetfall.

The last officers entered the shuttle. The hatch closed behind them.

Donalt heard the bay's inner doors close and the sound of
air being pumped from the sealed compartment containing the
craft. "This briefing doesn't sound good."

"What ever does in this navy?" Caron leaned her head
against the seat's headrest, closed her eyes, and sighed.
"There's no use trying to outguess them, or even worrying
about it. Whatever is going to happen, will happen."

"Some encouragement." Donalt finished strapping himself
in as the bay's outer door opened.

A metallic ringing reverberated through the craft when the
docking locks released. Weightless, free of the cruiser's artificial gravity, Donalt felt no sense of motion as the shuttle
slipped from the *Crispus Attucks* into space.

The craft rolled to a side. The turquoise, cloud-banked surface of Donalt's homeworld filled the porthole to his left. The
excited anticipation of planetfall had been replaced with a
rootless dread.

The spacecraft nosed downward. A brief roar of thrusters
rumbled through the passenger cabin. An invisible hand gently
pushed him into the seat's cushioning as the shuttle accel-
erated.

Donalt stared out the porthole and tried to lose his thoughts
in the spectacular entry into the planet's atmosphere. Not even
the beauty of the slow fall planetward could stop the doubts
that niggled at the back of his mind.

‹THREE›

A week on-planet! One lousy week!

Donalt forced himself to accept the announcement as the lights in the small auditorium dimmed. He was disappointed . . . but he had been disappointed before.

A hologram formed in the air above the speaker's podium. He should have guessed the emergency nature of the briefing the moment Admiral William Luister had been introduced to the assemblage of twenty officers. The chief of Chenoa naval operations was not known for welcoming back cruiser crews under his command.

Donalt had never suspected the *Crispus Attucks* would be reassigned so quickly. A week of double-shift crews working around the clock would barely complete the cruiser's battle damage repairs. The updating and refitting of the ship's equipment would be postponed.

Nor would a week give the surgeons the opportunity to perform the needed repairs on one Radman Donalt. Once in a hundred agains, the clone grafts would also be postponed.

Donalt glanced at his left hand. In the low light, the differences between flesh and blood and prosthesis were imperceptible. He shrugged and told himself the surgery was a matter of vanity and nothing more. The mechanical contrivances that served as his hand and leg had been sufficient to get him by for ten years.

"In light of what you have just heard"—Admiral Luister's voice drew Donalt's attention back to the podium; above the gray-haired officer glowed the Milky Way in miniature—"I must impress on you the unknowns you face."

Luister paused and his gaze moved over the seated officers.

"Whatever it is out there is equal in size and mass to our Mobile Command Modules. That makes it at least four kilometers in diameter. It's also jumping across the galaxy faster than any craft we or the Kavinites possess . . . *known* vessels, that is."

The admiral's head tilted back. A red arrow appeared within the holographic display near the galactic rim.

"Here in the Arvis system, one of our drone spy probes first detected the vessel's approach. The ship slipped into normal space for approximately two and a half minutes. It completed what appeared to be a test of its weapons systems, then punched back to tachyon drive."

Luister referred to an open folder on the podium. "Intelligence correlates the probe's data with an increased interest in the Arvis system by Kavinite High Command. This was gleaned from intercepted communiques over the past three standard months. From present indications, Intelligence believes the Arvis system represents a commencement point for a major assault on Lanatia."

Donalt straightened. A buzz of surprise whispered through the auditorium.

Had he heard correctly? During the twenty-five-year war, there had never been an offensive directed at the governmental heart of the Lofgrin Alliance. Lanatia lay too deep within Lof-Al space, was too heavily protected to make an attack feasible.

Luister raised one arm and quieted the assembly. "I assure you, my initial reaction was the same as yours. However, the LofAl Council and Naval Command concur with Intelligence. The consensus is that the craft represents a radical advancement in Kavinite weaponry—one the Kavinite High Command apparently feels is capable of bringing the LofAl to its knees with an assault on our capital planet."

The admiral allowed time for another wave of questioning whispers to roll among the officers. He looked back to the holographic galaxy above his head. A yellow glow superimposed over Lanatia. A series of five red arrows appeared within the display.

"The arrows designate star systems in which the Kavinite vessel has appeared since first detected. Each leap represents a hundred light-years in a standard twenty-four-hour period. . . ."

Donalt stared at the arrows. Luister understated the situation when he labeled the craft a "radical advancement" in weaponry. The Kavinites had managed to square present faster-than-light capabilities with whatever it was they had out there.

". . . the segmented green line indicates the vessel's projected trajectory. As you can see, it intersects Lanatia's orbit in three months." Luister pointed upward. "Here is where the *Crispus Attucks* will be deployed."

A circle of blue light appeared in the Bersh system directly in line with the Kavinite vessel's projected route. Donalt hastily calculated the fourteen days needed for the flight from Chenoa to the Bersh system. Add seven days for repairs on the *Crispus Attucks* and it equaled the same twenty-one days for the Kavinite ship to make an appearance within the star system . . . if the vessel continued on its present course.

Donald cursed beneath his breath.

"The *Crispus Attucks* and her crew will intercept the Kavinite ship within the Bersh system. If possible, capture it. If not, you are to destroy the vessel." Luister paused.

The silence conveyed the unspoken understanding that LofAl Naval Command considered the cruiser and its crew expendable.

Overhead, lights came on. The holographic Milky Way faded while Admiral Luister turned and walked from the podium. A junior officer replaced him to announce that copies of the Intelligence reports and official orders would be distributed within an hour.

Donalt pushed from his seat and hastened up an aisle toward the auditorium's exit. From the corner of an eye he saw Caron Watters wave at him; he ignored the Level Three Mate. He was in no mood to speculate on the assignment or to listen to the normal round of navy bitching. Neither really mattered. Not now. He needed time to assimilate and accept all he had heard.

A sickening cold sweat prickled at his body. An all-too-familiar darkness settled over his thoughts. *Is there no end to it?*

Twenty-five years and still humankind sought new methods to obliterate itself. If the Kavinite vessel's speed hinted at the ordnance it carried, humanity might have succeeded in discovering the long-sought key to genocide.

The futility of humankind's chosen path pressed around him, an invisible hand that squeezed tighter and tighter. *Homo sapiens,* the galaxy's pinnacle of evolution—born in

Earth's primordial slime to elevate itself to the position of lone
sentient creature among the stars.

Had the human consciousness altered since its first awareness? The noble human spirit had reached out from the lone
orb of its birth to conquer the heavens—but only after it
destroyed that womb. Now, humankind's every effort was
devoted to erasing even the most minute trace of its existence
from the stars it seeded.

And he remained a part of it. He willingly gave all to the
ceaseless "war effort." Which was the greater insanity?

Double doors at the end of the aisle silently opened. Donalt
stepped outside into the crispness of a Chenoan autumn. The
sweet chill of fall seeped into his lungs as he drew a breath.

It *was* insanity. He had seen that for years. If the fighting
continued, it would provide the ultimate conclusion, the final
conclusion, to the thin philosophical differences that separated humankind—a conclusion from which there would be
no return.

Yet, he knew he would be aboard the *Crispus Attucks* when
it faced the Kavinites' latest bid to seize the coveted crown of
madmen. No sense of loyalty—not by common definition—
directed him. A rational being could find nothing to be loyal
to during war. Evora's death had demonstrated that to him.
Death was death, whether doled out by Kavinite or Lofgrinist.

His obsession—though delusion often seemed a more accurate description to the psiotic—was an even greater futility:
the belief that his ability, the genetic quirk that allowed him to
mentally merge with the minds of others, could somehow provide a grain of sand atop the cosmic scales. And that grain
could shift the balance from madness to sanity.

A mirthless smile upturned the corners of Donalt's mouth.
That was perhaps the grandest jest of all.

The hum of a low-flying skimmer intruded into the maze of
the mind-merger's thoughts. He looked up to see a gun-metal
gray, eight-passenger limousine descend from the sky to gently
alight on the lawn in front of him. One of the vehicle's doors
swung upward.

"Donalt, Radman Donalt." An arm waved him toward the
skimmer. A head poked out from the craft's interior. "Move
it, Donalt! I haven't all day!"

‹FOUR›

Ten years older than Donalt and looking twenty, Thomas Pelsol carried ninety-five kilos on a one-hundred-eighty-four-centimeter frame designed to bear no more than eighty-two kilograms. The paunch of Pelsol's midriff was visible in spite of the loose-fitting business suit he wore.

Stationed in bureaucratic security behind the U-shaped desk/Con-Web console of his office, the Psi Corps director thoughtfully bit at his lower lip and listened while Donalt completed the report of Admiral Luister's briefing.

"I had hoped that the Navy was keeping more under its hat." Pelsol leaned forward and steepled his fingers atop his desk. "The only thing I can add is that Naval Command is deploying every ship they can spare along the projected assault route."

"If the *Crispus Attucks* doesn't succeed," Donalt mused aloud, "they'll keep throwing ships and men at it until something does . . . or it reaches Lanatia."

"Until they know more, there's nothing else they can do." Pelsol shrugged. "There're too many unknowns involved. Not enough facts to speculate with any accuracy."

"I've already heard that several times today." Donalt made no attempt to disguise his sarcasm.

The director ignored the tone of Donalt's voice. "You were ordered here immediately to meet Birgit Keller's replacement. A week isn't much time for a personnel transition, but it's all there is. You need to make use of every minute available."

"What about Michaela and Howin? All leaves have been canceled. The crew of the *Crispus Attucks* has been restricted to ship." Donalt imagined the complaints awaiting him when he returned to the cruiser. "And I'm supposed to shuttle back in three hours."

"You'll have to supervise linking Gosheven and Bickle with the new team member while en route to the Bersh system." Pelsol tapped the desk intercom and ordered the replacement clairvoyant into the office. "Since the crucial link in a psi team is merger–prescient, the psychiatrists want to monitor your first merges with Jenica. I've arranged for you to stay on-planet two days. The Navy won't allow more. Afraid of security leaks."

"Jenica?" It was the first mention of the replacement's name. Also the first hint at the sex of the new team member.

"Jenica Stoy." Pelsol ran a hand over his shaven scalp. "She's eighteen and a full Grade Ten prescient. She's been in our Development Program on Chenoa since her pre-teens. . . ."

Donalt nodded while the director summarized Jenica Stoy's qualifications. Quietly he contained the anger that knotted his gut. Jenica Stoy was another child thrown into the meat grinder of war.

He also gave no outward indication of his own disappointment. For once he would like to be teamed with an adult, a person who came within a decade of his own age.

That was too much to expect. The burnout rate for psiotics assigned to combat duty was high. Those who remained mentally stable beyond the age of thirty were a rarity. Their experience was a valuable asset that was thinly spread through the LofAl fleet.

". . . of course, she's been thoroughly tested and psychologically cross-matched with you and your team members. The psychiatrists feel the merger–prescient link will be especially favorable in this instance." Pelsol smiled.

Something in the director's overly pleasant expression made Donalt shift uneasily in his chair.

The door to the office slid open. Donalt started to rise. A young auburn-haired girl entered. His body went weak, unable to move. In the next instant, tension rigidly gripped every muscle in his body.

How?

Jenica Stoy stood an exact one hundred sixty-seven centimeters and tipped the scales at fifty-two kilograms. Her hair, styled so that it flipped upward slightly at her shoulders, was naturally auburn—no cosmetic enhancement. Her eyes were green, deep emerald, in hue. High cheekbones, a small up-turned nose, and a full mouth gave her face a coy, mischievous look when she smiled. Though only eighteen, she had the alluring form of a fully mature woman that filled the forest-green jumpsuit she wore.

"I blossomed early and was deflowered shortly thereafter— with no regrets."

Donalt recalled Evora's jest the night that they first bundled —remembered it as distinctly as he could envision the light brown mole directly beneath the nipple of her left breast.

"Radman"—Pelsol gestured to Donalt and nodded at the girl—"I'd like you to meet Jenica Stoy, your new team member."

An uncomfortable sensation wormed through the merger. Jenica Stoy was *not* Jenica Stoy!

"Mister Donalt . . . or is it Commander Donalt?" She extended a hand and smiled a smile that had haunted Donalt for ten years. "I understand the Navy can't adapt to Psi Corps informality and often confers unofficial rank on psi team members."

By sheer willpower, Donalt shattered the ice floe encasing his body. He stood. He accepted the proffered hand, his fingers closing around familiar warmth.

"Radman . . . or Rad." His name awkwardly worked its way up his constricted throat. With uncertainty, reluctant to break contact, he released her hand.

Did she know? Had they told her? Donalt's gaze shot to Pelsol, demanding an explanation. The director glanced away.

The bastard! The psiotic now understood his earlier discomfort when Pelsol had smiled. *He knew! The bastard knew all the time!*

"Radman, then." The gentleness of Jenica Stoy's voice drew Donalt back to the girl and that soul-rending smile. "Radman Donalt is something of a legend on Chenoa. I'm only sorry my selection for your team is shadowed by such unfortunate circumstances. I realize the difficulties inherent in accepting a new team member. But . . ."

"Difficulties have a way of appearing larger than they really are when you first step into a new situation. I'd never under-rate a Grade Ten prescient." His attempt to reassure the young woman sounded flat. How could it be anything else when he doubted what his eyes perceived?

"Thank you." Long lashes curled over emerald-green eyes as Jenica shyly lowered her gaze.

Emotions that vacillated between love and repulsion coursed through Donalt while he stared at, soaked in, the face that could not be. The slight blush of her cheeks, the sensuous invitation of her lips, the nuances conveyed by her eyes—he knew them. They were a part of him.

"Jenica, Brace wants you in the White Room," Pelsol said. "You're to be in alpha level when Radman merges. Radman and I will join you in a few minutes."

Jenica nodded and smiled at Donalt before she left the office.

The merger felt his hands uncurl. His fingers ached from the tension of his unconscious clench.

"Rad . . . I believe you deserve an explanation." Pelsol leaned back in his chair. "I recognize that Jenica is a shock for you, but . . ."

"You son of a bitch!" Donalt's fists doubled, although he contained the urge to launch himself at the man. " 'The merger-prescient link should be especially favorable!' Do you know who that was?"

"Yes, I do," Pelsol answered coolly. "But do *you*?"

"A clone, you bastard—Evora's clone!" Donalt made no attempt to stem his rage. "The Psi Corps . . . Naval Command . . . you've gone too far!"

Ten years of anguish welled within the psiotic. Something buried within him, guarded by the distance and the relative security of time, squirmed free. He trembled.

"She *is* a clone." Pelsol retreated to the aloofness of bureaucratic formality. "But Jenica Stoy is *not* Evora Garridan."

Donalt sank back to his chair, struggling through the morass of images that assailed his mind—rootless guilts he had harbored for a decade.

Evora and he were once again linked in alpha-level awareness, neither cognizant of the Kavinite destroyer that punched into normal space. Nor were they aware of the plasma barrage that tore into the heart of the LofAl cruiser *Victorious* to shatter the bulkhead above them.

Merged, two minds molded to one, they shared the agony of

their mutual death. Felt the rending of their bodies beneath the onslaught of hot, jagged metal. Like two finely polished mirrors that faced each other, the pain, the terror, the horror, rebounded between their consciousnesses, amplified to infinity.

This was what he had been unable to confront, to relive in his mind.

And the guilt, the soul-tormenting guilt stemmed from one fact. Donalt had not died.

He regained consciousness in the medical bay of the *Victorious* with prosthetic devices where legs, right arm, and left hand had once been. The ship's physicians pronounced him physically and mentally sound. But more than limbs had been taken from him. More than any prostheses could ever replace.

". . . get it into that thick psiotic skull. Physically, Jenica Stoy is Evora. There the comparison ends." Pelsol stared intently at Donalt. "Jenica has been carefully nurtured through our Development Program. Her personality, her attitudes, were molded by a different environment. She is not Evora Garridan . . . nor will she ever be. Can you understand that?"

"Then why?" The Psi Corps director's words penetrated Donalt's rush of unleashed memories. "Why a clone?"

"Evora Garridan was the best prescient ever to come through Chenoan Psi Corps Headquarters." Pelsol leaned forward and rested his elbows on the desk. "Eight years before you met Evora, she consented to the cloning. She was even present when the host mother gave birth to Jenica. Evora understood the necessity of what we did. She understood the importance of psi teams to the war effort."

War effort, the all-consuming war effort! Donalt's fist tightened.

"Are there more Jenicas? Are there any other Radman Donalts?" He suddenly recognized the possible—no, *probable*—scope of a Psi Corps cloning program.

For centuries, cloned organs and limbs had routinely been used to relieve human suffering. But never before had the process been employed to reproduce a living, breathing, sentient entity. Humankind had long ago resolved that utilization of biological duplicates directly conflicted with the natural evolution of the species.

The Psi Corps, however, had found a use for human clones and justified it with the all-encompassing rationale: "the war effort."

The Corps did not require the consent of its agents. The needed cells for cloning could be taken during any of the innumerable battery of medical tests given annually to psiotics.

Pelsol's mouth drew into a thin line. He offered no answer to Donalt's questions. The mind-merger needed no further confirmation to realize that somewhere a younger version of himself was being prepared to give life and soul for "the war effort." Perhaps to be teamed with another Jenica Stoy.

"Madness, Pelsol! Can't you see that?" They had gone too far, and Donalt had allowed them to take him with them. "Madness!"

"It's a method to provide the best possible psi teams we can assemble. That's my job, Radman. I'll do whatever is necessary to do it."

"Which doesn't mean I have to willingly support whatever perverted form of insanity you deem necessary." The Psi Corps was not the Navy. Donalt retained the option to turn his back on the whole operation and walk away.

"No . . . but you will. No matter what else you are, Radman, you are a moral man. A man with a conscience. If you shunned the smallest opportunity to bring the war to an end, you could never live with yourself. Guilt is the penalty one pays for having a conscience." Self-confidently Pelsol sank back into the chair's deep cushioning. His gaze moved to a chronometer on the desk, then back to the psiotic. "You've got ten minutes to be in the White Room. After that, I'll select another merger for the *Crispus Attucks* team."

Donalt rose and stepped toward the office door. "I wouldn't place any bets on my being there."

"I would." The Chenoan Psi Corps director smiled. "I would."

The door slid open and Donalt exited. A receptionist cast him a disinterested glance. Donalt strode past the man to enter a dropshaft at the opposite end of the outer office.

He felt like an insect trying to swim across a pond of oil. The morning's revelations—the Kavinite vessel, the apparent assault on Lanatia, Jenica Stoy, the clandestine cloning of psiotics, Evora—had come too fast to be grasped and sorted in so short a time.

And Pelsol—*the bastard*. Donalt cursed the Psi Corps director, who sat smugly in his office, certain of the merger's final decision, refusing even to consider the alternative.

Stupid son of a bitch! The expletive was for himself. Pelsol was right. He had no other option. Cosmic jester or not, he knew the Psi Corps offered the only avenue available to use his ability in finding a detour for humankind's head-on rush toward self-destruction.

And Jenica Stoy?

She *was not*, could never be Evora. The woman he had loved died a decade ago. With time, he could adjust to Jenica. She was, after all, a prescient, and he a merger, two members of a four-person psi team. Jenica Stoy was nothing more than the replacement for Birgit Keller.

Resigning himself to what had to be done, Donalt stepped from the dropshaft. He hesitated for a moment, then walked toward the White Room.

◀FIVE▶

Donalt stretched atop a sensor couch beside the one on which Jenica lay. He carefully matched his hands to the palm-shaped metal plates to each side of him.

A green light flashed on the control console to his left. Dr. Isas Brace and a psychiatric team, stationed in an adjacent room beyond the one-way mirror to Donalt's far right, were prepared to monitor the psi link.

Jenica lay with her eyes closed. After thirty-six hours and eight merges, Donalt no longer saw Evora Garridan when he looked at the young woman. He had dwelled within the fabric of Jenica's mind. The weave was totally her own, with no trace of Evora.

For a moment, he watched the signs of rapid eye movement beneath her eyelids. There were still memories of past intimacies when he looked upon this auburn-haired young woman, but even those lessened each time they met. Pelsol had explained that Jenica knew nothing of her true mother-sister, the woman who once possessed the body and face she now wore.

Donalt had made no mention of Evora to the prescient. Jenica remained overly self-conscious of the mental and emotional bonds the psi team had formed with Birgit Keller. Even without using his psi ability, he sensed Jenica's ever-present anxiety about replacing the dead clairvoyant. Were the young woman to learn of Evora, Donalt feared the psi link they had forged would shatter.

Donalt closed his eyes. Like generations of psiotics before him, he required conscious effort and physical immobility to attain alpha level. An ambulatory psiotic did not exist, although Donalt did not doubt that the Psi Corps had genetic engineering programs presently underway to achieve that end.

He relaxed each muscle of his body, beginning with his toes and working upward. Normal combat conditions did not allow such luxury, but this was a laboratory, and every detail of the merge was to be optimal. He subdued the input of his own senses and pulled within himself.

His mind isolated from all sensory contact with the antiseptic environment of the White Room, Donalt floated on the currents of unharnessed psi forces generated by his own brain. Alpha level! He gathered the random energies to him, molded them, wove them, and threaded the gyrating surges into a coherent tapestry that he focused, directed, and controlled.

He reached out.

He sensed rather than felt a slight tremor at first contact with Jenica's mind. It was a last vestige of resistance, a final barrier erected to defend the sanctity of the ego. Donalt waited until the last quiver of hesitation passed, then eased into the consciousness that was Jenica Stoy.

Gently, without disturbing the stream of her thoughts, he flowed, blended, and wove himself into the young woman's mind. Jenica opened. Her awareness became his, her emotions his, her sensations his—two minds linked, merged into one.

How easily he might transform the woman into an extension of himself, bending her will to his own. Such a possibility never fully formed in the seed of awareness that remained Radman Donalt.

As psi team leader, he was passive in his mind-merger role. His task was that of an observer. He was but an extra mind to interpret the prescient images within Jenica's mind—although during his years of Psi Corps service, his ability had been used for more than simply observing the minds of others.

A planted fear, a redirected thought, a momentary lapse of sensory input was as deadly as the energy bolt of a gun. Defensive programming against psi attack, which was supposed to protect combatants from mental invasions, had little effect in the heat of battle. Donalt had killed . . . more times than he liked to remember.

For this merge, Donalt remained the observer. He floated within Jenica's consciousness, adrift on the featureless dark streams of the prescient's alpha level. And he waited. Waited.

A pinpoint of white light.

It appeared in the distant blackness. A radiating diamond spun toward the mind's eye. It raced headlong in meteoric flight. A warmth, gentle and soothing, suffused Jenica-Donalt.

Soundlessly, the crystalline gem exploded. A myriad of fragments shattered outward in a dancing shimmer of kaleidoscopic splendor.

Love.

It caressed Donalt; cradled him tenderly. Light fingers of anticipation coyly taunted along his spine. He sought the source of the overwhelming sensation. It was undefined, an unfocused flowing.

Jenica?

The merger repressed a ripple of . . . he had no definition of the sensation that sought to intrude into his consciousness. He suppressed all personal reaction in the fear that it would be transmitted to Jenica and inadvertently influence her mental images.

Fire erupted across Jenica-Donalt's field of vision. Tongues of flame leaped as though some elemental force were embodied in the animated blaze.

Anticipation peaked within the young woman. The nebulous love intensified. Its source remained hidden.

Recognition!

A sense of familiarity transferred from Jenica to Donalt—at the center of the swirling fire, the quavering form of a man.

The flames, bejeweled with spinning fragments of shattered crystal, flared in splendor behind the silhouetted man. It was as though he flew through the vast darkness on wings of fire.

Donalt probed for an identity. There was none; the man was only an image of . . . Donalt faltered. The love, that overwhelming sensation of love, flowed not from Jenica as he had suspected, but from the man with fiery wings. Jenica extended herself toward the radiating love.

Closer. Jenica-Donalt floated across the void toward the fire-winged figure that greeted them from . . . from . . . the *stars.*

Old, older than old. More ancient than ancient. An aura of ageless age surrounded the man. Yet, he was young, as youthful as the woman he beckoned to his side to share . . .

Closer. The features of the winged man's face were masked by shimmering waves of heat. Closer. They, Jenica-Donalt, reached out to touch . . .

Darkness.

The prescient image vanished. Jenica's mind tumbled, lost, disoriented, sliding from the energy streams of alpha level.

Donalt withdrew. He pulled his awareness back into himself and extended his will to the flaccid bundles of muscles in his body. Gradually, his eyes opened to admit the glare of the White Room's overhead lights. Their harshness did not diminish the flaming image of the man who flew on wings of fire.

"I think of him as the starman." Jenica smiled at Donalt and shrugged lightly, as though she were embarrassed by the vision.

"Then you've seen this flame-winged man before." Donalt thought he detected a faint hum as they settled onto a couch in the waiting room outside Dr. Isas Brace's office. The merger gave the room a cursory examination, but could find no telltale optical sensors. If they were being holotaped, the equipment had been neatly concealed.

"The door's pressure plate, the sculpture on the table, and behind the grille of the air vent," Jenica said.

"What?" Donalt turned to the prescient. Her eyes flitted away from him as though he had caught her studying him. Pink, a hue deeper than normal, tinted her cheeks.

"The holocameras, that's what you're looking for, isn't it?" She smiled again when Donalt nodded. "I found them four years ago during one of my endless visits here. Brace and his psychiatrists will probably spend many delightful hours analyzing everything we say and do."

Donalt grinned at the thought of a precocious fourteen-year-old Jenica Stoy scampering about the waiting room until she had uncovered the holotape equipment.

"And, yes, the starman has visited before." Jenica's gaze remained on Donalt. "The first time was when I was thirteen."

"Puberty, when your prescience ability first manifested itself?" Donalt glanced away for an instant. A stirring of that undefined sensation he had experienced in the merge tickled behind his thoughts. It eluded examination.

"I didn't realize it was prescience at the time. I just thought it was a beautiful daydream like something out of a children's fairy tale." The hint of embarrassment in her voice was there again. "The starman seems a bit silly now."

Donalt caught himself before his expression revealed his doubt. Jenica had felt no foolishness during the merge. Nor had the love radiating from the starman seemed childlike. "And you're still having the same vision?"

"Once or twice a week." She shifted on the couch. "The starman has always been there. Doctor Brace isn't sure he's actually a true prescient image. He's speculated that the starman is something seeping out of my own subconscious fantasies."

"The vision is prescient," Donalt said with a shake of his head. "I was there, remember."

A pleased little smile touched the young woman's lips. "But it has never signified anything. The majority of my visions —beyond the normal meaningless images that all prescients receive—hint at something immediate. Something that will occur in the near future. I've never seen anything more than a day away."

Jenica's ability had the same limits as Evora's, Donalt noted. The immediacy of clairvoyant images was significant in weighing their importance. "And you have no interpretation of the starman?"

"No." Jenica glanced away as she shook her head. Her mouth tightened for an instant. Again she shifted on the couch. "Did you see anything I haven't?"

"Nothing." Why did he feel that she was hiding something? He felt her gaze on him again, as though she expected a revelation.

Donalt turned to her, unable to avoid the emerald green of her eyes. Something else dwelt within her gaze. Something that evoked that niggling, indefinable sensation.

He glanced away. It was his turn to shift on the suddenly uncomfortable sofa. He recognized the source of the sensation that taunted him, but refused to acknowledge it. It made no sense, not for him.

"Is there something wrong?" That familiar, coy, impish smile was on Jenica's lips. She gazed at him as though peering beneath the outer veneer that Radman Donalt presented to the world.

The door to Brace's office opened, and the psychiatrist entered the waiting room before Donalt could answer. The merger felt an inner relief at the intrusion. He pushed himself from the couch, perhaps a bit too hurriedly, to greet Brace.

From the corner of his eye, he saw Jenica's smile widen before he stood and turned to the psychiatrist.

"No time for a friendly chat," Brace said when the psiotics stepped toward his office. "Director Pelsol just called to say a skimmer will be outside in an hour to take you to the shuttle-port."

"Then I'm approved for the *Crispus Attucks* team?" Jenica asked.

"Full clearance by my staff." Brace nodded. "If your link with the remaining two members of the team is as smooth as with Rad, the *Crispus Attucks* should have a fully operational psi team within a week."

Jenica beamed. Donalt could see a portion of the insecurities about her role aboard the cruiser dissipate with Brace's pronouncement.

"Now, if there's nothing else on your minds," Brace said, "I suggest you prepare for your departure."

Without another word, the psychiatrist disappeared back into his office. Donalt waved an arm for Jenica to lead the way outside.

"It's going to work, Radman." She grinned as they walked down the hall toward a dropshaft. "It's going to work!"

"You never really doubted it, did you?" He returned her grin.

"Of course, I . . ." Laughing, Jenica threw an arm about his waist and gave him a joyous hug and kissed his cheek. "I'm going to be *the* best prescient ever to set foot on the *Crispus Attucks*. I guarantee that!"

Donalt's own laugh disguised his awkwardness at Jenica's unexpected display of affection. The warmth of her arm, the softness of her lips, lingered after she stepped into the drop-shaft ahead of him.

Reaching Psi Corps Headquarters third floor, they exited and agreed to meet on ground level in forty-five minutes. With a last wide grin, Jenica half-walked, half-trotted down the corridor to her dormitory room. Donalt watched the door to the room close behind her while he wrestled with the feelings the young woman had awakened in him.

He could not define his muddled emotions as he walked to his own room at the opposite end of the hallway. On second examination, the physical attraction he had felt for Jenica in Brace's waiting room, that evasive sensation that had briefly

eluded him, was not as mysterious as he first thought. Jenica
Stoy *was* Evora, physically.

The shock was that he felt anything. There, too, was a measure of guilt brought by the fact that the first physical stir-
rings his body had produced in ten years were for a woman
who had Evora's body. His physical reaction, no matter how
natural, seemed like a betrayal, a violation, of the love that he
and Evora had shared.

Palm to pressure plate, Donalt opened the door to his cubi-
cle and entered. Psiotics in transit needed little more than a
bed. Anyone in his right mind who was on-planet longer than
to receive new orders booked a room at one of the city's
numerous hotels.

From the room's closet, Donalt pulled a small flight bag.
He dumped his few toiletry articles into it, then folded a spare
jumpsuit atop them. Then he carefully placed two colorfully
wrapped gifts within the bag before closing it.

The gifts would not compensate for Michaela and Howin
being detained on the *Crispus Attucks*. Yet they might lessen
the venom of his team members' resentment. For Michaela he
had purchased a signed and numbered portfolio by the Chenoan artist Candra Wesh entitled *Polymorphic Flesh Dreams*.
Wesh's rediscovered art-nouveau style left something to be
desired as far as Donalt was concerned. But Michaela was an
avid aficionada of the woman's work.

For Howin he had found a new microfiche edition of the
complete works of Renol Ilgri, the renowned clavitar com-
poser. The volume, he hoped, would provide enough new
music to keep the receiver occupied for the next year or two,
adding them to his repertoire on the multivoiced instrument.

For himself . . . Donalt smiled wryly. He had no need of
bright new toys. Preparing the four-person psi team, molding
them into a functioning precision entity before arriving in the
Bersh system, would more than occupy his time.

A glance at the wall chronometer showed thirty minutes until the skimmer's arrival. He placed the flight bag by the door,
then stretched atop the bed to stare at the ceiling.

Jenica's excitement over her approval for the team worked a
shiver along Donalt's spine. He tried to repress his thought
before it was fully formed, with no success. The words
sounded in his mind: *More meat for the grinder.*

The futility of human endeavors within a universe torn by

war—there was no escape from its presence. The quixotic jester, the cosmic fool unshakable in his belief that *he* somehow could tilt the scales, continued onward. He let those who would, follow. No matter that they were only eighteen and had yet to discover a life of their own. No matter that they were the exact image of a woman he had once loved.

Evora . . . Jenica. The young woman was like a loud warning tone on a loop of holotape that announced the loop was once again beginning its continuous never-ending cycle.

Not again. If it were in his power, Evora's second physical incarnation would not suffer the same fate as her mother-sister. He owed that to Jenica . . . to Michaela and Howin . . . to the cloned duplicates of himself who had, or would, join "the war effort."

The mind-merger slowly shook his head and smiled ironically. *Grandpa Donalt to the rescue, single-handedly reunites the warring factions of humankind and places their feet firmly on the golden path of enlightenment.*

All the scenario lacked was a fair damsel to be snatched from the clutches of a slimy ogre before she faced a fate that was never worse than death.

A light knock came at the door. Donalt rose from the bed and answered it. Jenica stood outside, still grinning.

"I didn't have much to pack." She held up two flight bags similar to Donalt's. "I thought if you were ready, I could talk you into a cup of coffee in the commissary. There's still twenty-five minutes or so before the skimmer arrives."

"You talked me into it." Donalt stooped and grabbed his bag from the floor.

The dropshaft took them to the ground floor of Psi Corps Headquarters. The commissary was at the far end of a large foyer. Inside, twenty people sat scattered about the large servo-serviced cafeteria. Donalt approached the nearest of the machines, slipped his identcard into the appropriate slot, and punched out an order for two coffees.

"Enjoy it. It'll be your last *real* coffee for longer than either of us wants to think about." He handed Jenica the first cup. "The colored water served on the *Crispus Attucks* is synthetic. A poor substitute for the real thing."

"If that's the only problem I'll have, I'll accept it without complaint," she answered while they moved to a vacant table. "I've seen all the training films, read all the normal literature

. . . but I must admit, I really have no idea of what to expect aboard a naval cruiser.''

"Boredom." Donalt explained that a psi team's only official function aboard a naval vessel was to provide what information its psi ability could glean. "Except in combat, there is little to do beyond our daily, routine links. It's waiting, waiting, and more waiting for something to happen. Then, if you're lucky, nothing does."

Taking a sip from the steaming cup, he illustrated his point by noting that the team's receiver, Howin Bickle, was normally found assisting in the medical bay of the *Crispus Attucks* or engrossed in his study of classical clavitar. "Michaela Gosheven, our receiver-sender, has managed to attain a Grade Ten rating as a ship's mechanic during her three years on the cruiser.''

"Yourself?" Jenica's green eyes peered at him over the lip of her cup.

"Top grade jack-of-all-trades." Donalt chuckled. "I'm available for whatever needs doing. Not very glamorous, but it beats sitting and staring at the bulkheads.''

"Then there'll be time for me to get to know you . . . and the other team members.''

That same expectant expression he had noticed on Jenica's face while they discussed the starman was there again. Donalt shifted uneasily. Long-suppressed sensations stirred within him.

"Too much time." He grinned to hide his uncertainty. "By the time we reach the Bersh system, you'll probably have had an overdose of Howin, Michaela, and myself.''

"I doubt that. Two weeks isn't that long." A hint of mischief touched the corners of her mouth. "Give me at least a month.''

He smiled. "Maybe three weeks at the outside.''

His cup half drained, Donalt glanced around the commissary. He located a chronometer on the wall above the servo units. He tilted his head to draw Jenica's attention to the five minutes remaining until the skimmer's arrival. She nodded and quickly finished her coffee, as did Donalt. Flight bags in hand, the two psiotics rose and walked outside.

"Take a good look at it," Donalt said, eyeing Nidori's skyline and the fleece-white clouds overhead. "You won't see anything like this on the *Crispus Attucks*. Once we shift into tachyon space, you won't even see the stars. Nothing but monotonous gray.''

Jenica slowly turned a complete three hundred and sixty degrees. "I don't believe I'll miss it that much."

"Not the first time," Donalt said. "By the fourth or fifth time they lift you off-planet, you'll be missing it the moment you set foot in the shuttle."

The hum of an approaching skimmer drew Donalt's attention from the prescient. The aircar gently settled to the ground twenty-five meters away. The merger noted it was a white, four-passenger model from the LofAl's interagency pool rather than the sleek limousine Director Pelsol had sent for him after the naval briefing two days ago.

A similar lack of luxury awaited the two psiotics at the shuttleport. They found themselves seated in two of four passenger seats aboard an ancient cargo shuttle loaded with supplies for the *Crispus Attucks*.

Five minutes after strapping in, without so much as a courtesy warning from the pilot isolated in the control cabin, Donalt felt the familiar vibrations of pre-ignition. A second later the thunderous roar of the main rockets filled the craft. An invisible hand rudely shoved the merger into the padding of his seat. The gee-force doubled, tripled, quintupled, as the bulky craft climbed upward to escape the planetary gravity well.

As abruptly as it had grabbed him, the invisible hand was gone. Weightless, he sat in his seat, held there only by the harnessing straps. Beyond the one porthole provided for passengers, the mind-merger saw the kilometer-long form of their destination.

"The *Crispus Attucks*." He nodded his head toward the cruiser.

Jenica craned her neck to see the ship. She turned and grinned at Donalt. Warm, smooth, and very feminine, Jenica's left hand squeezed about his equally human right hand. The pressure of her grip grew tighter as they approached the cruiser.

◀SIX▶

Jenica lowered the microfiche reader to a knee, balancing it there while her gaze played over the Level Three recreational lounge. She visibly cringed at a sudden chorus of raucous laughter.

Impatiently, she twisted in her chair to locate the source of the outburst. Ten members of the ship's crew huddled around an Escher-table on the far side of the recreation area. They joked and talked as they placed bets on the time- and space-warped tumblings of a two-centimeter aluminum ball that shifted and gyrated through a constantly reversing force net.

Jenica glanced back at the microfiche, then nervously searched the room. From the corner of his eye, Donalt watched her while he maintained the pretext of viewing a holo-drama on a screen attached to the arm of his chair. Michaela and Howin, engrossed in a Chenoan version of chess called *Kei Cocheta,* were also in the room.

Jenica's head turned toward Donalt, catching his sideways glance. An embarrassed blush colored her high cheeks. Her eyes darted away as though she were a child caught in a forbidden act.

"Something troubling you?" Donalt switched off the holo-screen.

Jenica's gaze lifted, and she nodded hesitantly. The soft strands of her auburn hair stirred slightly.

"Prescience?" he asked, aware that clairvoyant images were not restricted to alpha level.

"Anxious about tomorrow." Doubt furrowed her forehead. "I don't know. Everyone seems so calm, and I've got a case of the jitters."

"So does everybody else. We've just learned to disguise our fear better," Donalt reassured her. "There's no one on this ship who wouldn't jump at the opportunity to be elsewhere!"

Jenica smiled, almost grinned. "Still, I wish I had something to get my mind off tomorrow. I can't stop thinking about the Bersh system . . . the Kavinite ship."

"And worrying about how you'll perform under combat conditions." Donalt watched her nod. "For the past two and a half weeks, we've linked three times a day. If I thought anything could go wrong, I would've said something."

He lied. Things could always go wrong under enemy fire. However, he was as certain as he could be of Jenica's capabilities. Neither Michaela nor Howin had voiced any doubts about her either.

Donalt edged away the holoscreen and rose. "I'm not much at zero-grav swimming or handball. But I could use a walk. Can I interest you?"

"I don't believe you could stop me from tagging along." Jenica stood and led the way toward the room's hatch.

Michaela looked up from the multicolored *Kei Cocheta* board as Donalt passed. The blond receiver-sender smiled coyly and winked. Donalt frowned, unsure of the gesture's meaning.

"Any particular direction, or just wander?" Jenica asked when they left the lounge.

"Wander, in that direction." Donalt pointed to a liftshaft that would deposit them on the cruiser's Level One.

"I never realized it would be like this when I was in training. It's so big." Jenica's gaze moved over the shaft's interior as they entered and drifted upward. She looked overhead to the exit, meters above. "I've only seen one other combat-class ship, a destroyer. It was docked a quarter of an orbit away from the Q3Z power station when the Corps shuttled a group of trainees up for weightless experience."

"And I've seen too many." Donalt smiled. One was too many.

"It really is larger than I ever expected." Jenica stepped from the shaft ahead of Donalt and walked toward a nearby observation bubble. "Nor did I realize the crew would be so distant."

"That'll take longer to get used to." Donalt recalled his first assignment aboard a naval vessel. Six months had passed before he shook the feeling that he was a carrier of a virulent strain of some exotic social disease. "Navy regulars are a strange lot. I don't believe there are any 'ten easy steps' to getting along with them. It's hard to get past that 'if-you-aren't-Navy-then-what-the-hell-are-you-doing-on-my-ship' attitude."

They walked into the bubble and paused by the railing. Outside the transparent fish-eye stretched the featureless infinity of tachyon space. Donalt turned to leave the gray monotony, but Jenica stared out into the faster-than-light nothingness.

"Do you ever wonder just how you got here?" she asked without turning to him.

"I know how I got here. I volunteered." Donalt stepped back to the rail. His gaze traced the gentle lines of her face.

He no longer saw Evora when he looked at her. The face, like her mind, belonged to Jenica. Evora and Jenica were separate and distinct individuals. He remembered his shock when Jenica had walked into Pelsol's office, his fear that he would never be able to work beside a living ghost. It seemed so distant in retrospect, as though the doubts had belonged to another man.

"My parents have a farm about a hundred kilometers from Nidori. I always thought I'd marry and live on a farm," she said.

"There's still time for that. The Psi Corps isn't an end to one's life." *Host parents,* he reminded himself. Jenica's biological parent had died a decade ago.

"Of course, my parents fully supported the war effort." She bit at her lower lip. "At thirteen, I was tested for latent psi ability. When they discovered I was prescient, I was placed in the Psi Corps Development Program."

A distant look shadowed her face. A look of loneliness implanted by those oh-so-cooperative, war-effort-supporting parents. Just how cooperative they had been, she would never know, Donalt thought.

Without spoken agreement, the two psiotics began to walk, meandering through tunnel-corridors. Crew members occasionally hurried past them to complete some required task in preparation for the cruiser's entrance into the Bersh system. Donalt consciously steered Jenica clear of the gun implacements that ran along the cruiser's outer hull. The fewer reminders of what awaited in the Bersh system the easier her sleep would be.

While they wandered he listened to Jenica's impressions of the *Crispus Attucks* and her first weeks of field service. He sensed a vulnerability in her he had not seen in her mother-sister. Her lack of confidence in her own prescient abilities haunted her.

Donalt also felt a lack of stability within Jenica that Evora had never displayed. He refused to place any weight on either observation. Jenica was still young. Youth required a certain amount of indecision about itself, to explore the alternatives that lay before it. Experience would eventually supply the confidence and lessen the hesitancy.

"To be honest," Jenica said, "I'm not sure what I would have done without you to talk to these past weeks. I don't think you realize how much I appreciate what you've done."

Donalt smiled as they entered a dropshaft that returned them to Level Three. He was amused by the warm, paternal glow her words elicited in him. He was equally amused by his reaction to the compliment.

Grandpa, he chided himself.

"Michaela and Howin have helped, too. But they have . . . an arrangement . . . each other." Jenica glanced up at him as they moved down a tunnel-corridor leading to the team's individual quarters. "They really would rather be left alone than having me underfoot. . . ."

And I'm a loner with an overabundance of available time. He did not like the bitter feel of the thought, despite the truth it contained.

"You've gone out of your way to see that I've felt like a part of the team." She stopped before the hatch to her room and placed her hand on the palmlock.

The entrance slid open to reveal a small compartment identical to those allotted the other three members of the psi team. Here and there on the walls, Jenica had labeled it as her own with holographs of family and friends. There were even three framed prints that Donalt recognized from the Wesh portfolio *Polymorphic Flesh Dreams.*

"I also want to thank you for the walk. I think I'm calm enough for bed now." Jenica turned back to him.

"Sleep's a good idea." Donalt felt awkward under her ex-

pectant gaze. "Captain Moven wants a full link an hour
before transition to normal space."

"I'll be there. . . ." Jenica abruptly rose on tiptoe to throw
her arms about his neck. Her mouth covered his, her tongue
probing intimately.

Donalt's arms hesitantly slid about her slim waist. He held
her to him lightly as though he cradled a fragile china doll,
uncertain, confused, but reveling in her womanly feel.

Then she was gone.

She edged into her room, shrinking from him. Her eyes
were wide, tinged with . . . uncertainty? Fright? He was not
sure. Had his reaction been more than she expected? He was
not even positive what he felt himself. Her kiss, its surprising
passion, had taken him off guard.

"Rad . . . I . . . I'm . . ." Jenica stumbled for words. Was
she afraid she had begun something she had not intended?

"I understand." Donalt smiled weakly. "It's all right."

He turned and walked down the tunnel-corridor, satisfied
he had gracefully given her the exit she had wanted. A sense of
quixotic chivalry filled him. He had done the "honorable"
thing by not taking advantage of the fair maiden's confusion.
The choice had been easy. His own confusion permitted
nothing else. Whatever it was he felt, it was not the paternal
glow Jenica had elicited moments before.

Donalt had moved several meters down the corridor when
he heard a soft hiss. He turned. A frown lined his brow. He
realized it was the sound of the closing hatch to Jenica's cabin.

◄SEVEN►

Donalt felt eyes watching him when he settled into a chair in the recreational lounge. He glanced up. Michaela and Howin studied him. The two young psiotics glanced at each other, nodded, and looked back at Donalt. Knowing smiles spread across their faces.

"It appears that you have been adopted, Grandpa." Michaela swiveled the chair around to face the mind-merger.

"What?" Donalt was not sure what she meant.

"Jenica," she replied. "Or are you telling us you haven't noticed?"

Before Donalt could answer, Howin said, "Come on, Rad. Jenica's constantly at your side. Has been since she came aboard."

"Jenica's frightened. It's difficult to be suddenly thrust aboard a naval cruiser." Donalt was not prepared to examine his muddled disarray of feelings. He needed time to quietly sort them, to put them in a proper perspective.

"And you've become her big brother, the father figure," Howin replied.

Donalt nodded slowly. Brother, father, they sounded distant. Somehow cold. "Why not friend?"

"The girl's got a crush on you, Grandpa," Howin continued.

Donalt's eyebrow arched. The "Grandpa" irritated him.

"That girl's not a girl. She's a woman and past the stage for crushes." Michaela glanced at her lover. "We're not talking about infatuation."

"She's eighteen," Donalt protested, unwilling to consider what they suggested. "I'm a forty-year-old man."

"Afraid of being accused of robbing the cradle?" Howin's casual jibe needled toward something that squirmed uncomfortably within Donalt. "Not from us. And the crew could care less."

Donalt picked up a microfiche reader, a signal the discussion had been concluded.

"Now he's telling us the attraction isn't mutual." Howin refused to let the matter drop. "Rad, you should have seen yourself these last weeks."

"A glow like that on a man's face isn't simply 'friendship,' " Michaela added.

"And I think you're both full of crap." Donalt waved them away. His tone was harsher than he intended.

"And I think you're a fool, Radman Donalt." A hurt expression fluttered on Michaela's face. She swiveled back to Howin. "If you can't accept what Jenica is offering you, you're the biggest asshole in the galaxy. A person can't stay locked away within himself for a lifetime. It's wrong. It's a damn waste!"

Taken back by Michaela's uncharacteristic outburst, Donalt stared at his two teammates. Neither paid him attention now, but sat half slumped in their chairs, heads hung over the *Kei Cocheta* board.

He started to speak. Instead he swallowed the half-formed words. He glanced about, suddenly at a loss to find a reason for remaining in the room. He could not find one. So he rose and strode from the recreational lounge. How could he explain? He wasn't sure himself. He walked down the tunnel-corridor toward his quarters.

He did not deny his attraction to Jenica. Until mere minutes ago, he had discounted it as an attraction to the physical appearance of her mother-sister. Jenica deserved better than some twisted form of necrophilia from him. Jenica was her own woman, not Evora.

He had not thought of the two in the same context for weeks, he admitted to himself. The emotions that befuddled him stemmed from Jenica, not Evora. He was . . . how difficult the words came after ten years of thinking himself incapable of ever feeling them again . . . in love. He loved Jenica.

But the years that separated them? The differences in their

lives? The experiences he had lived that were yet to be hers?

He stopped, standing alone and confused in the tunnel-corridor. In comparison to his forty years, Jenica was a child. No matter what Michaela said. There was more than affection in the nickname "Grandpa." It was a reminder of years that separated him from his teammates.

If you can't accept what Jenica is offering you, Michaela's condemnation replayed in his mind behind an image of Jenica. Those emerald eyes gazed at him, coy, expectant.

Expecting *what*? He knew, perhaps had always known, but had been too frightened to accept. It was difficult to shed a decade of insulation from human contact, to discard the illusion of total self-reliance and isolation.

Donalt glanced around, aware for the first time that he was standing in the center of the tunnel-corridor. He stood facing the entrance to Jenica's compartment.

Had he misinterpreted the fright he had read in her face earlier? Had he placed it there to protect himself from the love he felt and had refused to accept?

Of its own volition—another lie, he told himself—his hand reached out and rapped lightly on the hatch. With resolution, he knocked harder.

The entrance slid back. Surprise in the form of a demure smile widening to a grin on Jenica's face greeted him. "Radman . . . I thought . . ."

He stepped forward; his arms encircled her and drew her to him. There was no hesitance, no indecision. They kissed. For a moment that lingered to minutes, they clung to one another. They parted only long enough for Jenica to edge him into the cabin and close the hatch.

Their mouths met again, softly as though savoring the sensation his reluctance had denied them. Her lips and playfully nibbling teeth were at the corner of his mouth, his neck, his ear. She whispered disbelief at his return, that she had feared she frightened him away, misjudged what appeared obvious to her.

"The shock on your face when I kissed you . . . I thought that I was wrong . . . that I had made a mistake."

Hands tenderly cradling the beauty of her young face, his lips quieted the fears, the doubts. Her mouth opened to the taunting insistence of his tongue. She pressed closer to snugly nestle the very feminine contours of her body against his. Arms tightened, hands languidly stroked, soaking in the marvelous texture of the moment.

Jenica eased away again three eternities later. She lifted his hands to the open neck of her jumpsuit. Fingers unwarrantedly steady, Donalt ran a hand down the static strip which bound the front of the suit. It opened with a whispered sigh.

Her eyes, lit with expectation, anticipation, gazed into his. He grasped the open edges of fabric and inched them wider to ease the jumpsuit off her shoulders.

That enticing, coy half-smile uplifting the corners of her mouth, Jenica let the cloth slowly drift down her body to gather about her ankles. She stepped from the jumpsuit and stood before him unashamed.

Donalt's fingertips rose to lightly brush the small brown mole beneath the nipple of her left breast. She trembled at the momentary contact. For an instant, an image of Evora fluttered within the merger's mind. A bittersweet hint of déjà vu possessed him. A decade was lost in the single caress of his eyes.

As abruptly as it came to him, it dissolved. Jenica Stoy, not Evora, opened her arms to him. Familiar, yet totally new, were the body, the mind, the person she offered.

Fumbling, together they opened his jumpsuit and took it from his body. If the years that separated them mattered, he could find no trace of it in Jenica's radiant expression.

"Jenica, I . . ." He wanted to assure her with words. He felt the need to somehow vocalize the love and desire that filled a part of his being that had been vacant for far too long.

"Hush." She touched a fingertip to his lips, then replaced it with her mouth.

Jenica's hands, cool and soothing on his back, slid down to cup his buttocks and guide him to her bed. Together they sank onto the sheets, lost in the revel of skin on skin.

The need for words had passed. His eyes lovingly traced the beauty of her face. His fingers combed through the silky cloud of auburn that spread atop the pillow beneath her.

Her fingers lightly danced over his cheeks, glided over the bridge of his nose, and roved across his lips as though to memorize the feel of his face.

"I *did* surprise you when I kissed you, didn't I?"

He took her fingers in his hand and kissed their tips. "I'm a forty-year-old man, and . . . I couldn't believe . . ."

"Believe," she said. "I *do* want you."

She eased beneath him and guided him into her body. There was a brief instant of resistance that Donalt neither expected nor was prepared for. Jenica winced, stiffening for a moment.

He stared at her while his mind accepted the full measure of what she gave him. He leaned down and kissed away the hint of moisture from the corners of her eyes. "I didn't realize."

"It doesn't matter now," she said, smiling up into his face. Then her arms were locked behind his neck and she drew his mouth to hers.

He lost all meaning of time as he lay there bathed in the luxury of her body. His hands, radiating all the tenderness he felt, stroked and caressed to reassure her. When her fingers once again stroked over his back, he moved to bring their bodies to a gentle, rocking rhythm. Neither asked nor strove for more from this first union.

Man and woman, woman and man, they touched and were touched. They kissed deeply. They clung to each other. They drank every moment of this most intimate of sharings. They harbored each other, sheltering themselves from the insane universe in which they dwelled. In the lulling rhythm of their lovemaking, they renewed their right to exist, to live.

Donalt felt tension tauten the suppleness of her body as the moment of release approached. He reached out, merging his mind with hers. There was no resistance. She opened to him, he to her. Sensation, emotion, man, woman, melted together in a single entity of total sharing. He was she. She was he. They were both in the same instant.

Together, the mutual consummation of their desire swirled outward, inward, careening wildly from one mind to the other. Together they rode the crashing waves of their bodies' release.

Slowly, ever so slowly, Donalt eased from Jenica's mind, reluctant to sever the union of their merge. He mentally stretched within himself. He searched for any nagging guilt or lingering doubts. There were none, only a realization of being alive, of being whole. He smiled as he joyously lolled in the contentment he had denied himself for a decade.

A shudder! He sensed-felt the quaking shudders that ran through Jenica. He heard the choked sounds of her sobs. His eyes opened to stare at the tears welling in her eyes.

"Jenica?" he whispered, and reached out to touch her cheek.

"You bastard! You bastard!" Anger twisted the gentle beauty of her face. She shoved him from her, then pushed out of the bed. Arms rigid, fists clenched, she glared. "You knew! You bastard! You used me!"

"Knew?" Donalt tried to rise. Jenica's arms thrust out, slamming into his chest. Off balance, he tumbled back to the sheets. "What the hell? What . . ."

"*Evora,* you bastard! I'm not Evora. I saw her in your mind. I'm not her. I won't be her for you. I won't." Donalt saw more than rage in her features. He saw the pain, the hurt. "How could you? How could you use anybody the way you just used me?"

"Jenica, if you saw, then you know it wasn't Evora I made love with. It was *you.*" He tried to rise again, ducking when Jenica swung a fist at his head. "If you saw, then you know. Jenica, you know what I feel is for *you.*"

Her anger was undiminished. "Convenient, wasn't it? Just pop into bed with the . . . the . . . *clone* of . . ." She broke down, her sobs racking her body.

Donalt pushed from the bed and took her in his arms. "It's not me, is it? It's you, and Evora, isn't it?"

Palms against his chest, she shoved from his arms. She stood staring at him, looking lost and bewildered.

"Jenica, I'm here. I can help. You saw my mind, you know." He stepped toward her, arms outstretched.

The young woman retreated. Her head moved from side to side. "I don't know. I need time. I need to think."

"We can talk. It's easy when someone is there. You showed me that. Let me be here for you."

Once again she shrank from him.

"No." Her body stiffened with determination. "I need to be alone. I need time to think. I can't be sure of anything right now. Not even you, Radman."

"Jenica, please. I can help." Donalt pleaded for himself, for her.

Her head shook. "Please . . . give me time. It would be better if you left now."

"Jenica, you need to talk this out. *We* need to talk. You can't contain something like this."

"Radman, I want you to leave." She pointed to his clothes

on the floor. "Get out! Leave me alone."

She turned from him, walked to the far corner of the bed, and sat on its edge. When he moved toward her, her eyes darted up at him, fired with anger once again.

Donalt scooped his jumpsuit from the floor and dressed. Perhaps time was what she needed now, an opportunity to sort through all she had found within his mind. When she did, she would realize the love he felt was real—for her.

He walked to the cabin's hatch and opened it. Turning back to Jenica, he said, "When you need me, I'll be there."

She said nothing, just stared at him, though Donalt sensed she no longer saw him. Her mind was elsewhere, juggling the unexpected revelations of her past.

Donalt stepped outside. The hatch closed behind him. Feeling like a man who had discovered paradise and lost it in one instant, he moved through the dim light of the tunnel-corridor, in the artificial night aboard the cruiser, and entered the suddenly cold solitude of his own cabin.

◄EIGHT►

Michaela's eyelids opened to reveal glazed, blue irises. She stared at Donalt as though unable to see him. She blinked, once, twice, to shed the last traces of trancelike alpha state. Light returned to her eyes.

"Howin's on the command deck ready to relay anything Jenica might pick up." The receiver-sender glanced at the younger woman in the reclined couch to her left. "Ready?"

Jenica took a deep breath. "Ready."

Donalt watched the prescient close her eyes to prepare for her immersion in alpha level. He resisted the temptation to shake his head in doubt. Jenica had disappeared that morning and only reappeared in Psi Team Operations thirty minutes before the scheduled link. Her behavior was unchanged; there was not the slightest hint that anything had happened between them the night before.

Donalt did not question her attitude. Jenica's discovery of her cloned life, what they felt for each other, had to be shuffled into a corner temporarily until after they confronted whatever the Kavinites were throwing at Lanatia.

If there were an "after."

Donalt took the vacant couch beside Jenica and pressed the recline button on the side of its right arm. While the seat tilted into position, he closed his eyes and pulled within himself to drift on the streams of alpha state. Practiced time and again for three weeks, he opened himself to merge with Jenica.

Resistance met his mental probe. Surprised by the determination preventing his entrance, he withdrew, waited, then reached out again. The conscious mental barrier Jenica had constructed gradually dissipated. He merged to enter the featureless void of prescience alpha state.

In turn, Michaela's receiver-sender ability allowed her to tap the merger-prescient awareness and simultaneously transmit their shared visions and reactions to Howin. The receiver waited on the *Crispus Attucks* command deck to relay any information gleaned from the link to the cruiser's captain. This was the psi team at full capacity, four individuals—minds joined as one.

Donalt's total attention focused within Jenica's mind, ready to interpret the visions that formed atop the jet tapestry of alpha level.

In the distant blackness, a pinpoint of white light flared into existence.

The diamond. He recognized the jewel that raced forward. It was the same he had first viewed on Chenoa through Jenica's mind's eye. Warmth, the tenderness of love, surrounded the merger's senses. He felt a faltering, a momentary thrust of resistance as though the young woman sought to expel him from her mind. Then the love was there again.

From the jewel? Jenica?

Mentally Donalt stumbled. The enfolding sensation was as overwhelming as the love Jenica had given him freely last night. Was it for him? Did it flow outward from Jenica? He could not pinpoint the radiating source.

The diamond shattered into shimmering, careening fragments. Tongues of fire exploded in glorious profusion. The starman appeared. Flames fanned behind his silhouetted form like wings.

There was no doubt to the source now. Donalt was engulfed by the love that enclosed Jenica in its tender embrace.

Light, actinic in its harshness, shredded the harmony of the silent psi stream. The starman faded, dimmed to nothingness. A maelstrom of fury swirled. Darkness undulated across the light to leave a blackness studded with distant stars. Closer, the yellow-white orb of Bersh. Jenica had no knowledge of the star. Donalt did. He had seen it five times during twelve years.

The *Crispus Attucks* winked into existence, leaving tachyon space. Apprehension railed through Jenica.

Bees! The single word formed in her mind. *Bees!*

Bees the size of on-planet skimmers swarmed over the surface of the kilometer-long spacecraft. Their yellow-and-black bodies blurred in the rage of their flight. Needlelike stingers

stabbed at the cruiser's scarred hull, seeking an exposed softness in which to embed their venom.

The bees . . .

Jenica's eyes flared wide to shatter the prescient images.
Donalt moaned with her.

The merger withdrew and eased back into his own mind. He
force-fed his will into senses and muscles abandoned, but . . .
he had no sense of the time that had passed while linked.
Struggling against the leaden lethargy of his eyelids, he opened
them. Fuzzy vision cleared.

Jenica sat on her couch. She stared at Donalt. Her hand
shook as she reached for his.

"The *Crispus Attucks* . . . did you see *them*?" Her voice
was two octaves above its normal range. "They attacked the
ship!"

"I saw." Donalt's fingers tightly closed around her hand.
"I saw."

"Howin wants to know what the hell that was all about?"
Michaela pushed to her elbows. "*Bees*? What were they?"

Jenica's head moved from side to side with doubt.
Michaela's questioning eyes shifted to Donalt.

"That was all I got . . . giant bees in *space*." Donalt pulled
at his lower lip. "Whatever . . . they attacked. Tell Howin to
convey everything we saw."

Michaela leaned back. Her eyes closed.

"And, Michaela, tell him, it's danger. There's no other interpretation of the attack."

Jenica nodded in confirmation.

"Got it." The receiver-sender lay still as she returned to
alpha state.

"It was so distinct . . . so clear." Jenica's voice still
quavered, though it had regained its normal level. "I've never
seen anything like it before."

Donalt squeezed Jenica's hand in reassurance. Her eyes
lowered as though noticing that he held her hand. She looked
up at him. His fingers went limp; she withdrew her hand.

Michaela stirred, drawing Jenica's attention. The receiver-
sender's head rolled to her teammates. "Howin broke contact.
He's relaying everything to Captain Moven."

Donalt tilted his couch upright and ran a hand through
gray-salted hair. The command deck felt a light-year away. He
wanted to be there to convince Moven of the cruiser's danger.

The wall intercom crackled. "Commander Donalt, Captain Moven here."

"Donalt here." The psiotic crossed to the intercom grille.

"Bickle informed me of the prescient's vision," the cruiser's captain said. "I want confirmation on the interpretation."

"Definite attack," Donalt replied.

For several heavy, silent moments, the intercom was dead. Donalt turned to his companions. Their attention was riveted to the wall grille.

"There's no possible way to divert our present course, Rad." Moven's voice returned to the intercom. "I've ordered tachyon transformation exactly two seconds prior to our scheduled punch-through. That'll place the *Crispus Attucks* kilometers short of its original transition point. With luck, there'll be no bees waiting for us."

The intercom went dead again. Despite the attempt at levity, Donalt recognized the weight Moven placed on the prescient vision. Alterations in preprogrammed jumps were a rarity aboard a naval vessel.

Donalt looked up at the wall chronometer. Forty minutes remained until the cruiser's return to normal space. There was nothing to do, but wait.

Choking back the rush of bile that forced its way up his esophagus, Donalt swam through the waves of nausea. Over and over he drew lungfuls of air through his nostrils in an effort to combat the effects of below-light transformation.

An alarm screamed.

Donalt concentrated on the holoscreen image that materialized to fill half a wall of Psi Team Operations. A destroyer, its metallic hull agleam with Bersh's yellow-white light, drifted across the star-speckled blackness. The ship's sleek design was unmistakably Kavinite. From its underbelly swarmed . . .

. . . *Bees!*

Equipped with full close-range armaments, the yellow-and-black painted Swarmers carried more sting than the giant insects of Jenica's vision. Each attack vessel contained a one- to four-person crew. It would be a matter of minutes before they were all over the *Crispus Attucks*.

Had it not been for Jenica's perception, Donalt realized, the cruiser would not have those minutes to prepare for the attack. The *Crispus Attucks* would have slipped from tachyon space to find itself englobed by the attack vessels.

Five bolts of plasma energy shot from the destroyer's nose while the merger counted thirty-five small ships slicing toward the cruiser. Flaring red obscured the holoscreen when the globes impacted the LofAl vessel's defensive shield.

The glare dissipated. A line of twenty one-man ships, naked metal adorned with a lone blue-and-white rondelle aft of the canopy, shot from the *Crispus Attucks*. They were outnumbered and outclassed by the Kavinite assault wave.

A crosshatched web of green energy blasts rent the blackness. The ordnances of destroyer and cruiser lashed across space. Five Swarmers in the small flotilla homing in on the *Crispus Attucks* disintegrated when their trajectories intersected the energy beams.

Brilliant blossoms of violet splattered across the holoscreen —the explosions of stealth floaters striking the force field. Three of the LofAl assault ships winked into oblivion, caught in the second wave of plasma bolts the destroyer unleashed.

"Any aid you can provide against those *bees* would be greatly appreciated, Commander Donalt," Captain Moven's voice called over the intercom. "My weaponry crews have their hands full with the destroyer."

Donalt acknowledged the command and glanced up as the hatch to Psi Team Operations opened. Howin entered.

"Moven said I'd be of more help here than getting in the way on the command deck. That destroyer is carrying about twice the firepower we've got."

Donalt glimpsed the terror that shadowed Jenica's face. He wanted to comfort her, to tell her everything would be all right. But there was no time for lies. He turned to Michaela.

"Feel up to causing some confusion?"

Without a word, the receiver-sender reclined her couch and closed her eyes. Somewhere beyond the cruiser's defense shield a Swarmer pilot, his concentration focused on the destruction of the *Crispus Attucks,* found his brain bombarded by commands to turn his weaponry on his companions.

"Howin, you and Jenica give Moven what support you can."

Donalt closed his eyes and drifted toward alpha level. Monitoring the prescient streams would take Jenica's mind off the holoscreen. Howin was needed to sense any psi emanations from the Kavinite destroyer directed at the crew of the *Crispus Attucks*.

Sensory input eliminated, Donalt reached out. He moved past the minds of the cruiser's assault ships to the occupants of the Kavinite Swarmers. He touched a mind.

Gingerly he wove past the mental warnings implanted by the psi training given every combatant, Kavinite or Lofgrinist. Beyond, he induced a momentary lapse of memory within his host. The maneuver was not foolproof, but this time it worked. He merged with his host, totally, completely.

A woman . . . Swarmer assault ship Able-Three . . . master sergeant Grade Two . . . bond-mate Chal Lanu—awareness inundated Donalt's consciousness. Through the woman's mind, he saw the *Crispus Attucks* and its faltering shield.

The psiotic exerted his will. He commanded the woman to draw the laser cutter holstered to her personnel armor. He directed the weapon at the Swarmer's Con-Web and squeezed her finger around the trigger.

Donalt did not wait for the discharge that sent the ship careening out of control into the depths of space. He withdrew and reached out again.

The mind he touched repelled the merge. The psiotic wasted no time, but moved on to slip into the consciousness of a man piloting a four-person Swarmer. A fingertip brushed over two toggle switches, and he swerved the craft into the path of a sister ship. Donalt barely escaped sharing the death agonies of his host when the two assault vessels collided and were transformed into a twisted meteor of debris.

Three Kavinites blocked his entrance to their psyches before he found a new host—the female pilot of a two-person Swarmer that was locked securely against the hull of the *Crispus Attucks*. The cruiser's defensive shield had been penetrated.

Donalt repressed a rush of panic. Through the woman's eyes, he saw five other vessels nestled to the metallic shell.

He felt the cutter in his host's hand and shifted its barrel from the cruiser's hull to the pilot's companions. Six armor-clad invaders died before the woman's fire was returned. Donalt did not escape the searing flame that dissolved her abdomen, nor the glimmering recognition that she had been controlled by another human being.

Guilt and shame suffused the merger when he withdrew to

touch another mind. The war, the killing—the very things he dedicated his existence to ending—were Radman Donalt. He was but another weapon in Naval Command's arsenal.

Donalt caught himself. Later, alone in his cabin, he would free the nightmares his actions created. Survival, only survival mattered now.

Rad!

Michaela's thoughts, urgent and demanding, resounded within his brain.

Rad, break off. The ship's been breached! Break off now!

‹NINE›

The warning alarm undulated persistently inside Donalt's skull. His three teammates crowded around him. A flurry of arms and hands pulled and tugged, urging him from the couch.

"Move it, Grandpa!" Michaela's arm around his waist dragged him to his feet. "We've got to get the hell out of here."

"Kavinite assault forces have penetrated to Level Three." Howin slapped an energy pistol into Donalt's hand, then passed weapons to Jenica and Michaela. "Evacuate to the shuttle bay."

Comprehension sifted through Donalt's clouded mind. "Where'd they breach?"

"Aft." Michaela stepped to the hatch and slapped its pressure plate. An explosion echoed in the tunnel-corridor outside. She looked over a shoulder at her companions. "Close. Let's go!"

Howin darted through the hatchway before Michaela finished. He dropped to a knee in the middle of the tunnel. With a two-handed grip, he leveled his gun before him to provide cover. Michaela ran out the exit and raced toward the ship's prow and the dropshaft that led to the relative safety of the shuttle bay.

Donalt started toward the hatch. Howin's head twisted to him. "Jenica?"

Pivoting sharply, Donalt faced the prescient. Jenica stood in the middle of the compartment, eyes wide and wild. "Move it!"

Jenica remained immobile as though his command were in-comprehensible or had gone unheard.

"Get the hell out of here." Donalt waved Howin after Michaela. "I'll get her."

The receiver disappeared down the tunnel-corridor in a hasty backstep. Donalt's attention returned to Jenica, who stood in the same spot, eyes closed and swaying.

Damn! He recognized the familiar signs of alpha state. *There's no time . . . not now!*

In two strides, Donalt crossed the room and caught Jenica in his arms as her knees buckled beneath her. He cursed the nonambulatory limitation shared by all psiotics while he low-ered Jenica to the deck.

Not now, damn it! Not now!

Her eyes fluttered; incoherent mumblings came from deep in her throat. Donalt felt flaccid muscles tauten as she re-exerted control of her body. She blinked. Recognition lighted her eyes.

"The Kavinite destroyer . . . its number two bay . . ." She sucked a deep breath and managed to stand with Donalt's aid. "I saw three stealth mines penetrate the destroyer's shield. The tachyon drive is located above the destroyer's number two bay. I saw it, Rad!"

Donalt activated the intercom without question and relayed Jenica's vision to the command deck. A sizzling burst from an energy pistol erased all thought of the captain's reply from his mind. Donalt swirled.

Jenica, legs wide in a defiant stance, stood facing the hatch. Her gun was extended before her. Two Kavinites in yellow personnel armor stood in the tunnel-corridor outside. The molten remains of what had been a laser cutter pooled at the feet of the first intruder, evidence of the prescient's marks-manship.

Jenica's finger squeezed the trigger again . . . again. Noth-ing happened.

In a deceptively awkward waddle, the nearest Kavinite wedged through the entrance, movement hampered by the bulky armor. A yellow arm swept back.

Donalt leapt. Arms wide, he caught Jenica about the waist. They tumbled to the deck.

Overhead came a sucking sound as the invader's arm slashed harmlessly through empty air. The Kavinite needed no weapon. The armor was a mechanical extension of its wearer that amplified normal movement. The blow had been meant to take Jenica's head off at the neck.

Donalt rolled to his feet, swung his pistol upward, and fired. A burst of green light speared into the attacker's armor-protected midriff. A smoking scar of melted metal and flesh appeared where an abdomen once had been.

The Kavinite took an uncertain step. His helmeted head, faceplate mirrored opaque, twisted to one side. Then he collapsed to the deck.

Donalt had no time to wonder about the face hidden within the helmet. He stared into the wide muzzle of the second invader's energy weapon. The mind-merger reacted rather than thought. He leaped to the right, away from Jenica.

The sizzle of discharge resounded within the compartment.

Pain!

Nerve-searing pain lanced through the psiotic's left hand. Unconscious of his reaction, guided only by the burning agony, Donalt dropped his pistol and grasped his left arm.

Numbness.

The pain died as quickly as it had been born. He had no left hand. The melted remains of his prosthesis smoldered, reduced to a blackened stub. The sensor-nerves of the device had been burned away. There was nothing left to transmit sensation to his brain.

The Kavinite's pistol swung toward Donalt. He did not wait for the second shot. He launched himself forward beneath the deadly muzzle.

His left shoulder screamed in protest when it struck the unyielding shell of yellow-enameled armor. The Kavinite staggered back under the weight of the unexpected impact. Donalt clung to the encased attacker, willing the armored man-machine to fall.

He did not. The Kavinite regained balance and swung an arm downward to brush away the psiotic like an annoying insect.

Releasing his hold on the intruder, Donalt dropped to the deck. The Kavinite's blow pounded uselessly into his own armored thigh.

Something large and metallic slammed to the deck beside the merger's head—the Kavinite's cutter, jarred from its holster by the invader's own blow.

Donalt rolled, grasped the tool's handle, and depressed a single black button inset in the hilt. The cutter hummed. The Kavinite pivoted surprisingly fast. The attacker's pistol once more swung toward Donalt.

The cutter's blade of amplified light danced out to slice. The Kavinite's gauntleted hand, still wrapped about the butt of the pistol, dropped to the deck.

Donalt drew the cutter upward in a looping backstroke. Its beam slashed the belly of the yellow suit. Solid metal ran molten; crimson seeped in a trickle from the smooth-edged rent. A scream resonated from the armor shell.

The Kavinite staggered back like a disjointed marionette blundering toward the hatchway. He did not reach his destination before collapsing face down on the deck. He lay there unmoving.

Donalt released the cutter's activation button. Its hum died. His eyes moved over the bodies of the two invaders.

A movement he caught with the corner of his eye drew him to Jenica. On hands and knees, the prescient searched beneath his desk, trying to retrieve his fallen pistol. He called to her.

Jenica glanced up, auburn hair in tangled disarray. Her gaze riveted on the fused stub of plaskin and metal at his left wrist. Questioning, she stared at him while she picked herself up off the deck.

"A prosthesis." He shrugged, unable to think of anything else to say. "The med-crew will have a hell of a time replacing it."

"It might have been a *real* hand." She moved to him and took his left arm and held it, trembling. Her words were taut and strained when she spoke again, as though she struggled to prevent herself from taking that last step into hysteria. "You could have been hurt! It looks bad. Should you be in the med-bay? Is there anything I can do? What is . . ."

Donalt's right arm encircled her and drew the prescient tightly to him. She had faced the enemy, met him without faltering. The crisis passed, the implications of what-might-have-been struck home. Before there had been no time for fear; now, in the aftermath, the terror and horror of the ordeal dilated with her expanded awareness.

"Shh." His palm stroked the back of her head, soothing. "It's over. I'm all right. It's—"

"It's not all right!" Her neck craned back so that she stared up at him. "You could have been killed! We both could have been killed!"

He leaned down and his lips lightly touched hers. Her arms slid around him as she pressed herself to him. The tenderness of their embrace mounted to a passionate grasping for reaffirmation that they still lived, that both had stared into the mocking face of death and survived.

Abruptly, Jenica's palms were flat against Donalt's chest. She shoved away. "No, Rad, no. It's wrong!"

The merger released her. Confused, he stared at her as she backed away from him. "Wrong? Is it still last night? Evora?"

"Yes . . . no . . . I don't know." Her head moved from side to side. "Rad, I just don't know. I want . . . I don't know what I want. It's happening too fast. It's all jumbled in my head."

"Jenica, I love you. *You!* Do you understand that?" He took her hand. She did not pull away.

"I want to believe that. I think I believe that, even knowing about Evora. And I lo . . . I want to love you. But I can't, not now. Not until I'm certain." Her eyes pleaded for him to understand. "I have to be certain. I have to be."

"And you're certain it is not Evora?" He tried to understand.

"No, I'm not. You can't expect me to accept what I saw last night with a snap of my fingers. To be in the arms of a man who claims to love me, then to learn that I'm a clone . . . a clone of the only woman he's loved . . ." She paused and took a deep breath. "Last night, I felt betrayed, used."

"I *loved* Evora. I *love* you. You saw that last night," he said, frustration welling within him.

"I saw. But you, the Psi Corps, had hidden Evora Garridan from me. What else are you hiding? Can I be certain you aren't holding something else from me?" The tone of her accusation revealed the depth of the pain that he had unwittingly caused. Yet, her hand squeezed tightly about his. Tears welled in her eyes. "Rad, I do love you. Something within me wants to share that love. But I can't. Now now. Not while . . ."

"Is there someone else?" He felt a fool asking that, like some third-rate actor in a poorly written holodrama. Yet, he had to know.

Her chest heaved and doubt furrowed her unlined brow.

Her lips parted as though to speak, then closed hesitantly. She glanced away from him. "I don't think you'll understand."

"Try me," he answered. "I want to understand."

Her eyes rose, hesitantly. "The starman."

"The starman? Your vision?" She was right; he didn't understand.

"You've felt him, the love he carries," Jenica continued. "You've felt that love reaching out to me. Since coming aboard the *Crispus Attucks,* the starman disappeared from my visions. Since Chenoa, since we have grown to know each other, he hasn't been there. I knew what I felt for you . . . sensed you felt the same thing. I thought . . ."

Her words trailed off, and her head turned from him. Donalt needed no further explanation. Jenica had carried the starman with her since her prescient ability's first manifestation. For five years, she had basked in the love that radiated from the vision of a man who flew on wings of fire. The love the mind-merger had sensed when the vision began, he realized, now had a source. It had flowed from Jenica, outward to greet the starman, to welcome him to her.

"I am not a vision." Donalt stared at her. "I'm a man. What I feel is real. It's now."

"I know . . . I know. What I feel for you is real. It *is*," Jenica said softly. "But what I feel for the starman is real. He's waiting somewhere in the future. I have to find him, Rad. Then, and only then, will I be certain. Can you understand?"

"Jenica, I don't . . ."

"My god!"

Donalt's head jerked to the hatchway. Michaela and Howin stood there, staring at the two dead Kavinites that blocked the entrance. They looked up at Jenica and Donalt. Michaela's gaze moved between the two psiotics.

"I was about to say you missed all the excitement," Howin said, "but I believe you've had more than your share."

"Excitement?" Donalt was uncertain what the receiver meant.

"The destroyer," Howin answered. "Moven just announced there will be commendations for our newest teammate. Seems Jenica told her how to shove several floaters down the destroyer's gullet."

Donalt turned to the holoscreen. The Kavinite destroyer was

gone. In its place floated an artificial asteroid of melted slag. Gone, too, were the Swarmers. It was over. While the *Crispus Attucks* had fought for its life, he had . . .

"We lost ten of our attack vessels. There's at least another ten dead or injured from the five Kavinites who breached the hull." Howin glanced at the two dead, armored figures on the floor. "The ship is now secure and repair crews have started patching her up again."

Michaela started to step over the bodies, then pulled back. "Moven wants us on the command deck. The Kavinites' *big* surprise is due to punch into normal space in the next . . . Rad! Your hand!"

"Merely an inconvenience." He held up the blackened stub. "I'll check into the med-bay for replacement as soon as we get a breather."

The wail of a general alarm reverberated through Psi Team Operations.

‹TEN›

The gargantuan sphere hung in space like a miniature planet of human-crafted metal. Its immensity crowded the command deck's holoscreen, dwarfing those who stared at the awesome sight conveyed by the *Crispus Attucks* optical scanners.

"Naval Command underestimated its size." Captain Vedis Moven glanced at the four psiotics she had summoned. "It's five kilometers in diameter."

Moven was Donalt's age, but she appeared ten years older. The Kavinite assault followed by *this* had tightened the features of her thin face. She stared up at the ship that had sat motionless since the *Crispus Attucks* had transmitted standard identification queries. The vessel had taken no hostile action, nor had it answered the queries. It just sat there twenty kilometers off the cruiser's prow.

"Preliminary sensor sequence shows no biological readings from the ship." Moven ran a hand through her short-cropped black hair.

She touched a turquoise button on the console before her. A three-dimensional Con-Web schematic blinked on a small monitor screen above her hand. "Here's what the scanners read so far. Very similar to our Mobile Naval Command Bases."

As his teammates crowded around him, Donalt watched the display peel back each of the vessel's inner levels. The size of the ship was mind-boggling. A new level, a sphere within a sphere, had been constructed every hundred or two hundred meters. The ship was more than a spacecraft. It was a world, worlds within worlds.

"Crew quarters, med-bays, galleys, command level, large

64

recreational areas . . . it's all there. And it's empty.'' Moven
looked at the holoscreen and ordered full telescopic magnifi-
cation from the optical scanners. "Then, there's this.''

Donalt followed the wild zoom toward the craft. The hull of
the gigantic ship appeared immaculate, unmarked by the normal wear and scarring common to all starships that had seen
more than a month's service. By surface indications, the vessel
had been recently commissioned.

The telescoping optics homed on what appeared to be identification markings stenciled on the polished metal hull. Donalt's companions chorused the merger's own sharp intake of
breath.

"It can't be." Jenica's head jerked to Moven. "We were
told it was a Kavinite ship!''

"Could be a ruse." Moven nodded. "It also could be why
it's just sitting there. We've located ten similar markings on its
hull.''

For the hundredth time in an equal number of seconds,
Donalt read the unmarred letters and numbers painted on the
spacecraft:

LOFGRIN ALLIANCE EXPLORATORY VESSEL
NX263Y

"There's no such vessel within our Con-Web reference
files.'' Moven ordered the optical scan to its former position.
"Our scanner and sensor readings are being fed back to
Chenoa. They're running a registry records check on NX-two-
six-three-Y.''

"Captain, bio readings.'' A lieutenant in a brown jumpsuit
looked up from the displays he monitored. "Two of them
within what appears to be a shuttle bay in the southern hemisphere.''

Jenica, Michaela, and Howin edged closer to the team
leader, necks craned for an unobstructed view of the screen
and its schematic display at Moven's fingertips. There was no
north or south in space, no up or down, no left or right. Direction was relative to the observer. For the convenience of its
human operators, the Con-Web labeled a point on the spherical vessel "north" and an opposite point "south.''

The screen winked. A localized schematic of the southern
hemisphere appeared. Outlined in red amid the ship's yellow

curves was the shuttle bay. Two pulsing plus signs beside each other marked the source of the sensor readings. HUMAN LIFE-FORMS: INACTIVE flashed across the bottom of the monitor.

Donalt smiled to himself. Unless the gargantuan ship carried an animal cargo, the identification message was not needed. Although humankind had encountered an exotic variety of lifeforms among the billions of stars within the Milky Way, it had yet to discover another sentient entity. No intelligent alien, hostile or friendly, had appeared to share the wonders of the galaxy, in spite of the years of countless speculations.

There had been hoaxes over the centuries. More than one had required Psi Corps involvement to uncover the sham. But the genuine article remained elusive. Scientists had long ago discounted the possibility of sentient contact within the Milky Way. Only philosophers and dreamers pondered the possibilities held within neighboring galaxies.

"Picked up another reading on NX-two-six-three-Y command level," the lieutenant in brown called to Moven.

The monitor screen blinked again to display one of the ship's innermost levels. A single plus sign blipped; HUMAN read the identification. Beside it was the designation ACTIVE.

"Someone's alive and moving in there," Moven said as though to herself. She called to her left, "Repeat full identification sequence and see what we get this time."

A young, red-headed woman turned to the captain and announced that Con-Web had interfaced with NX263Y's onboard logic system. The monitor at Moven's fingertips replaced the schematic with an analysis of the system it had discovered: CRYSTAL LATTICE COMPUTING AND ANALYTICAL MODULE.

Donalt heard a barely audible grunt of surprise from the cruiser's captain. He looked back to the holoscreen and the metal monster that filled the viewing area.

It made no sense for a ship as new as an NX263Y to be fitted with a system as outmoded as a Crystal Lattice C/A. The seminal Control Web Logic Systemry, with its integration of crystal molecular and biological memory, had replaced Crystal Lattice C/A two centuries ago.

Donalt looked back to Captain Moven. "Do you want a psi probe of the three humans aboard the ship?"

Moven sucked at her teeth. "Until I get clearance from

Chenoa, all I can do is sit here and keep an eye on NX-two-six-three-Y.''

"Chenoa can't be serious." Howin Bickle vocalized the disbelief on the faces of the psi team. "There must be a glitche in their memory retrieval system."

"It's been double-checked with Lanatia and they pulled hard copy on the ship—the original registry documentation." Captain Vedis Moven ran a hand through her black hair. "NX-two-six-three-Y is the *Seeker*."

The sudden appearance of a two-century-old exploratory vessel was incredible, in spite of Naval Command identification. Donalt scanned the Con-Web readout once more. He tried to dredge up vague history lectures from his early Psi Corps training.

The *Seeker* had been launched to explore a distant galaxy two hundred years ago. The ship and its two-thousand-person crew had never been heard from again.

The Con-Web identified the *Seeker* expedition as a LofAl Council endeavor under the direction of the Psi Corps. The mission's directives were to contact and formalize relations with an alien race, the Erna, in galaxy REV90732P.

Erna? Alien race?

Something niggled at the back of Donalt's brain but eluded his attempt to bring it forward. He read a footnote from Con-Web: ERNA—BELIEVED TO BE A SENTINENT LIFEFORM COMPOSED OF UNIDENTIFIED ENERGY. It also labeled REV90732P an echo galaxy, a radio phantom.

The readout disclosed that alleged alien contact had occurred on Earth and the planet Morasha. It had been made by Psi Corps field agents Caltha Renenet, a receiver, and Nils Kendler, a mind-merger. The alleged contact on Earth was a result of a LofAl time exploration effort known as Retrieve.

Donalt recalled a brief mention of Retrieve in his history classes. The program had been intended to reclaim humankind's homeworld after its destruction during the Holocaust of 2123 and the Global Wars that followed. Earth was to have been transformed into a planetary park divided into living sections showing stages of the planet's evolution.

LofAl Council interest in and funding for Retrieve eventually dwindled. Retrieve died from neglect, producing Earth's

second death. A third death came early in the present Kavinite–LofAl conflict. Kavinites established a galactic rim command base on the planet. The base operated for a standard
year before it was assaulted and destroyed by LofAl forces.
Thus the insanity continued, Donalt reflected bitterly.

He read that the legendary director of the Psi Corps, Kate
Dunbar, the woman who had developed the Corps into a full-
fledged, influential branch of the LofAl government, had
been responsible for the forty-year round-trip flight of the
Seeker. Dunbar, who held the Corps' helm for seventy-five
years, had died shortly after the launch of the *Seeker.* The
woman had been survived by a grandson and a daughter,
Caltha Renenet, the same Caltha Renenet, who, with Nils
Kendler, commanded the ill-fated mission of the *Seeker.*

The readout concluded with the information that, subse-
quent to Dunbar's death, the evidence of the Erna's existence
was reexamined by a LofAl Council board of inquiry. The Psi
Corps' evidence was determined to provide no valid conclu-
sions to have justified authorization of the exploratory mission. The board also intimated that the Erna were a Kavinite
hoax of undetermined nature.

Donalt's earlier elusive memory wiggled to the surface. The
board of inquiry had been one of the few political black eyes
ever given the Psi Corps. At the time it had been convened,
various branches of the LofAl had been embroiled in political
infighting for control of the LofAl Council. The board's finding subsequently limited the Psi Corps' influence for nearly
two decades.

"Our directives prohibit a psi probe of the *Seeker,*" Moven's voice intruded into the merger's reflections. "Chenoa's
been beaming everything we've sent directly to Lanatia. The
big boys at Naval Command are calling the shots now."

Moven turned from the psi team to glance at the giant vessel
filling the holoscreen. "Naval Command Lanatia is as skeptical of the *Seeker* as I am. It's just *too new.* However, Kavinite ruse or not, they want the ship boarded."

Looking back to the psiotics, she explained that the *Crispus
Attucks* would be brought within a hundred meters of the hull
of the *Seeker.* Four five-person teams would enter the ship
near the shuttle bay from which the two lifeform readings
originated. Level Three Mate Caron Watters would command
the teams.

"Your personnel, along with Watters, will compose the first of the four teams," Moven said to Donalt. "Lanatia wants you there to detect possible psi emanations."

The boarding presented unnecessary risks for the psiotics, who could perform the same task by probing the *Seeker* from Psi Team Operations. Moven's pained expression indicated she recognized this fact, but that the decision was out of her hands.

Donalt nodded. There was no fighting Lanatia.

"The other teams are waiting for you at airlock B-two," Moven said. "I'll have a crew ready to suit you when you get there."

◄ELEVEN►

One hundred meters across the infinitely yawning chasm of space, the airlock of the *Seeker* opened. An orange-suited figure exited where five had disappeared inside three minutes before. The figure waved; static popped within Donalt's helmet.

"The air's fresh and clean inside." An anonymous male voice spoke from the miniature speaker in the merger's helmet. "The lock can hold all of us. Team One first, then Three and Four."

A white-suited Caron Watters tapped Donalt on the shoulder and pointed toward the giant sphere. Attaching the spacesuit's left shoulder ring-clamp to a monofilament tether line that ran between the two ships, Donalt used his legs to shove into space. Momentum carried his weightless body along the line.

Ordinarily, a tunnel-corridor would have been extended between the ships to provide a sealed and secure passage. This boarding was anything but ordinary. Other than the three blinking plus signs on Con-Web's display screen, no one knew what awaited within the interior of the *Seeker*. Even with good air inside, the teams were under orders to remain fully suited.

An orange-clad arm reached out and wrapped around Donalt's midriff as he entered the spherical vessel's airlock, halting him enough for the soles of his static-grip boots to contact the deck. Donalt unsnapped from the tether and moved to the airlock's inner hatch to await his companions.

Ten minutes later, the outer doors closed to seal sixteen space-suited sardines in the airlock's cramped confines. Donalt heard the hiss of inrushing air that replaced the vacuum about him. A green light blinked overhead a moment before the lock's inner door slid open. Team Two's suit lights greeted him as he entered the *Seeker*.

"Somebody find some light." Caron Watter's voice crackled over the merger's helmet speaker.

Suit lamps marking their movements, the teams spread out along the nearest bulkhead to search for lighting controls.

"This could hold the *Crispus Attucks*." Jenica's voice now came from the speaker.

Donalt turned. She was behind him, her suit lamp beamed into the shuttle bay's interior. His own beam was lost in the darkness before it reached the bay's opposite wall.

"Rad," Michaela called to him. "There's something over there."

The receiver-sender stood to Donalt's left. He followed her light to what appeared to be a blunted snout of steel thrusting from the darkness. Donalt's beam cut beneath the metallic nose to find tripodial landing struts jutting from a shadowed belly.

"A ship," Jenica whispered the obvious.

Light, white and blinding, exploded around the psiotics. Donalt heard several gasps and felt his own body stiffen in anticipation of the worst.

"Wayne," Caron called to one of the team members, her voice a bit shaky, "next time, warn us before you hit the lights."

Donalt blinked, his eyes accustoming themselves to the transition from total blackness to harsh light. Then he comprehended the immensity of the bay. With a ceiling two hundred meters overhead, the bay stretched at least two kilometers beyond where the mind-merger stood. The interior bulkhead was two hundred meters to his right.

The machinery needed to service the shuttles *Seeker* once carried stood abandoned about the bay. Rows of work tables were neatly laid with tools for nonexistent hands.

"Son of a bitch." Donalt heard a woman mutter. The sounds of sucking breaths and surprised whistles chorused the remark.

"Rad, you better take a look at this." Michaela summoned him toward the rounded nose of the lone ship within the bay. "It's Kavinite . . . some type of scout ship."

Donalt and the rest of the boarders gathered about the shuttle-size craft. There was no mistaking the imperial rondelle stenciled to the ship's hull.

"Team Two, check the interior," Caron ordered. Five orange-suited figures opened a hatch beside a bubble turret on the scout's underside and disappeared within. "Teams Three and Four, follow your designated search patterns."

Donalt watched the two teams exit the bay. Jenica's face, distorted by the faceplates of their suits, caught his eye when he turned back to the Kavinite ship. She wore a pained expression. "Anything wrong?"

"The bay, it isn't right," she replied. "It's too clean . . . no grease . . . no dirt on the floor . . ."

She was right. The shuttle bay appeared as new and unused as the exterior of the *Seeker*. There was no trace of men ever having walked the deck. Apprehension played along his spine like an icy fingertip.

"There's a man and woman in the control bubble!" A voice crackled inside the merger's helmet. "They're out cold."

"Bring them out," Caron answered, relaying the discovery back to the *Crispus Attucks*.

"The Con-Web in here is dead, frozen solid. Even the clock is lock—" The voice on the speaker stopped abruptly. A curse followed. "If this clock is right, the Con-Web went down twenty-six days ago."

Donalt gazed at the Kavinite scout. Twenty-six days ago the *Seeker* had first been detected in the Arvis system.

Two orange-suited men dropped from the ship's belly hatch. Two limp bodies, clad in flight jumpsuits, were passed down and placed on the deck at Caron's feet.

"They've got pulses . . . barely. It's as though they're in chemo-sleep," one of the men said while Donalt read the names labeled to their jumpsuits—Kaveri and Loundon. "It would take chemo-sleep to keep them alive in there for over three weeks."

If the two had been within the ship for that long, Donalt thought. He looked at his teammates. "Anything from these two?"

"Nothing," both Michaela and Howin answered, indicating that neither the woman Kaveri nor the man Loundon were emanating psi energy.

"Matthews, Taylor, stay with these two," Caron said as the three remaining members of Team Two dropped from the scout. "The rest of us will proceed inward to the command deck."

And to the final plus sign—the one Con-Web designated "active,"—Donalt thought as he followed the Level Three Mate from the shuttle bay into a darkened tunnel-corridor.

Beams from eight suit lamps flashed into the various compartments the boarding party found open along the corridor. From their general appearance, the rooms were work areas of one type or another. As with the bay, none showed any trace of ever having contained a human being. The sounds of the *Seeker,* the internal mechanical operations that kept the vessel alive, echoed in the darkness.

A quarter of a kilometer from the bay, Caron located a dropshaft. One after another the eight boarders stepped in to drift down two levels before the shaft abruptly ended. Outside and a quarter of a kilometer through a second abandoned tunnel-corridor, the group entered another dropshaft that took them inward three levels before stopping.

After the fourth shaft transfer, Donalt realized the shortness of the tubes delineated the various spin sections of the *Seeker.* In flight, the various sections would rotate independently to create the centrifugal force needed for the illusion of gravity on each level.

The levels, tunnel-corridors, and compartments shared three similarities. They were dark, deserted, and *new*.

It was as though the eight members of the group had descended into the depths of an ancient tomb or had discovered a self-contained world whose population had abruptly vanished, leaving the material proof of their existence behind unmolested by the passage of two centuries.

One of the boarding party spoke. It was a whisper, spoken as though the sound of a voice would violate the emptiness, or would summon the shades of the two thousand crew members who had once inhabited *Seeker.*

In the flickering light, the merger saw the shadowed faces of his companions. The drawn tautness of their mouths, their wide eyes, the nervous movement of their heads were like mirrored images of his own visage.

Inward, ever inward, they went down level after level until they reached the tunnel-corridor that ringed the command deck of the *Seeker.* Caron Watters halted and waited until teams Three and Four reached the corridor. Then her hand touched a pressure plate that opened the command level hatch onto the brain of the *Seeker*. No one mentioned that this was the only closed hatch that they had found aboard the ship.

Donalt's gaze took in the array of multicolored lights that winked and glowed on the consoles of the ship's logic and computing unit. Monitors displayed various views of the *Crispus Attucks* hanging a hundred meters beyond the *Seeker*'s outer hull. Other screens were lighted with images of the boarding party. Optical scanners had apparently tracked their progress through the vessel.

Silhouetted against the dim glow of the consoles' light stood a lone figure—a man.

"Identify yourself." Caron Watter's voice shattered the silence.

Five members of the party leveled pistols at the unmoving shadow.

Lights flared overhead, flooding the command deck. Donalt blinked and squinted.

Tall and slim, the man stood there, his dark eyes calmly staring. The merger could not easily discern the features of his face; they were half hidden behind a thick shaggy shock of coal-black hair that covered his forehead, and an equally thick jet beard that bushed over cheeks and chin. Thirty to forty, Donalt estimated his age. He wore a tan jumpsuit that appeared as new as everything else on the ship.

"Identify yourself," Caron repeated.

"Nils Kendler, Psi Corps, co-captain of the Lofgrin Alliance Exploratory Vessel NX-two-six-three-Y, the *Seeker*," he answered in a deep, distinct voice.

Kendler?

Donalt's mind rejected the man's words. Kendler had been forty-six when the *Seeker* was launched. Despite the average human lifespan of one hundred thirty years, the man could not be alive. Not after two centuries.

"LofAl?" Caron asked skeptically. "Why were our identification queries ignored? Why is there a Kavinite scout ship in the shuttle bay?"

The man who claimed to be Nils Kendler stared at the officer. He offered no answer.

"Where the hell is the crew? Mister, you've got a shitload of explaining to do."

"Dunbar, Kate Dunbar," the man said with the same

unwavering resonance. "I will explain everything to Kate Dunbar."

"Dunbar? Is this guy serious, Grandpa?" Michaela stepped closer to Donalt. "Kate Dunbar has been dead for at least a hundred and seventy-five years!"

The mind-merger turned to answer the receiver-sender. His comment was left unspoken. He saw the expression on Jenica's face.

The prescient's eyes were locked on the man in the tan jumpsuit. Even behind the distortion of the helmets' faceplates, Donalt could see her face. It was . . . he could only think of a single word . . . ecstatic.

Donalt's eyes narrowed, shifting to the man who identified himself as Nils Kendler, then back to Jenica. He could almost feel—he shook his head, uncertain what it was he sensed.

"Kate Dunbar," the solitary survivor of the *Seeker* repeated. "I demand to be taken to Kate Dunbar."

‹TWELVE›

Donalt wiped a hand over his face. It did nothing to relieve his burning eyes nor ease the fatigue of thirty-six sleepless hours. His body ached and his thoughts came slow and fuzzy.

He stifled a yawn and stuck a brown-stained mug beneath the shining spout of a servo unit. The brown-black sludge that oozed from the unit tasted vile, bitter, and over-cooked. He slugged it down anyway; he needed caffeine, not taste.

"The son of a bitch looks as cool as Chenoa's polar ice-caps." Caron Watters' mouth twisted in disgust when she joined the merger at the servo. "You'd think that he'd just awakened from a week's sleep rather than being locked in here for sixteen hours."

Caron looked anything but fresh. The bruiselike circles beneath her eyes and the tangled disarray of black hair, a result of frustrated fingers repeatedly combed through the short strands, evidenced her bone-weariness.

Donalt tried not to picture his own appearance. The stubble on cheeks and chin, and a general grimy feeling, told him that he was long overdue a shower and a shave.

And eight hours undisturbed sleep.

"Any word on the two Kavinites?" Donalt turned back to study the man seated at the center of the small cabin.

No two-century-plus-old man had the right to look like that, the mind-merger thought, especially not after sixteen hours of interrogation by a four-person team. But Kendler—Donalt called him Kendler for lack of any other name—did.

With armed guards to each side, Kendler sat casually in the same chair he had occupied since Lanatia had given orders for him to be brought aboard the *Crispus Attucks.* Not even a trace of sweat ringed the armpits of his jumpsuit.

Nor had Kendler's expression altered during that time. If the calm, relaxed muscles of the man's face could be categorized as an expression. Only his dark eyes moved from one interrogator to the other.

Kendler steadfastly ignored questions pertaining to himself, the *Seeker,* its missing crew, the ship's mission, the alien race *Seeker* had been sent to contact, or the two Kavinites and their scout ship. Time and again, he repeated his demand to meet with the long-dead Kate Dunbar, assuring everyone all questions would be answered then.

"Did you say something?" Caron asked after a long sip from her own coffee.

"The Kavinites," Donalt answered. "Any word on them?"

"Nothing new." Caron took another sip. "Both are catatonic and dehydrated. The meds are pumping liquids into them intravenously. No indication of how or why they're in the state they're in."

To the left, the hatch to the cabin opened. A yeoman entered and crossed the room to Caron. Donalt saw two armed guards stationed in the tunnel-corridor. Beyond them Jenica leaned against the bulkhead.

He smiled, walked to the hatchway, poked his head out, and raised his eyebrows in question.

Jenica pushed from the bulkhead. "Just wondering if there was anything I could do for you, or get you?"

"You could get me a good night's sleep." Donalt grinned. "Other than that, they're fairly considerate of slaves on this galley. They feed us, water us, and occasionally allow us use of the toilet facilities."

"Are you sure there's nothing I can do?" Jenica moved to the hatch. "You've been in there a long time."

"At least three weeks." Donalt's grin faded when he noticed her peer into the compartment. A hint of a smile uplifted the corners of her mouth.

"Has he said anything more?" Jenica intensely studied the bearded man.

"He's as tight-lipped as he was when we found him."

Donalt found himself irritated by Jenica's obvious interest in Kendler. Doubly irritated at his own questioning of that interest. Everyone aboard the cruiser wanted to know about the man who had been resurrected after two centuries.

"Captain Moven's trying to get permission for a merge from—" Donalt began.

"Rad," Caron interrupted. "Moven wants us on the command deck as soon as possible. Some sort of briefing."

Donalt followed the officer through the hatchway. "Jenica, best get some sleep. Tell Michaela and Howin to do the same. Unless I miss my bet, sleep will be a rare commodity around here for the next few weeks."

Jenica smiled and nodded as Donalt started down the tunnel-corridor toward the command deck. When he reached a sharp bend in the corridor, Donalt glanced back at her. She stood at the hatch and stared in as it shut. He pushed the partially formed questions from his mind. He was too tired to even consider them now.

Lanatia, in two months. At the *Crispus Attucks*'s top speed, the journey would take a standard year. Few Chenoa-born had ever set foot on Lanatia. Contact between the two worlds was usually limited to tachyon communications.

Now, the cruiser's chief engineer, Cohid Adigun, proclaimed that a few modifications in the *Crispus Attucks* propulsion system would permit the ship to reach Lanatia in two months. The faster-than-light drive of the *Seeker* could be adapted to the *Crispus Attucks* system.

And Naval Command Lanatia had agreed to those modifications.

Donalt listened to Adigun and attempted to understand the "phase shift" in that, the "polarization" of this, the interface here, and the sync-mating there. It sounded like so much mishmashed engineering jargon. In the end, he accepted Adigun's assurance that the "slight modifications" would do what they were intended to do.

The question that seemed more important, which everyone gathered within the small conference room seemed to consciously overlook, was *who* had originally made the modifications aboard the *Seeker*. Donalt let the matter pass. He was too exhausted to throw a verbal monkey wrench into the engineer's newest toy.

". . . three days, four at the most," Adigun concluded, "and my crew can complete the modifications."

While the engineer assured Moven that the present interface between the cruiser's Con-Web and the Crystal Lattice C/A aboard the *Seeker* would allow David to control Goliath via remote control from the command deck of the *Crispus*

Attucks, Donalt's attention wandered. The twenty officers looked as haggard as he felt. At least his teammates were lost in sleep by now. If Jenica had conveyed his orders.

Jenica wedged herself into the forefront of Donalt's thoughts. He wanted to talk with her, needed to talk with her. Her revelation about the starman had cut the ground out from under him. But he could not press her and risk forcing her into a corner. That corner might exclude Radman Donalt.

The memory of the prescient's face when Kendler was discovered on the *Seeker* drifted across his mind's eye. What had he really seen there? Was it just the distortion of the faceplates?

Donalt pushed the unanswered question away in time to hear Moven and Adigun agree that a five-person team from the cruiser would be assigned to the *Seeker* during the journey to Lanatia "should unforeseeable difficulties arise."

Neither elaborated on those "difficulties."

Nusa Ir, chief of security, rose to assure the officers that the *Seeker* contained no "secret weapons," nor was it booby-trapped in any detectable manner. After he finished, the cruiser's communications officer rose, followed by Dr. Anthea Tegner. One by one the cautious officers stood to convey information they considered relevant to the *Seeker.*

Donalt listened and tried to place the fragments into a recognizable pattern. They would not fit. There was information, but no answers. Why were the Kavinites and their scout ship in the *Seeker*'s shuttle bay? And how and why did a two-hundred-year-old ship suddenly appear without one blemish to mark the passage of those centuries? Where was the crew? How could Nils Kendler still be alive?

And the Erna—did the alien race exist?

The answers lay within the head of Nils Kendler. And Kendler refused to talk to anyone except a woman who had been dead for a hundred and seventy-five years.

Donalt focused on the briefing again as Caron Watters briefly summarized their long hours of interrogation. ". . . he has been informed of Kate Dunbar's death. That has not deterred his insistence on meeting her."

"Hmmmm." Moven sank back in her chair. "It seems Kendler will get the chance to do just that when we arrive at Lanatia."

Donalt's head twisted toward the ship's captain. Had the

Psi Corps cloned the long-dead director as they had Evora?

"It seems this Kate Dunbar is still alive," Moven continued, "or, at least, her brain is . . ."

Donalt realized instantly what the captain was saying. From what he had read about the stiff-necked Corps director, it was something that she would have approved of, with or without prior consent. After the fact, it would not matter.

". . . prior to her death, Dunbar donated her brain to the Psi Corps' seminal Con-Web research," Moven explained. "With most planetary Control Web systems, the original systems are never eliminated, just modified, added to. In effect, Kate Dunbar never died. Lanatia reports she, her brain, has several hundred years of life left to her . . . it."

Kendler would have his meeting, Donalt thought. Then, perhaps, there would be the answers to the countless questions.

"Radman?" Moven nodded toward the psiotic.

It took a moment for Donalt to comprehend that the captain expected a report from him. "I have nothing to add to what Caron said. I do repeat the recommendation that my team be allowed to probe Kendler's mind."

"Lanatia has taken the request under advisement," Moven answered. "Considering the unusual circumstances, I believe you can understand the delay in making that decision."

Donalt did; a merge with a resisting host always carried the risk of insanity. However, if Kendler was who he claimed, a mind-merger himself, the merge . . .

A mind-merger himself—a thought intruded like a distant, half-formed shape. It wavered, no more than a phantom, then faded.

Donalt struggled to retrieve that fleeting thought before it slipped back into his subconscious. He cursed; it was gone, lost for the moment. Only the catatonic Kavinites Kaveri and Loundon remained adrift in the weary blur of his brain.

"Rad," Caron nudged his shoulder, "best get some sleep."

Donalt glanced up to find that Moven had dismissed the briefing. He nodded to the Level Three Mate. Kendler, the *Seeker,* the nagging questions, each breeding new questions, would have to wait. At the moment, all he wanted to think about was sleep.

‹THIRTEEN›

Donalt flexed the fingers of his left hand—his new left hand—new prosthetic left hand. Abnormally alert for aberrant sensation, he held it up, turned it over, stared intensely at its back, and flexed it again.

"You were damn lucky," said Anthea Tegner, the cruiser's chief physician, while Donalt swung his legs over the side of the med unit and sat on its edge. "There was no tissue damage, nor did the blast touch the neuro-bionic interface. It was a mechanic's job."

Plaskin sheathing microsensors, mini-servos, a skeleton of stainless steel—the device imitated the movement of musculature and bone. Except to a trained eye, the prosthesis—four fingers, an opposing thumb, palm, and heel—appeared to be Donalt's hand. Even the graft of new plaskin to old was imperceptible.

"Looks like the real thing." An approving smile moved over Donalt's lips. "Right down to the fingernails."

Tegner chuckled. "Only you never need manicure those."

Donalt grinned at the woman. He lowered the hand to his side. After a month without a prosthesis, the replacement felt heavy and obvious dangling there. "Any operating or maintenance instruction?"

"Don't go sticking it into any energy beams. Those things are a pain in the ass to replace." Tegner eyed her handiwork with satisfaction. "Now, if you'll get the hell out of here, I'll attend to five crew members who need to be administered aspirin."

Donalt raised his left hand, thumb and forefinger in a circle, and winked. He walked to the med-bay exit. "Thanks for giving me a hand, Doc."

With the physician moaning loudly behind him, the psiotic ducked into the tunnel-corridor outside. A blinking chronometer inset on the curved wall caught his attention. For a moment, he considered ignoring his daily visit with Kendler. Instead he proceeded to Level One of the *Crispus Attucks*.

Kendler's month-long reticence was a continual source of irritation. The man responded to neither direct interrogation nor casual conversation. He ate and slept within the confines of his guarded cabin, never offering more than his name and the repeated desire to speak with Kate Dunbar. Any time spent in the attempt to pry one further syllable from Kendler's lips was wasted.

Donalt shrugged. What else was there to waste while slicing across the galaxy in tachyon space?

Donalt greeted the two armed guards outside Kendler's cabin, then reached for the pressure plate. Before his fingers made contact, the hatch slid open. He stepped back to allow Jenica and Michaela to exit the room.

"Good afternoon." Donalt tipped an imaginary hat with his new left hand.

Neither of the women noticed. So much for his self-consciousness about the device.

Michaela gritted her teeth and shook in an exaggerated expression of anger. "That man! He just sits there . . . and gazes at you. He doesn't even stare!"

"Give him time." Jenica shot a reprimanding frown at her teammate. "He's as uncertain of us as we are of him. He'll talk with us eventually."

"I gather our friend displayed his normal cooperative attitude." Donalt noted Jenica's eyes rose to him for support, then dropped at his comment. A rootless twinge of guilt needle-pricked at him.

"Nothing! The same as every other day. . . ." Michaela shook herself again. "The bastard doesn't even make polite chitchat."

"How would you react if you were abruptly returned to humankind after two centuries?" Jenica's voice was tight and strained. "How would you feel if you were continually interrogated by people who are supposedly friends?"

Michaela's mouth twisted in disgust. "I think he burned out on his way back from wherever he's been."

"Or is maintaining a charade," Donalt suggested. He watched Jenica out of the corner of his eye.

She winced visibly at each of the remarks.

"I don't intend to give up. It's too important," Jenica said firmly. Her gaze shifted between her companions.

"No one's giving up. But I'd like to receive a 'good morning,' a 'nice day,' or a 'get fucked' for all my effort." The receiver-sender took a calming breath. "What I need is a cup of coffee, or perhaps something stronger. Join me?"

"I think I'll pass." Jenica looked at Donalt, then Michaela. "I've been doing research on Kendler and the *Seeker*. Maybe I can find something."

Every member of the psi team had been over the reports and personnel files Lanatia had relayed to the cruiser—at least a hundred times. They had provided nothing. Donalt could not understand Jenica's refusal to accept their uselessness. He watched her walk toward a dropshaft that would take her to Level Three and Psi Team Operations.

"How about you?" Michaela asked.

"I'll take a raincheck," Donalt replied to the coffee invitation. "How long was she with Kendler?"

Michaela shrugged. "She was in there before I arrived. I was with him for an hour."

Donalt frowned. Jenica's attempts to talk with Kendler were more frequent than even his own daily visits. Getting through to the man had become an obsession with the prescient. Was it another manifestation of her youthful insecurity? A task through which she could define her purpose aboard the cruiser?

"You know what bothers me about Kendler?" Michaela stepped across the tunnel-corridor and leaned against the bulkhead. "Neither Howin or I have received a hint of psi emanations from him. Even without being in alpha level, a receiver gets bleed-off flashes from people they're constantly around. It's especially intense with an active psiotic. Kendler's mind seems to be as closed as his lips."

"We need permission to probe his mind." Donalt leaned against the wall beside her. "Lanatia maintains a hands-off policy, despite my request to link with Kendler."

Michaela stared at the deck silently for several moments. "What about Jenica?"

"Jenica?" Donalt realized the receiver-sender had shifted in her train of thought.

"Jenica and you." Michaela eyed him questioningly. "You've lost your constant companion. You two have a fight?"

Donalt gave no answer; he had none. For the past month Jenica had avoided talking about "them" beyond admitting she accepted that his love was for her and not transferred feelings for Evora. She had asked for time, and he was giving her that. Their intimacies never exceeded an occasional meal together or a friendly stroll about the decks of the *Crispus Attucks.*

Should he maneuver their conversation from a neutral path, he would immediately sense tension in Jenica's voice. The three times he had ignored the limits that she placed on their behavior and pressed for answers, the results had been anger and frustration. Now, he just waited, allowing her the time to come to a decision.

"You're about as talkative today as Kendler." Michaela bit her lower lip when Donalt shrugged. She took his right hand and squeezed it. "If you ever feel the need to talk it over, you know where you can find a sympathetic ear."

Donalt grinned. "Won't give up playing the matchmaker?"

"Never," Michaela said. "Too few good men around to waste one."

Releasing her hand, he waved her away. "You've got your hands full with Howin. Grandpa Donalt can take care of himself."

"Sometimes I wonder if you can, Radman Donalt." Michaela's gaze homed in on the prosthesis. She smiled. "It looks good."

"Now I can wring Kendler's neck if he continues to be so cooperative." Donalt laughed as he stepped back to the hatch and pushed the pressure plate. "Later, Michaela."

"Later," the receiver-sender repeated when he stepped into Kendler's cabin.

The sole survivor of the *Seeker* mission lay on his back atop a standard bunk attached to the compartment's bulkhead. Kendler did not stir at Donalt's entrance.

"Good afternoon." Nor did the mind-merger's greeting bring a response.

"You're doing your best to drive away two very attractive women, Nils." Donalt seated himself in one of the cabin's four chairs. "I think common courtesy would warrant a 'hello' when they come to visit."

Kendler's eyes opened. His head rolled toward Donalt. "All your questions will be answered when I speak with Kate Dunbar."

"And your name is Nils Kendler." Donalt did not disguise his disgust.

"My name *is* Nils Kendler," the man echoed.

There was nothing else. Kendler popped back into the universe of the living after two centuries aboard a forgotten ship; his crew was missing; his wife and co-captain, Caltha Renenet, was gone; there was nothing else.

Donalt studied the man who gazed at him. A gaze—not a stare, he remembered Michaela's description. There was something missing from Kendler's facial features. Something he could only describe as expression.

Kendler's head rolled back. He gazed at the ceiling, then his eyes closed again. He lay there and ignored Donalt.

Donalt felt frustration well. The war continued in the galaxy beyond tachyon space, and he was here attempting to make small talk with a man who couldn't care less that he was in the room.

What answers were locked away in Kendler's head? Donalt bit at his lower lip. The propulsion system aboard the *Seeker*, outstripping anything held by the Kavinite Empire or the Lofgrin Alliance, would undoubtedly provide LofAl Naval Command with an unexpected military advantage. It would hasten an end to the fighting, something Donalt had attempted, with no success, for twenty-two years of his life. Now it seemed so close, yet locked behind a transparent barrier beyond the touch of his fingertips.

That barrier was the man who claimed to be Nils Kendler. What other secrets did he hide? What other technological advances were contained in his brain?

What was the source of those advances? The Erna?

The existence of an alien race remained the province of philosophers and dreamers. It was too much for Donalt.

However, the original crew of the *Seeker* might have colonized a planet in the REV90732P galaxy. The reports from Lanatia said the crew, even the fifth-grade grease monkeys, were selected for intelligence and latent psi ability. Such a concentration of human potential might produce anything—everything—when their efforts weren't directed at the destruction of humanity.

Donalt stared at Kendler again. Was his mind playing games? Or was the possibility real? Could Kendler's brain hold such secrets?

Would anyone ever know?

There is a way. . . .

An uneasy tremble worked up Donalt's spine as he allowed his mind to reach the conclusion it had been laboring toward for days.

There is a way.

He refused to consider the possible consequences for himself, were he to fail . . . or if his actions were discovered. The consequences did not matter. Kendler's mind had to be unlocked. There was only one person aboard the *Crispus Attucks* who could do that.

Donalt inhaled a deep breath to steady himself and sank back into his chair. He had never before totally disregarded orders. This time he had to.

He closed his eyes. The tension lingered endlessly, refusing him access to the psi streams of his mind. Methodically, like some metaphysical guru slipping into a meditation, he concentrated on the rhythm of his breathing. He focused the flow of air that entered his body.

Inhale through the nostrils—deeply into the lungs—exhale through the mouth—empty the lungs. Inhale—exhale—inhale—exhale—inhale—exhale . . .

Gradually, the lulling monotony unclasped the taut fingers that bound his muscles.

Donalt relaxed, closed his sensory input, and drifted into alpha level. He focused the random psi streams and reached out to the mind of Nils Kendler.

Nothing!

Donalt retreated, shocked by the lack of contact. He gathered himself and probed again.

Nothing.

No!

He felt something—an insubstantial illusion of nothingness.

On the surface the deception intended to prevent his merge was perfect. It was the nothingness of a blank, that one-in-a-billion freak of nature whose mutated genes left him devoid of any psi channels within his brain. A vague, undefined hint of psi emanation underlay the illusion.

Donalt extended a weaving feeler through the nothingness in search of the source that molded the illusion. Blind within the void, without mental references to guide his path, Donalt delved.

Mocking amusement.

He sensed it about him. The emptiness dissipated.

Pain!

Donalt slammed head-on into a wall. Pain lanced through his awareness. He recoiled from the solid barrier that rose before him.

The pain vanished the instant contact was broken. What had he touched? He had never encountered such a mental defense within the human mind. The pain, what had caused it?

Donalt stubbornly refused to abandon the attempt to link with Kendler's consciousness. He reached out for a third time, his mental probe no more than a silken thread adrift on a gentle breeze.

Agony sizzled through his head when he brushed the invisible barrier surrounding Kendler's mind. Donalt jerked away, reeling from the intense pain.

Again all sensation disappeared when contact was broken. Donalt immediately rammed forward in a concentrated effort to shatter the wall of resistance.

Pain like molten metal rained through his consciousness. He withdrew and threw himself forward, again, again, in search of one small chink, a solitary, vulnerable niche in Kendler's armor of indefensible pain.

There was no chink, no niche. Only the burning agony.

Defeated, his senses frayed from the unrelenting assault, Donalt pulled back into himself and sank from alpha level.

He opened his eyes.

Across the cabin, Kendler lay flat on his back, eyes still closed as though in sleep. The man had not stirred. He displayed no hint that they had met and fought. He gave no indication that he had totally defeated Donalt.

Body shaking, legs threatening to fold beneath him, Donalt

pushed from the chair. He staggered to the hatch and leaned against the bulkhead. His head throbbed in pulsing reminiscence of the pain imparted by Kendler's defensive barrier. What had he encountered? What other psi abilities did the man control?

Donalt opened the hatch and exited the compartment. Only when he reached his own cabin on Level Three did he allow the frightened weakness to return to quake within his body.

‹FOURTEEN›

The ghosts filed by in an unending procession. Their faces, devoid of all expression, belied the jeers that contemptuously writhed from unmoving lips. They mocked Donalt with the continuous repetition of their names. A mere murmur at first, their phantasmic voices mounted to an incomprehensible roar that rumbled the foundations of his soul.

Donalt attempted to turn from them. There was no escape. They surrounded him, pressed closer, demanded the reason for their deaths. The reason for his life.

He felt their cold breath on his flesh as icy as death itself. It swirled to engulf him, intent on drawing life from his body—life that would give the legions rebirth. He welcomed the vampiric breath. He willingly surrendered himself to the shades.

They vanished.

One moment they drank his very life. Then in his acceptance of their hunger, they rejected him.

Michaela stood before him now, blond hair softly tucked about her implike face. With an arm locked about the receiver-sender's waist, Howin stood at Michaela's side. A stride behind them was Jenica.

"Meat for the grinder?" Their voices came as one, a whisper that was an offering of their lives rather than a question.

"No . . . no." He extended his arms to gather them to him, to shield them.

Vanished.

Only taunting laughter echoed around him.

A whine, undulating, persistent, rent the vision. Darkness spewed from the torn fabric like blood gushing from an open wound.

Donalt cried out; he ran before the onrush of black ink that sought to drown him.

The whine shrilled as it rose through the octaves.

Donalt awoke to find himself sitting upright in his bunk. Sweat, clammy and oily, rolled from his naked body. He groaned trying to shed the remnants of the dream.

The whine, diminished to an annoying buzz, continued.

He blinked, forced his eyes to see beyond the film of sleep clouding them, and then reached out to depress the intercom switch on the bulkhead beside the bed.

"Donalt here," he mumbled.

"Rad, it's Moven," the voice of the cruiser's captain answered. "Doctor Tegner needs your team in the med-bay immediately. The Kavinites have come out of their comas."

"Tegner, med-bay, Kavinites." Donalt's sleep-blurred brain accepted fragments of what Moven had said.

"I want a full team probe of these two, Rad," Moven said. "You've got an hour, maybe ninety minutes before Tegner will file an official report with Lanatia. I want that probe completed before Naval Command has the opportunity to answer."

"Understood!" Donalt switched off the intercom. He swung from the sweat-drenched bunk with a wide smile on his face.

Moven was sticking her neck out. She wanted the probe before Lanatia had the chance to deny them the opportunity of searching Kaveri and Loundon's minds.

He had told Moven of his attempt to merge with Kendler three weeks ago, and she had remained silent about the incident. Now she was giving him a chance to redeem himself. With luck, at least the question of what two Kavinites and their scout ship was doing aboard the *Seeker* would be answered.

Donalt stretched across the bunk to reactivate the intercom and awaken the rest of the team.

"They're through that door." Anthea Tegner pointed to a hatch at the end of the med-bay. The single word ISOLATION was stenciled in black on its white surface.

"Two nurses are with them at the moment. I had to place the patients under sedation. They were like madmen, trying to climb the walls," Tegner added, her brow furrowing.

"The nurses?" Donalt asked.

"If the patients are immobile, you can tell them to leave," Tegner replied. "Say I want to see them in my office, if you need an excuse."

"Aren't you going to be present during the probe?" Donalt glanced questioningly at the physician.

"What probe?" Tegner said simply. "What I don't see, I can't report. As far as I know, you four are here simply to observe the patients."

"We'll keep the nurses if you don't mind. I don't think any of us would care to be in alpha state with wild men loose." Howin placed his hand on the small of Michaela's back and steered her toward the white hatch.

"Might be best," Tegner agreed.

Donalt nodded his thanks and turned with Jenica to follow their teammates past the two armed guards into the isolation room. The two nurses, one for each patient, stood by the Kavinites' beds, spoon-feeding them what appeared to be warm cereal.

A cold finger tapped at the base of Donalt's spine. Kaveri and Loundon accepted the food mindlessly, unaware of the portion that dribbled from the corners of their mouths. Their eyes stared blankly ahead of them, unfocused.

"These two don't have all their oars in the water," Michaela whispered to Donalt. "Tegner must have them doped to the gills."

Donalt made no comment, but silently agreed. Neither Kaveri nor Loundon appeared to be aware of anything other than the cereal being shoveled into their half-open mouths.

The merger motioned to four chairs placed in one corner of the room.

"Michaela, Howin," he directed as the team seated itself, "key on Kaveri first, then move to Loundon."

The two closed their eyes immediately to begin the transition to alpha level. Donalt looked at Jenica. "Just drift in alpha state. I don't know if anything will come of this, but something might spark. At the moment, *anything* is more than we have."

Jenica smiled. "Understood."

Donalt watched her prepare herself. He repressed the urge to reach out and take her in his arms. This was neither the time nor place to interject personal feelings. Though with Jenica there never seemed to be an appropriate time for anything beyond the friendly formality that had existed since their one night together.

Donalt closed his own eyes and rapidly achieved alpha level. He reached out. There was no resistance as he flowed into Kaveri's mind. The woman's senses opened to him.

He shuddered inwardly. Taste dominated the Kavinite officer's sensations. That taste was oatmeal. Donalt shuddered again. The cereal was one of the few foods he could not tolerate. He excluded the sensory input of the woman's mouth and nose.

The psiotic moved inward to weave himself along the pathways of the woman's consciousness, then opened himself to her.

Chaos engulfed him. A swirling maelstrom of insanity sucked at him and dragged him downward. Donalt offered no resistance, but blended with it, accepting the whirling madness.

Simultaneously, he shielded a seed of the identity that was Radman Donalt at the core of his awareness. To have struggled against the raging incoherence that filled Kaveri's consciousness would have unraveled the threads of his sanity and left him stranded within the Kavinite's fragmented personality.

Images, in a blurred procession, raced before Kaveri's mind's eye—a child. *Hers?* It came and disappeared too quickly to be grasped. A LofAl cruiser exploded—lips hovered close—the lid of a casket closed—a sunflower blew in a gentle breeze—a hand closed upon a breast—a woman laughed—a man cried—crowds pushed into a—the sharp dogleg of a tunnel-corridor.

Ceaselessly the barrage of unrelated images flashed like a kaleidoscope, shifting, bending, blending into one another. There was no logic, no rationale, only a mind gone mad, a jumble of disoriented pieces in a puzzle that would never fit together.

Donalt focused his consciousness on the seed of identity he harbored and shut out the visual bombardment before he withdrew from Kaveri's mind. For some moments, the merger drifted within his own mind to allow himself time to shed the sensation left in the wake of the contact. He stabilized the reality of his own ego, then reached out again.

The barest contact with the sergeant's mind was all he needed to confirm it lay in the same shambles as Kaveri's consciousness. Loundon's mind contained a flashing parade of images that were strung together without logic or reason. Insanity was its own self-defining logic.

Deeper, Donalt probed in search of the source of the man's madness. There was no beginning, no ending. The insanity was continuous loops within loops within loops that fed and generated on themselves. Time and again, he entered Loundon's consciousness only to be deluged with the shattered reflections of the Kavinite's brain.

Each attempt to locate the reason for the man's madness frustrated, Donalt accepted his inability to unlock Loundon's mind. He withdrew. Once more he allowed himself the time needed to gather his own sanity and re-exert control of his body and senses. He drew a deep breath and opened his eyes.

Michaela and Howin sat beside him. Their expressions revealed the fruitlessness of their probes. Michaela shrugged as though saying "sorry." Donalt sucked at his teeth and shook his head. He turned to Jenica.

The prescient's cheeks reddened; she glanced toward the deck. "The starman . . . I saw the starman. He came close, closer than . . ."

Donalt tuned out her voice. The last thing he wanted to hear about now was Jenica's recurring vision, his intangible competition for her love.

In their beds, Kaveri and Loundon accepted spoonful after spoonful of oatmeal. Donalt stood with disgust and walked to the Isolation Room's hatch. Moven had to be told she had placed her neck on the block for absolutely nothing.

◀FIFTEEN▶

Donalt's gaze wandered around the oval-shaped conference table, resting for a moment on each of the ten men and women, as he paused to let his comments penetrate. They were top brass from the LofAl Council, Naval Command, and the Psi Corps. The air was rarified where he stood now, but that did not alter what he had told them. During the past month on Lanatia, he and a team of two other mind-mergers had made daily attempts to penetrate the barrier surrounding the mind of Nils Kendler. The results had been exactly those achieved during his clandestine attempt aboard the *Crispus Attucks*— nothing.

"Kendler possesses a mental defense system that is impenetrable. And even knowing its effects, we have been unable to duplicate it."

"Recommendations?" The question came from Arland Loma, director of Psi Corps Lanatia. This was only the second time Donalt had seen the man since the *Crispus Attucks*'s arrival at the Lofgrin Alliance's capital planet.

"Allow Kendler access to Con-Web and Kate Dunbar," Donalt replied. "There's no other option available. That is, if we intend to unlock the man's mind."

Donalt was the fifth team leader that morning to advise the gathered heads of state to proceed with the Kendler–Dunbar meeting. For the past month Kendler had successfully fended off every attempt Psi Corps and Naval Command had made to breach the mental barrier surrounding his mind. Drugs, hypnosis, chemo-hypnosis, psiotics, electronic brain probes—all had failed. Kendler would not break, or even crack. He simply sat and gazed, not stared, about him, accepting everything that happened as though he were disassociated from it.

"Thank you . . . uh . . . Radman." Loma dismissed the merger while glancing at a piece of paper before him on the table. "Our last report is from Dr. Simuel Iacuzzi, who heads the Biological Investigation team."

While Donalt returned to his chair at the back wall of the conference room, Iacuzzi rose and stood at the head of the table. The man dropped a bound report eight centimeters thick atop the table. The heavy cracking sound brought up every head in the room.

"There are copies of this report for everyone present. Your staffs can dissect it at their convenience," Iacuzzi began. "I see no reason to subject you to the boring results of countless urine analyses, brain scans, EKGs, muscle-eye coordination tests, stool analyses, and a barrage of other tests that have been repeated time and again for a month."

The man paused to give his audience the opportunity to object. None did.

"The final line is, this man is Nils Kendler. Retina prints, voice prints, fingerprints, DNA patterns, et cetera, et cetera, et cetera, are those of the Nils Kendler whose personnel file may be found within the Psi Corps Con-Web."

Iacuzzi paused again for questions. "Extending an individual's life for two hundred and fifty-six years is presently medically impossible. Yet, if we are to accept that this is Nils Kendler, we also have to accept his age."

The biologist continued with the suggestion that two possible explanations might account for the age discrepancy. The first was some Einsteinian warping of time and space in which Kendler's age was relative to the observer. The second was the possibility that this was a clone of the original Nils Kendler.

"The first possibility was not within the parameters of my team's investigation and has already been rejected during Dr. Peterson's report. So has the clone possibility."

"Are you telling us this *is* the Nils Kendler who headed the *Seeker* expedition?" a woman who carried the rank of admiral on her sleeves and shoulders asked. Donalt had never seen her before.

"Down to the minutest physical description in Kendler's file, including a millimeter scar on his left upper eyelid. A minor injury Kendler sustained during the construction of the *Seeker*," Iacuzzi replied. "There is one major exception, however. This man's body apparently absorbs Kirlian energy rather than radiates it."

"Kirlian energy?" Belva Julian, chairperson of the LofAl Council, asked the obvious question.

Iacuzzi held up his hands. "Kirlian energy lies in the area of the metaphysical as far as I'm concerned. Dr. Kote will give you an overview on the subject. My team concerned itself only with the physical identity of Nils Kendler."

"Wasn't this Kirlian energy supposedly the source of life for the alien creatures the *Seeker* expedition was to have contacted?" asked Director Loma.

"I yield the floor to Dr. Kote." Iacuzzi stepped back to his seat to allow a small, bald-headed man to stand before the conference table.

Donalt smiled. The *Seeker* and the Erna were still sore spots within governmental circles, even after two hundred years. The expensive blunder was a stigma with which no one wanted to be branded.

"Perhaps . . . I can . . . shed some light on Kirlian energy." Kote appeared no more eager to discuss the subject than did Iacuzzi. "No one is exactly certain what this energy is, though it can be photographed under laboratory conditions as an 'aura' that surrounds all lifeforms."

Kote explained that Kirlian force had been a popular concept with many mystical movements throughout humankind's history. It had been called by various names—odie force, bioplasmic energy, life energy, prana, mana, magnale, n-rays, animal magnetism, psychotronic energy, bioenergy, chi, toliner force, atta.

Donalt listened while Kote reeled off the seemingly endless list of names. He saw no value in the recitation.

"During several periods, science has seriously explored the significance of Kirlian force." Kote paused to nervously clear his throat. "The most recent period preceded the launch of the *Seeker*. It was a direct result of an assignment on which Nils Kendler and his wife Caltha Renenet were involved. At that time, it was discovered that pyramidal constructions conforming to the proportions of an ancient Terran pyramid named *Giza* produced Kirlian energy that corresponded to certain psi wavelengths."

Donalt's head came up, as did every other head in the room. Kote stammered, apparently taken back by the unexpected interest in his report.

The man outlined a research program instigated by former

Psi Corps Director Kate Dunbar that was intended to develop a psi generator or psi enhancer. No conclusive results were achieved; the project was canceled after Dunbar's death.

"This Giza pyramid, Kirlian energy, and the Erna . . . what's their relationship?" Chairperson Julian asked.

Donalt could feel Dr. Kote's internal squirming as the Erna was brought back into the discussion. The man tugged at the high collar of the coat he wore. He cleared his throat again.

"According to Con-Web memory files, the Erna, a term used to describe both the race and an individual, was a pure energy entity. This creature was alleged to have existed both on Terra and on the planet Morasha. The latter was destroyed in a nova about the time of the Psi Corps' renewed interest in Kirlian energy. Allegedly, the Erna dwelled within a pyramid on both planets. The pyramids generated the Kirlian energy required for the alien's existence," Kote explained.

The "allegeds" continued, Donalt noted. Kote had no desire to be associated with the Erna. It was humorous, but of little import. The relationship of Kirlian energy and psi was!

If they were indeed the same wavelengths, and if Kendler was capable of absorbing Kirlian energy, Kendler might have gained the capability of boosting his natural psi ability via Kirlian energy, thus successfully blocking the attempts to probe his mind.

When asked for their recommendations on the Kendler-Dunbar meeting, Iacuzzi offered no objections. Kote straddled the fence and presented no opinion at all.

"Director Loma." The woman with all the naval braid turned to the Psi Corps Director. "I'm not certain I understand the purpose of Dr. Kote's report. Is the Psi Corps suggesting a connection between the man Kendler and the existence of the Erna? If so, may I remind you that the Erna was declared a hoax."

Loma shook his head and smiled. "I had Dr. Kote prepare a report to provide us with a bit of background, to point out some correlations that exist between the situation two centuries ago and now."

"I believe we have drifted from our purpose in being here," said Belva Julian. "That is, do we allow Kendler access to the Kate Dunbar mode of Con-Web?"

"Agreed," Loma conceded. "Based on the recommendations of our advisory staff, I cast my vote in favor of access."

One by one, the vote continued around the table with each of the participants elaborating on the reasons for his or her decision, pro or con. Donalt kept a mental tally of the vote. Belva Julian completed the circuit with her final comments and "aye," granting access by an eight to ten vote.

"In two days, then, Nils Kendler will have his meeting with Kate Dunbar." Julian rose then turned to Psi Corps Director Loma. "Are facilities available for this committee to view that meeting?"

"I'll arrange for audio-visual sensors to be placed within the room where Kendler will be," Loma assured the head of the LofAl council.

Filled with a sense of relief, Donalt stood and waited while the others exited. Two days, and if Kendler had been telling the truth for the past months, the questions about the *Seeker* and its crew would finally be answered. And . . .

The Erna?

His skepticism about the existence of a sentient alien culture had not lessened.

The minor logjam at the door to the conference room thinned. Donalt glanced around and found a chronometer on the wall: noon. He had two full days until the Kendler-Dunbar meeting. He smiled as he left the room. He was not certain what Lanatia offered in the way of recreation, but it was bound to be superior to confinement in Psi Corps Headquarters.

"Rad," Jenica called to him. "Rad."

Donalt turned. He grinned, perhaps too widely, too eagerly, when he found her standing down the corridor. In his month of Psi Corps' imposed separation from his team, Jenica had grown even more beautiful to his eyes. He felt his pulse increase like a grammar school adolescent's.

"Jenica!" Without realizing what he did, Donalt moved down the hall and greeted her with a joyous hug. To his surprise, she returned the gesture and lightly kissed his lips.

"Damn, but it's good to see you. Can I interest you in lunch? How's Michaela and Howin? I've wanted to check in on you three, but Psi Corps has demanded twenty-four standard hours a day from me."

"Answer to question two, Michaela and Howin are fine. And, yes, lunch sounds great, as long as it's not in the commissary. There's a restaurant fifteen minutes on the slidewalk from here—a real restaurant, human cooks and waiters, no servos,'' she said. ''And I'll even allow you to pick up the tab.''

Arm about her waist, still no objection from Jenica, Donalt escorted her to the nearest dropshaft. Perhaps the month's separation had given her the time she needed for her decision, Donalt speculated. Was that why she had come? To tell him she had missed him as much as he had missed her? His pulse doubled its tempo. He tried to calm himself and not read his own desires into Jenica's unexpected appearance.

It did not help. When the Psi Corps directive had arrived, placing him in a four-person merger team assigned to the Kendler investigation, he had quietly hoped the imposed distance from Jenica would prove that his feelings were merely the infatuation of an older man for a younger woman.

Now that he saw and touched her, he realized the opposite was true. If it were possible, he loved her more.

They took the slidewalk outside Psi Corps Headquarters to Jenica's suggested restaurant and ordered their meal. The prescient gave him a thumbnail sketch of the rigors of Psi Corps training the majority of the *Crispus Attucks* psi team had been put through. For the most part, the courses had been reorientation programs for field agents, and a total waste of time as far as Donalt could judge.

''There are some new ideas and theories on prescience interpretation,'' Jenica said while they waited for their meal. ''We made copious notes for our team leader to study when he finally gets back to us.''

Donalt chuckled. ''Sounds like Grandpa Donalt has a month's catching up to do.''

''Do you have to call yourself that?'' Jenica gave him a disapproving frown. ''It's bad enough that you let Michaela and Howin do it. I've never thought of you being any older than the rest of us.''

''No more Grandpa,'' he said, tilting his head in acceptance. Maybe he was being oversensitive about the difference in their ages. Apparently, Jenica did not care. Or was he once again trying to read something into what she said?

''Good.'' A smile brightened the beauty of her face. ''Now for the real reason I'm here. I've managed to wiggle a bit of information out of Psi Corps . . . that you've got a couple of days off.''

Donalt nodded, again trying not to anticipate or hope.
"Well deserved, if I do say so myself."

"Those two days just happen to correspond, thanks to some
conniving on the part of three psiotics you know and love, to
two days they have off." Jenica's smile widened impishly. "I
am here to invite you to spend those days at a nearby mountain lake resort with your old teammates."

Jenica hastily enumerated the various recreational facilities
available at the resort, ranging from floater skiing to swimming in a hot spring-fed lake.

"We've already made reservations for the four of us.
Though Michaela and Howin have asked me to apologize in
advance if you don't see much of them. The corps have kept
them separated in sexually segregated dormitories for the last
month."

"Which will leave you and me." Donalt emphasized his
comment.

Jenica's expression remained unchanged. Donalt ignored
the momentary sinking sensation in his stomach. No matter
what else, the next two days would give them the opportunity
to talk.

A waiter with a tray balanced in one hand interrupted the
conversation to serve their meal. After that, Jenica returned to
discussing the training sessions.

Donalt considered maneuvering toward a discussion of
Jenica Stoy and Radman Donalt, but discarded the idea. The
timing was wrong. Later, at the resort when they were alone,
would be far better.

"Atop everything that Psi Corps has been running us
through, we've felt cut off from what's really going on,"
Jenica said while she sliced a thick steak that the menu proclaimed was raised on the hoof rather than coming from a
recombinant DNA culture tank. "Since planetfall, no one will
tell us what's going on with Kendler. It's as though we're supposed to forget something that we've been involved with for
months of our lives."

"It hasn't been much better at headquarters." Donalt swallowed his first bite of meat. If the steak were cut from a real
side of beef, he could not tell the difference. "Everything has
been on a need-to-know basis. Except for what I've been per-
sonally involved with, I have no idea what is going on."

He could not tell her about the morning's meeting. The

"need to know" had not been extended to anyone outside that conference room, and would not be until the powers-that-be declared it so.

"But you have seen him, haven't you?" Jenica stared expectantly across the table.

"Huh? Seen who?" Donalt deferred a raised forkful of baked potato dripping with sour cream.

"Kendler," Jenica said, her own meal forgotten for the moment. "You've seen him, haven't you?"

"Yes. I've seen him more than I really want to, at least twice a day." Donalt studied the furrows creasing Jenica's brow, deeper than normal curiosity would warrant. Or were they? Was he so insecure with her that even a mention of Kendler posed a threat to him?

"Then, he's all right?"

"Medically, as far as anyone can tell, he's perfectly healthy," Donalt replied. The steak was suddenly tasteless and tough. "There has been no change in him since coming to Lanatia. He just sits there and accepts everything around him without a word."

"Have they decided to allow him access to Kate Dun . . . the Con-Web?" she continued.

"I'm really in no position to say," Donalt lied. "Like I said, everything pertaining to Kendler is hush-hush."

Jenica glanced away. A distant expression transformed her face to a mask Donalt could not read. When her attention returned to the meal, she lifted a fork and aimlessly poked it at her baked potato.

Donalt asked for more details on the mountain resort. She began to list the other facilities that would be available to them for the next two days. Her earlier enthusiasm was missing.

Her mood had totally reversed itself without warning.

When they finished and left the restaurant to meet Michaela and Howin at a skimmer rental agency, Jenica remained within the shadow of whatever was occupying her mind.

Donalt's earlier optimism vanished. What had he said to cause the abrupt shift? He could not recall anything. However, he could not escape the feeling of dread that seeped into his chest. These next two days were not going to be what he expected or what he wanted.

‹SIXTEEN›

Donalt waved as the skimmer rose. Its three occupants waved back for a brief moment, then turned their attention to the sky. Donalt watched the aircraft move toward the west, feeling abandoned and lost.

In spite of everything that had been said, or left unsaid, for two days between Jenica and himself, the psiotic had not realized how much he actually missed the members of his team. Now that they were gone again, he could sense a bout of loneliness that would be in full swing by the evening.

He turned from the departing skimmer and walked toward the entrance to Psi Corps Headquarters. The far-too-short vacation had been worse than he had imagined. To be sure, all the recreational facilities Jenica had promised had been available. But they seemed of little consequence then or now.

He had hoped the time together would clear the air between Jenica and himself. It had not. The situation, his emotions, and apparently Jenica's, were just as muddled as they had been aboard the *Crispus Attucks*. Again and again the opportunity to talk had presented itself. Jenica repeatedly dodged any attempt to broach the subject of their love.

Last night, while Jenica and he had lounged beside an indoor swimming pool, he finally pressed her for some indication of what she felt. Once again, she asked for time.

"I do love you, Rad. Please believe that. But I'm uncertain that it's right. I need time until . . ."

Until what, she never said. Nor would she elaborate. The old frustrations, the fears of total rejection had risen, and Donalt had backed off. Two days that had started so promisingly now left him hollow and depressed.

102

Inside headquarters, Donalt stepped into a dropshaft that took him to the tenth floor. A "yes" or a "no" from Jenica was all he wanted. The indecision held him suspended on a frayed thread between heaven and hell. The next time they were alone, he would demand an answer, something solid he could grasp.

Donalt entered the conference room and took his designated chair along the wall. While he watched the committee and members of the advisory staff enter, he admitted his false mental bravado. He was not willing to force the issue with Jenica. It was easier to wait. Waiting, at least, held hope.

The last committee member took his seat, and portable holographic and audio equipment was wheeled into the room. A few moments later, the equipment was switched on, and a one-to-one scale image of the small room in which Kendler would confront Kate Dunbar appeared at the far end of the conference room.

Except for a single chair, the holographic room was empty. That chair faced a wall lined with row atop row of Con-Web components. A lone optical sensor, black and lifeless, provided cyclopean sight for the cybernetic logic and computing system.

The lights in the conference room lowered when a dark blob blurred the foreground of the hologram. The image focused. Kendler, escorted by an armed guard on each side, entered, and took the chair to face the optical sensor. The angle of the holographic image shifted so that those in the conference room viewed the sole survivor of the *Seeker* from the side. The guards left and closed the door behind them.

"As Kendler requested," Psi Corps Director Loma's voice came from across the conference room, "he is alone with Kate Dunbar."

Donalt, anticipation rising, watched Kendler. The man had not even turned when the guards exited; he gazed, not stared, at the Con-Web.

"Nils," a woman's voice, gravelly with age, yet containing the tone of one accustomed to authority, came from the hologram, "it's good to see you again."

Loma spoke again, "We matched Dunbar's voice prints with the Con-Web's verbal enhancer. Kendler and we are now hearing the voice of Kate Dunbar."

Kendler's head lifted. His eyes searched for the owner of

Dunbar's voice. "Kate? Kate, is that you?"

"Yes, Nils. I understand you've wanted to talk with me," the Con-Web's Kate Dunbar mode replied.

Kendler glanced about him. "First I must have the privacy I requested."

Audio to the projection died. There was no slow fading, but an instantaneous disruption.

"What the hell!" Donalt heard Loma hit the intercom on the conference table to report the equipment glitche.

In the next instant, the projection itself winked out.

Loma's palm slapped the intercom again as the room's lights came up. A distant voice tried to answer his demands for the audio-visual link to be reestablished immediately. The director's cheeks reddened. "Then get a console in here!"

The intercom's voice was silent for a long, heavy moment. When it returned, its words were indiscernible to Donalt. Loma paled visibly; his fingers slipped from the intercom. Those within range of the voice turned a sickly ashen hue.

Loma's gaze slowly rose and moved over those in the room. "An energy shield of an unknown nature is englobing the room containing Kendler. Not only has the field disrupted our projection, but it has also isolated the Dunbar mode of the Con-Web. There's no interface between Dunbar and the rest of the system."

"Get the guards down there and burn through the door," Belva Julian demanded. "We can't allow Con-Web access under these conditions."

Loma shook his head. "The guards were under orders to do just that in case of emergency. Their energy weapons have no effect on the field. The shield absorbs the blasts."

"What's the next move, Loma?" Julian glared at the director with obvious contempt.

"I could call for plasma weapons and take out this building and at least two others around it." Loma made no attempt to conceal his irritation with the LofAl chairperson. "Other than that, we do nothing . . . except wait."

Which is what they did, deaf and blind while Nils Kendler and Kate Dunbar had their conversation in the total privacy Kendler originally had requested.

The energy field englobing the room faded five minutes later. The holographic projection returned in time to witness the guards, ten of them, move through the door and surround Kendler.

Donalt watched, uncertain of what he saw as the guards escorted Kendler back to his detention quarters. What he thought he saw was a sly smile on Kendler's lips and a wink to greet the guards.

‹SEVENTEEN›

Two hours after Kendler had been locked in his room with triple guards, Donalt was reassigned to Psi Corps reorientation along with the other three members of the *Crispus Attucks* psi team.

He immediately experienced the isolation Jenica, Michaela, and Howin had endured for a month. No matter how many requests he made to Psi Corps for information on Nils Kendler, he was politely informed he was not presently cleared for such information.

He did learn through the normal intra-office grapevine that five teams of Con-Web technicians had worked around the clock for three days checking, rechecking, and rechecking again the Kate Dunbar mode. They verified that the system had in no way been tampered with.

What had transpired within the energy-shielded room during those five minutes never passed beyond Director Loma, top Naval Command brass, and the LofAl Council.

Nor did his daily proximity to Jenica diminish the tension between them. While obviously happy to have him back with the team, Jenica returned to the friendly, formal attitude she had exhibited aboard the *Crispus Attucks*.

Donalt's attempts to breach that invisible wall were coolly rebuffed. After two days, he simply acquiesced to her wishes. Following the line of least resistance lessened his emotional turmoil somewhat, although he felt disgusted with himself for giving in so easily.

At the end of a week, the team was ordered to Psi Corps Director Loma's office. Donalt led his teammates through the doors into Loma's bureaucratic inner sanctum an hour after receiving the orders.

There were no formal introductions. The thin, red-haired director began by giving Jenica, Michaela, and Howin a sketchy briefing on all that had occurred the past five weeks, including the Kate Dunbar meeting.

"What you will see today is an accurate record of what occurred during Kendler's access to Con-Web." Loma leaned back in the chair behind his desk. "It's been thoroughly verified by five teams of engineers."

"The energy shield is still of an undetermined nature?" Donalt asked.

"The source has been determined. I believe the presentation will provide a better explanation than I can with words." Loma tapped several buttons on a Con-Web console to one side of the desk. "Con-Web, audio-visual file A-oh-oh-oh-five-oh-six, Kate Dunbar mode, voice actuated."

"*Kate* will be sufficient," the gravelly voice of Kate Dunbar answered from a speaker inset in the office ceiling. Donalt smiled when he noticed Loma's raised eyebrow at the reply.

"Run file A-oh-oh-oh-five-oh-six, Kate," Loma continued.

"A bit of common courtesy would be considered appropriate, Director Loma," Dunbar's voice answered. "While I may be no more than a small cog in what you refer to as Con-Web, my personality is still intact. And I *did* once sit in the chair now occupied by your backside."

"What the hell!" Loma swiveled in his chair. His fingers punched a series of buttons on the console's keyboard. There was no response to his commands. He reentered them.

"A-oh-oh-oh-five-oh-six must be accessed through me," Kate Dunbar said from the overhead speaker. "A simple 'please' preceding or following your command will achieve the desired results."

"Run file A-oh-oh-oh-five-oh-six . . ." Loma swallowed. Nothing occurred. "Please."

"Thank you," Dunbar replied.

The office lights dimmed. The far wall was replaced with a holographic projection of the room in which Kendler had been given access to the Con-Web. As before, Donalt watched two guards seat Kendler in the room's only chair, then leave. Once again Dunbar's voice greeted him.

Unlike the original attempt to view the meeting, the projection did not blink off. There was no need for the audio portion of the recording. There was no sound.

Kendler stood. He reached out and placed both of his palms against the face of Con-Web. For a moment, he just stood there and stared into the solitary optical sensor. Then he stepped back to the center of the small room.

Donalt scooted to the edge of his chair. He heard his companions do the same. An aura, white and shimmering, appeared around Kendler.

"What is that?" Howin asked. If he expected an answer, he did not get one. The attention of the other four people in the office was riveted to the holographic display.

The aura expanded. Like a crystalline bubble it grew around Kendler. It moved outward, touching the Con-Web, the walls.

Donalt's brain staggered in an attempt to reject the image transmitted by his eyes. Kendler—*Kendler!*—had generated the force field!

It was not possible. No man was . . . *man?* Donalt's eyes widened. *Man . . . no. Kendler was not a man.*

A ripple of light shimmered through the solidity that was Nils Kendler. Like a holographic image burned out by an abrupt flare of light, Kendler vanished. In his place, floating at the center of the room, was . . .

Donalt's descriptive abilities failed him. Kendler—*it*—was a sphere of light, a living, constantly changing orb of light. Shaftlike rays lanced from the sphere and thrust through the face of the Con-Web, leaving the metal surface undisturbed.

"Kate, explain, please," Loma said.

"A direct energy interface," the Dunbar voice of the Con-Web replied. "The Kendler entity read and understood my tetradecimal computing arrays and memory files, then communicated via Con-Web language."

For five minutes, Donalt sat and watched the "Kendler entity" talk in absolute silence to Kate Dunbar. Light beams flashed and darted between the sphere and Con-Web. The light globe turned and spun as it subtly shifted through the spectrum.

Then it was gone.

Nils Kendler once more stood at the center of the room. Ten guards rushed through the door, energy pistols leveled at the man. Donalt sat back. Kendler *did* wink at the men who led him away.

"End of file A-oh-oh-oh-five-oh-six," Dunbar announced, and the projection faded. The office lights came up once again. "Will there be anything else, Director Loma?"

A liquid sensation of weakness suffused Donalt when he turned to the others in the office. The guards who came rushing into the room—those standing outside Kendler's quarters at this very moment—deceived themselves with their weapons. If Kendler, or whatever it was, decided it did not want to be confined—it would not be confined.

"What was that?" Michaela was the first to disturb the silence within the office.

"An Erna," Dunbar replied.

"An Erna?" Howin repeated as though he were unable to accept the answer.

Donalt's mind stumbled again attempting to relocate solid ground.

Erna?

He listened while Kate Dunbar explained that the supposed alien hoax was no hoax. The Erna did exist. Nils Kendler and the *Seeker* had made contact with the alien race in the REV90732P galaxy.

"An alien race." Awe filled Michaela's voice. She turned and looked at her fellow team members.

"A sentient alien race to be exact," Dunbar corrected. "A race whose natural state is pure energy. The same aliens I launched the *Seeker* to contact two hundred years ago."

"And the Kendler form?" Loma's expression revealed he already knew the answer.

"When the *Crispus Attucks* contacted the *Seeker*, the Erna assumed the form of Nils Kendler," Dunbar explained. "Its original human contact resulted in a hostile attack. It was reluctant to appear in its natural state until contacting a LofAl authority with which it was familiar. Being Nils Kendler's superior at the time of the *Seeker* expedition, it sought me. Had I not existed, it would have presented itself to the current Psi Corps director, Director Loma."

At Loma's request, Dunbar told of the *Seeker*'s appearance in the Arvis system. There it encountered the Kavinite scout ship that contained Kaveri and Loundon. When the smaller vessel attacked, the Erna incapacitated its two-person crew, then brought the scout into the shuttle bay of the *Seeker.*

"Apparently, the psi contact with the Erna was too much for their minds," Loma said. "The resulting insanity from that contact has now been corrected by the Kendler-Erna. Both Lieutenant Kaveri and Sergeant Loundon are presently in the custody of Naval Command Intelligence."

Donalt recalled the Nils Kendler reports he had read a hundred times aboard the *Crispus Attucks.* Kendler and Caltha Renenet had originally contacted an Erna on the planet Morasha where the psi emanations of its dying agony had been responsible for a planetwide mass insanity. Kendler and Renenet later used the LofAl's time travel program, Retrieve, to contact the alien while it dwelled within the Giza pyramid on Earth at an earlier time. Both psiotics had been rendered unconscious by the mental contact with the energy creature.

"The crew of the *Seeker*?" Donalt asked. "What happened to the two thousand men and women on the expedition? What happened to Nils Kendler?"

"Kendler, my daughter, and the rest of the expedition remain with the Erna," Kate Dunbar answered from overhead. "Though successful in contacting the Erna on their homeworld, that very contact was a tragedy, a disaster."

Dunbar explained to the psi team that the Erna was a lonely race. While the first one-celled creatures struggled to cope with their newfound life on Earth, the Erna searched the galaxies for other sentient lifeforms. Their efforts to make contact were fruitless until the sentinel placed on Earth encountered Kendler and Renenet.

"Perhaps that should have forewarned us of what to expect when the *Seeker* reached REV-nine-oh-seven-three-two-P," the Kate Dunbar mode continued.

Did Donalt detect an inflection of regret in the electronically created voice?

"Consider the psi force harnessed by one Erna," Kate Dunbar postulated. "Now consider the Erna as a race, twelve billion such energy entities covering the surface of a planet the size of Lanatia . . . twelve billion separate minds united in the communal awareness that is the Erna. The Erna, a single mass consciousness amplified by the individual minds of its race. The power held by that communal entity is beyond comprehension even to the Con-Web. To the human mind, confined within its 'self' concept, isolated from true contact with its fellow creatures, the seemingly unlimited force controlled by even one Erna would make that creature appear godlike. . . .''

Donalt tried to visualize it. A planet of energy creatures, sentient beings, any of which held the power capable of driving a world insane, was impossible to conceive. He still had not assimilated the fact that other intelligent lifeforms did exist within the universe. That they harnessed such psi force was incomprehensible.

''. . . consider the aeons of loneliness the Erna endured among the stars while they waited for another sentient race to evolve,'' Kate Dunbar's voice floated down from the ceiling speaker.

''Take the awe, the excitement, the joy you are presently experiencing at the realization that sentient aliens do exist. Multiply that by the awareness of one Erna. Then raise that to the power of the communal mind of the Erna race. Now you have the joy, the eagerness of the Erna when the *Seeker* slipped from tachyon space into their star system.''

A shivery chill ran along Donalt's spine to dissipate the glow of anticipation. He saw a similar reaction on the faces of his team members.

''As a communal entity, a single consciousness, the Erna surged from their homeworld to greet the *Seeker*. They rushed forth to welcome the human crew, to share a complete union with them,'' Dunbar continued. ''The union the Erna offered in its welcoming was complete, a sharing of mind, body, and spirit.

''No one aboard the *Seeker* was prepared for that greeting. They were overwhelmed. Engulfed. The contact was too powerful for the human mind. Identity could not survive beneath the surging joy of the Erna. The Erna did not comprehend this fact until it was too late. In a matter of seconds, the *Seeker* and its crew were literally absorbed into the mind and body of the Erna.''

They remain with the Erna . . .

The full weight of Dunbar's earlier comment drove home to Donalt. Two thousand men and women had been absorbed by an alien being, beings. Mass converted to energy in seconds. Living, sentient mass to living, sentient energy. The mind-merger's temples pounded.

''The Kendler-Erna?'' Jenica looked up at the ceiling

speaker. "What is his purpose in being here?"

"The Erna has adapted itself," Kate Dunbar answered. "The Kendler entity is an envoy extending an invitation from its race. The Erna has prepared itself to greet humankind again."

"Repeat and explain, please," Loma requested.

"The Erna has adapted itself for human contact," Dunbar reiterated. "It awaits humankind's second voyage to REV-nine-oh-seven-three-two-P . . ."

The expectant expressions on the faces of his companions mirrored Donalt's inner feelings. An alien intelligence waited among the stars!

"As a gesture of its sorrow for what occurred on the *Seeker*'s original arrival, for the loss of the crew," Dunbar said, "the Erna offers this . . ."

The office lights went down. A holographic display materialized at the far end of the room. It was a technical schematic that meant nothing to Donalt.

"What is it?" He turned to Loma.

"Dunbar will explain," the director replied. "However, a staff of Naval Command engineers have verified the feasibility of what you're seeing now. Dunbar, please elaborate."

"The schematic displayed is a proposal for a new tachyon transition drive that outdates presently existing systems," Dunbar answered in her gravelly voice. "The drive consists of ten polarized, crystal . . ."

"Keep it nontechnical, please," Loma said.

"Simply put," Dunbar said after a brief pause, "the drive will permit a voyage to REV-nine-oh-seven-three-two-P in sixty days rather than the twenty years required for the original voyage of the *Seeker*."

Again Donalt thought he detected an inflection in the electronic voice—mild disdain.

The projection blinked out, and the lights came on again. The four psiotics' heads swiveled toward the Psi Corps director.

The red-haired man nodded to confirm what they had heard. "Naval Command has estimated the new drive can be constructed within a month by modifying the *Seeker*'s present propulsion system."

The man paused and lifted four envelopes from his desk and passed them to Donalt, who distributed them to the team.

They immediately began to open them.

"Read them later," Loma said. "Basically they say the crew of the *Crispus Attucks* is now assigned to the *Seeker*, which includes the cruiser's psi team. Naval Command wants another month to test the drive within the star systems neighboring Lanatia. Then, if all the glitches have been worked out, the *Seeker* will begin its second voyage to REV-nine-seven-oh-three-two-P...."

War effort or not, Naval Command, the LofAl Council, and the Psi Corps could not allow such an opportunity to pass. Cynically, he realized that all three branches of the government hoped that any knowledge gained from the Erna would provide an advantage over the Kavinite Empire. Certainly the new propulsion system itself would be a major turning point in the twenty-five-year war.

"Donalt," Loma stood. "You and your team will immediately report to Naval Command and receive shuttle assignments to the *Seeker*."

When the psiotics rose to leave, Kate Dunbar's voice once again came from the ceiling speaker. "Good luck."

‹EIGHTEEN›

Donalt halted at the junction of tunnel-corridors on the *Seeker*'s Level One—the sphere surrounding the vessel's innermost level, the command deck—fighting the urge to slink back and conceal himself.

He repressed the irrational reaction, but could not bring himself to step forward and join the couple standing at the entrance to the liftshaft.

Neither Jenica nor the Kendler-Erna noticed him when they stepped into the tube. The man and woman were . . . Man?

Alien and woman? Did an Erna truly have a sex? Was it capable of performing as a man while in its Kendler form—a form that it had taken from a human being who had been absorbed into the communal body of its race?

Petty.

Donalt shoved aside the unwarranted thoughts. Neither Jenica nor the Erna deserved his bitterness. His resentment was generated by a fear that Jenica had finally come to a decision and was attempting to break it to him as gently as possible.

Since the *Seeker* had begun its voyage fifty-nine days ago, Jenica had behaved like an acquaintance, not like a woman who claimed to love him. She did not avoid him; in fact, the friendly formality of their relationship continued. She sought his company whenever she had time. There just never seemed to be much time.

Outside her normal psi team duties Jenica had become the unofficial liaison for the Kendler-Erna. She was constantly at his—its—side. What was known of the Erna culture, Jenica had gathered and disseminated to the rest of the crew. The job was needed, necessary, but . . .

"I'd say strange bedfellows," Michaela said from Donalt's left, "but they don't share a bed. I know; I was nosy enough to ask."

Donalt's head jerked around. The receiver-sender stood across the tunnel-corridor from him. He felt chagrined. "How long have you been there?"

"Long enough to see the look on your face." Michaela bit her lower lip, started to say something, then closed her mouth.

"Is it that obvious?"

"Worse. Even Howin has noticed. Generally, he's blind to such things. Not that my muscle-man is insensitive. It's that he's not observant at times." Michaela paused and smiled. "Speaking of Howin, have you seen him?"

"In operations about five minutes ago," Donalt replied. "He's a bit nervous about the Erna contact tomorrow."

"He's not the only one." Michaela's smile faded to a somber expression. "Rad, if you need someone to talk with . . ."

Donalt shook his head. "Things will work themselves out one way or another. Either way, I'm a big boy now and will manage to survive."

Michaela tilted her head affirmatively, then turned toward operations. For a moment Donalt watched her walk away, then moved to the liftshaft and entered. He floated toward the command level and the final briefing on the *Seeker*'s arrival within REV90732P. Tomorrow, after two months under tachyon drive, the spherical behemoth would punch its way into the slower-than-light reality humankind called "normal" space.

Donalt's apprehension about what waited within the Erna's home system equaled Michaela's and Howin's. The aliens possessed the psi force to banish the human brain irretrievably to the realms of insanity. The Kendler-Erna had vividly demonstrated that with the Kavinites Kaveri and Loundon.

The first voyage of the *Seeker* had ended with its crew being completely absorbed by the communal mind and body of the Erna. The only assurance that there would not be a repeat of the disaster was the Kendler-Erna's claim that his race had adapted itself for human contact.

The mind-merger edged aside his personal jealousy of the

alien's monopoly on Jenica's time. The Erna had given no indication that he was anything other than what he represented himself as—a friendly ambassador from an alien race.

The Erna had been constantly available during the two-month flight and openly aided those who requested his help. A thousand technical modifications had reshaped every major piece of equipment aboard the *Seeker*.

Through daily sessions the Kendler-Erna prepared its human companions for their contact with its race. It opened to them, reaching out to touch their minds. In these sessions, Donalt experienced a sincere sense of caring, of gentleness, of desiring human interaction. The sensations were almost loving. He had only felt such overwhelming emotions while merged with Jenica during her starman visions.

However, Donalt secretly had attempted to merge with the alien on five different occasions. The same fiery force shield he first met aboard the *Crispus Attucks* flared to prevent the psi link each time.

It was as though the energy creature who had assumed the shape of Nils Kendler permanently shielded its awareness from true human contact. On Lanatia, the Erna had explained that a merge would scramble the human brain beyond recognition and leave a merger totally insane. Perhaps it was racial chauvinism that refused to admit the inferiority of humankind, but Donalt could not accept the explanation.

The Erna touched their minds but would not allow them to touch his. It was a locked door that Donalt wanted to open wide. One he would have battered down, if it were in his power.

Donalt stepped from the liftshaft and turned toward Captain Moven's quarters. Ahead in the tunnel-corridor Jenica walked beside the Kendler-Erna. Of the four members of the psi team, only she seemed to have no qualms about what they would face tomorrow. Donalt prayed that she was right.

Jenica reclined on a couch within Psi Operations. She smiled as Donalt took the couch beside her and pushed a button on its arm to recline it. "Ready?"

Donalt glanced at the wall chronometer. Two hours before the *Seeker* entered REV90732P. They were right on the schedule Moven had set for the team during yesterday's briefing. He felt uncomfortable without Michaela in the operations room.

Moven had requested that the receiver-sender, as well as Howin, be on the command deck when the pretransition prescient probe was made. Moven felt it would expedite communications between the team and her. Donalt had made no objections to the departure from normal procedure.

"Ready," he said as he glanced at Jenica and watched her close her eyes.

He did likewise and drifted to alpha level, to merge with Jenica. The blackness surrounded him. Through Jenica's consciousness he felt the nothingness of the empty prescient currents. He waited.

Stars, individual pinpricks of unblinking light, winked into existence across the dark field until they were as thick as the very heart of the Milky Way.

REV90732P?

The linked minds that were Jenica and Donalt did not know. They simply were observers of the images that bled back in time from a future that would be.

A solitary rose, dew-jeweled petals undamaged by the vacuum of space, floated across the psiotics' field of vision, then faded away. A warm breeze, scented with freshly mowed hay, caressed their mutual cheek. The blackness transformed into a background of pleasing pastel green.

White, fluffy, and silky soft, a kitten appeared atop the green. Clear blue eyes looked up. Jenica-Donalt reached out a disembodied hand and ran it gently over the animal's back. The kitten curled and purred contentedly.

The sensation of tenderness enfolded the psiotics. As they stroked the kitten, the sensation cradled them.

The blackness, the void, slowly returned. The moments of prescience had passed. Jenica descended from alpha level.

Donalt withdrew from her mind and specifically formed a mental message for Michaela to inform Moven that he would contact her after discussing the images with Jenica. He then made his own descent from alpha state. When he opened his eyes, Jenica stirred on her couch, a beautiful, young woman awakening from a restful sleep.

Her eyelids opened to reveal the two emeralds of her eyes. She smiled. "It was beautiful, wasn't it?"

"But it didn't make much sense." Donalt righted his couch

and swung it around to face the prescient.

Jenica eased her couch toward him. "Not the individual images, but the feel of it did."

Donalt cocked his head to indicate she should continue. He had no arguments with the vision's "feel."

"I accept visions like this for what they appear to be without trying to interpret them." Jenica shrugged as though she were unable to define what she wanted to say beyond that. "This felt good. The rose is my favorite flower. When I was a child, they used to grow outside my bedroom window. They were especially beautiful on spring mornings when the dew clung to them like small diamonds."

"And the white kitten?" Donalt asked.

"That's a bit harder to explain," she said. "That was Wumpus, a kitten my parents gave me when I was six years old. I loved it more than anything a six-year-old child could love. It died of distemper a week after I got it. I cried for two days. My father bought me another kitten, as white and as pretty as Wumpus, but it wasn't the same."

Donalt studied her. "But that was twelve years ago. How could Wumpus be part of prescience?"

"I don't know. That's what I can't explain." She shook her head. "I know that a dead kitten existing in the future doesn't make sense, but that was Wumpus."

Jenica's gaze rolled downward almost shyly. She sat silently for several moments as though quietly sifting through her thoughts. When her eyes rose, a smile beamed on her face.

"Rad, the vision is like an omen, an indication that the future holds only good for us." The smile spread to a grin. "It's a feeling that something is about to happen to us, something that will dim all human experience with its brightness."

"The Erna?"

"I think it's the Erna," she replied. "But I'm not certain. It's like something you've known will happen all your life, something good, but you've never known what it would be or how to express it."

Donalt smiled as he remembered a younger Radman Donalt who once had held similar feelings. The war had erased those as thoroughly as it had erased countless lives.

He reached out, took Jenica's hand, and squeezed it before he realized what he had done. Her gaze searched his face.

"Jenica . . ." Whatever he intended to say slipped irretrievably from his mind. The emotion he had held in check for far too many months welled within him, seeking an avenue from which to flow.

Loving, caring, wanting, needing, Donalt stood, and Jenica stood with him. He eased her into his arms. She came without resistance, her eyes on him while his gaze caressed every minute detail of her face.

"Rad . . ." Her lips parted, trembling.

"Jenica, I love you." His voice was soft but firm. "I love you."

He leaned to her, his mouth covering hers. His arms drew her against him, to revel in the closeness he had been denied since their one night together.

His fingertips read her quivering uncertainty as their mouths opened to each other. His palms tenderly stroked over the young woman's back to soothe and quiet.

Hesitant at first, then with growing desire, Jenica's hands crept about him to press and clutch.

"No!" Her lips wrenched from his. Her palms were flat against his chest, thrusting from the embrace.

Her eyes were wide and confused where they had contained a soft invitation but seconds ago.

"Jenica?" He reached for her, bewildered by the sudden transformation.

The prescient backstepped. Her head moved slowly from side to side. "Please, Rad. You're confusing me."

"Confusing *you*?" He left mention of his own confusion unspoken. "Jenica, I love you. There's nothing befuddling about that. It's very simple. A moment ago, you understood, and you returned that love. It was right. What else is there?"

"You don't understand. You just don't understand." There was an undercurrent of desperation in her voice. Tears blurred her eyes. "Don't you see? I love you. But I love him, too!"

"The starman?" Donalt could no longer contain himself; he pressed for an answer, a decision.

"Yes!" Jenica said, the desperation more evident. "I have to know . . . I have to!"

"Damn it! The starman is just a *vision*!" Frustration boiled up within the mind-merger. "He's not real. He's an image you've retained from your childhood!"

"No . . . I don't know. That's what I have to find out. Can't you understand that?" Jenica trembled now, her eyes wildly searching Donalt's face. "The Erna . . . Kendler . . . I have to be with him."

Jenica gave him one last pleading stare, then pushed past him and ran from the room.

Kendler . . . the Erna?

The original paradox of Kendler's age, old but young—the Erna's transformation to its natural form on Lanatia, the glowing globe spreading behind Kendler's form like fiery wings—the daily contact with the alien's mind aboard the *Seeker*—each might have come directly from Jenica's starman vision.

Stunned by the obvious similarities, Donalt stared after Jenica, too numb to react.

Why had he been so blind? The Kendler-Erna—the starman! It had been there all the time, only he had refused to accept it. He still could not accept. The Erna was an alien. Not a man.

"Jenica!" Donalt's mind railed. He thrust aside the weight of the revelation. No matter what the surface appearance, it could not be! It couldn't! "Jenica."

He started for the door to go after her, to . . . He was not certain what he would do when he found her. How could he convince her that she was wrong? That the vision was wrong. If it were wrong? Yet, he had to do something, anything.

"Rad," Michaela's voice called from the intercom. "What's going on? Moven wants your interpretations of Jenica's visions."

Donalt stopped in mid-stride, pivoted, and reached for the intercom. His fingers hesitated a centimeter from the switch. He had forgotten all about the vision. He ran a hand over his face, swallowed, then touched the switch.

"Tell the captain," he answered, pausing for a steadying breath, "Jenica's images apparently have no direct bearing on the *Seeker*'s entrance into REV-nine-oh-seven-three-two-P. There was no indication of any imminent danger. . . ."

Was that a certainty? Could Jenica's expectations of the starman have colored her prescience? "No, Michaela, tell Moven, the vision is invalid and has no bearing on the ship's situation. Tell her that I believe personal interests are interfering with Jenica's clairvoyant abilities."

"Personal interests?" Michaela questioned.

Donalt did not answer, he turned and left Psi Operations to

find Jenica. It was no longer a matter between a man and a woman. It involved the safety of the *Seeker*. If her desire to find the starman was somehow effecting her psi capability, Moven needed to know. There was only one way to ascertain that fact: another merge.

Michaela called after him as he ran down the tunnel-corridor outside.

‹NINETEEN›

Donalt returned to Psi Operations empty-handed fifteen minutes later. The effort had been a total waste of time. The *Seeker* was too immense a ship in which to find a woman who wanted to hide. He berated himself for letting Jenica flee in the first place. If only her starman revelations had not jerked the rug out from under him.

The intercom buzzer greeted him as he ducked through the hatchway. Reaching the grille inset in the wall, he tapped its switch. "Donalt here."

"Rad, what in the hell is going on?" Michaela sounded on the verge of panic. "Moven is ready to keelhaul you without a spacesuit for cutting us off. She wants a more exact explanation of your interpretation of Jenica's vision."

"Michaela, I can't elaborate further. At the moment, I doubt the validity of any of Jenica's visions." He did not have the time to impart a detailed review of the prescient's starman obsession. "I need a full merge with her before I can clarify what I've said."

"Then merge, goddamn it!" Moven replaced Michaela. "This ship is due to slip into normal space in ninety minutes, and I'd like to know what to expect."

Donalt concocted a spur-of-the-moment lie about Jenica and he having an argument that concluded with her storming out of Psi Operations.

"I'll . . ." Moven began. Her words abruptly cut off.

In the background, Donalt heard Michaela mutter, "Oh, my god!"

Moven's voice returned to the intercom. "Donalt, I think

you'd better get to Level Two mess immediately. Bickle has found Stoy. She's unconscious."

"On my way." Donalt flicked off the intercom and bolted through the hatchway.

The mess—he had not checked there, but had searched for Jenica in the opposite direction before he realized the futility of a one-man search of the vessel.

Unconscious?

His mind ran in ten different directions simultaneously. Each path ended in a far worse speculation that the previous one.

Howin stood at the hatch to the Level Two mess. His head jerked around at Donalt's approach. "I've called the med-bay for help. Moven sent me to find out why you weren't answering. When I passed the galley, I happened to glance in and found her with him."

"Him?" The merger's question was answered when he stepped into the galley.

Jenica lay on the floor. Her body twisted and contorted in convulsive spasms. Her mouth was open, lips twisted unnaturally. Incoherent sounds rose from her throat.

Above her stood the Kendler-Erna. It gazed down at Jenica as though completely removed from the scene, no more than a disinterested observer.

"What happened?" Donalt shot a glance at the alien, then his attention returned to Jenica.

Abruptly Jenica's body went flaccid. She lay still on the floor. No sound came from her lips. Donalt dropped to a knee beside her and pressed two fingers to the carotid artery. It pulsed ever so slowly.

"What in hell happened to her?" Donalt asked, feeling totally helpless.

"It's psi related." Howin knelt beside him. "Can't you feel it? The emanations are still strong."

Donalt sensed nothing except the panic churning within him. Where were the medics? What was taking them so long? He looked up at the Erna in human form. "Were you here when it happened?"

It nodded and started to walk away.

Donalt was on his feet. His arm shot out to wrench the alien around before it took a complete step. "What happened? What caused this?"

"She asked to see my mind," the Kendler-Erna replied, its voice flat and montonous. "She said she loved me. She said she had to know if that love was shared. She asked to see my mind. She begged to see it."

Donalt's temples pounded; his stomach tied itself in knots. Jenica had come professing her love, had come in search of her starman.

"I allowed her that," the Kendler-Erna said. "I allowed her to see my mind."

The naked psi energy the alien harnessed in its awareness —all focused into Jenica's mind! The Erna knew what would happen. Why had it . . .

Donalt could not contain his rage. His right arm jerked back as he prepared to flatten the nonhuman nose that disguised the alien.

He never got the chance to throw the punch. Howin's arm shot out. Viselike fingers clamped around the mind-merger's wrist, stopping it before it could strike.

"Rad! You can't help Jenica by pounding his face." Howin jerked the team leader around. "You can't hurt him. But you might be able to help her!"

The receiver's words penetrated the anger. Donalt stared at his teammate for a long, silent, rage-trembling moment before the meaning to the words sank into his skull.

I might be able to help Jenica!

"A merge," he mumbled. He looked down on Jenica lying still on the floor. "Maybe it's not too late."

"Do it," Howin urged. "I'll keep an eye on him. Hurry, do what you can."

Donalt disentangled himself from Howin's arm and stretched out on the floor beside the unconscious prescient. He forced through his anxiety, used the familiar deep breathing to bring a semblance of relaxation that allowed him to rise to alpha level.

Gently, with all the love and care he held for Jenica, he reached and touched her mind. Cautiously, ever so cautiously, he entered, and waved himself into her awareness.

He opened himself to her, and her to him.

A torrent of images bombarded his consciousness.

Flashing, spinning, careening off one another, they flew at him from all directions only to shatter into a barrage of other contorted images. Donalt trembled as he fought to maintain a seed of his own identity, a slim thread which would allow him to climb back into himself. Slowly he sank into the maelstrom of madness storming within Jenica's head.

The Kavinites', Kaveri and Loundon, minds had been like this. Had the Erna allowed them a glimpse of its awareness? A cold ice floe moved through Donalt's thoughts. Is this what he had courted in his attempts to breech the defensive wall that surrounded the Kendler-Erna's consciousness?

The face of a child hurled head-on at Jenica's mind's eye. It exploded, raining down a thousand mirrored images of Radman Donalt. The miniature psiotics swirled, coalesced into a single rose. The one of Jenica's prescient vision? Blood welled from the flower's petals to transform into prismatic butterflies with light-refracting wings.

Donalt floated within the eye of the tornadic array. He made no judgments, simply observed, searching for the source of the endless images. Fear, lust, joy, love, need, hate, guilt, panic, euphoria, shame—the spectrum of human emotion streamed through the shared awareness.

Deeper, deeper, he sank, delving for the core of her insanity. Nothing, he found nothing.

It was as though the consciousness that had been Jenica Stoy had been stripped from her and in a single instant jumbled, then crammed back into her skull. As he had found within the minds of Kaveri and Loundon, there was no logic, no center of the madness at which to anchor reality.

Desperately, he extended his will into Jenica's mind, exerting himself. In that instant, he felt his grasp of sanity slipping. The wild torrent of images and emotions was too overwhelming. He pulled back to cling to the seed of ego he sheltered.

There was nothing else he could do. He, the man who had controlled the minds of others, had driven countless men and women to their deaths, was helpless. He could not save the mind of the woman he loved. He withdrew, pulling back into himself.

An hour, a second, a year? Time meant nothing as he huddled deaf, dumb, and blind within the fleshy shell that was Radman Donalt. He had failed. Jenica was lost to him, lost to herself.

Listlessly, he re-exerted control of his body. He opened his eyes. The blur focused into the concerned faces of Michaela and Howin. Other faces hovered above them. He recognized Anthea Tegner, the ship's physician.

"Are you all right?" Howin reached out and helped Donalt rise. "You've been merged with Jenica for over an hour."

Donalt glanced around. The other faces belonged to two nurses. Jenica now lay stretched atop a floater gurney. The Kendler-Erna was no longer within the galley.

"Where is the Erna?" Donalt's head jerked around, searching for the missing alien. "She's like the Kavinites. Only the Erna can help her. He helped Kaveri and Loundon. He can help Jenica."

"Moven had the Kendler-Erna placed under armed guard when she found out what had occurred," Michaela answered.

"I've got to get to him," Donalt said, as he tried to push his way through the people surrounding him. "He's got to help Jenica. He's got to."

A warbling warning echoed through the galley.

Donalt's head jerked around. The ten-minute warning that the *Seeker* was about to slip from tachyon space. "God!"

The full weight of what that warning meant descended on Donalt like a sheet of lead. He had to warn Moven! Had to stop the transition before it was too late!

‹TWENTY›

Captain Vedis Moven listened without interrupting to Donalt's hasty evaluation of Jenica's encounter with the Kendler-Erna and the chaos he had seen within the prescient's mind. When he concluded, she rubbed the back of her neck and nodded.

"Agreed. I was going to delay tachyon exit by ten minutes if you weren't out of the merge." She turned and called for "Abort 2B" to be fed into the Con-Web.

An intercom buzzer sounded and Moven touched a white button on the side of her chair.

"Captain, Jaenes here." The man's voice came from a grille inset in Moven's headrest. "We've got a problem. The Kendler-Erna is gone."

"Gone?" Moven's head jerked around. Her eyes narrowed.

"It was here—sitting on the bunk—looking at the four of us. There was a flare of light, and it was gone. Vanished into thin air."

Moven ordered the guards to search Level Two, then nodded to Donalt. "It's taken an energy form. Suggestions?"

Donalt shook his head. "Just don't bring the *Seeker* below light speed. Whatever the Erna is up to, it wants this ship at its homeworld—or else it wouldn't have crossed galaxies to get us. If you can keep that away from it, then we might find out what the hell is going on."

A woman called to Moven from the command deck. "Captain, the Con-Web won't accept the abort command. We're locked into sublight transformation in oh-seven minutes."

"Manual override," Moven ordered.

"Override fails to respond," the woman answered.

"Webber, sever Con-Web interface. I don't care what you have to do," Moven said, her face strained with tension, "but kill the transition program and keep us in tachyon space."

Donalt stared at the arrays of blinking lights on the Con-Web's face. "We've discovered where the Erna disappeared to."

"If it's trying to control the Con-Web on this ship like it did on Lanatia," Moven said, "then we're in for a hell of a lot of problems. We can stay in tachyon drive without Con-Web. But if we're ever going to drop back into normal space, we must have it for the transition."

The *Seeker* needed Con-Web to track its course while traveling faster than light. When and if the ship ever obtained sublight speed again, the main question would be where in the universe were they?

The intercom's annoying buzzer sounded. Moven tapped it and was answered by Jaene's voice again. "Captain, it's the psiotics Gosheven and Bickle. We found them in Psi Operations. Both are unconscious . . . passed out on the floor."

Michaela and Howin!

Donalt leaned closer to the speaker while the guard recounted his unsuccessful attempts to revive the two psiotics.

". . . It's like whatever got the prescient got to these two," Jaenes said, then signed out when Moven ordered him to take the psiotics to the med-bay.

"Captain," Webber called from the command deck, "the Con-Web can't be overridden. I can't disrupt the interface. The ship won't respond to any command."

A warning alarm sounded, drowning out whatever Moven had intended to say. It didn't matter. Ten seconds later, the *Seeker* entered transition to sublight—normal space.

◄TWENTY-ONE►

Donalt threaded his way through the waves of nausea brought by the sublight transformation. He breathed deeply and worked his jaw. His ears popped unmercifully, but the quivering sensations that sought to work up from his stomach into his throat subsided.

He heard Moven shout, but couldn't comprehend her meaning for what seemed like an eternity. When he did, he looked up to see the holoscreen filled with a radiant white globe.

"The Erna's homestar?"

"Homeworld." Moven tilted her head toward right corner of the screen and a smaller blue-white orb suspended there. "That's the star. . . ."

"Captain, the report on the star." A man leaning over a Con-Web monitor called to Moven. "Its mass exceeds the Chandrasekhar limit. The star went supernova thirty-five thousand years ago. . . ."

Donalt fumbled through half-forgotten astronomy lessons to recall that the Chandrasekhar limit for a dying star was one point four solar masses, the mass at which degenerate electron pressure can contain a star's collapsing core of oxygen and carbon and allow it to die a slow, peaceful, smoldering death. The Erna's star was a neutron star no more than thirty-two kilometers across. A single teaspoon of its substance weighed over thirty billion tons.

". . . star's mass exceeds two point five solar masses," the man continued. "To be exact, two point nine five seven five solar masses. Captain, the star is on the verge of collapsing."

"We should be dead right now. The gravitational force of

that star should have twisted this ship into knots the moment we exited tachyon space," Moven said. "How can a planet exist in this system? The supernova would have disintegrated any planet orbiting it."

"The Erna," Donalt said to himself as much as Moven. There was no other explanation. No one had even suspected the true extent of the power the Erna controlled.

"Commander Donalt's correct, Captain," the man at the monitor said. "The *Seeker* is englobed by a force field of some kind. Its source is the Erna's planet."

"We've got a welcoming committee on the way." Donalt pointed to the holoscreen.

Like a serpentine tendril, a thin, glowing, white thread lifted from the planet's surface. It extended through space toward the *Seeker*.

Moven's gaze left the optical sensor image to run across the command deck. There was uncertainty on her face, but not in the steadiness of her voice.

"Con-Web command for tachyon transition, Webber. Pop out of here and bring us back to normal space a light-year away. The Erna can meet us in neutral territory."

The woman responded immediately to encode the command. A warning alarm, high and ear-piercing, sliced the air to announce the imminent transformation.

Nothing happened. The *Seeker* remained "normal."

"What the hell!" Moven shouted at Webber.

"No response, Captain." The woman's face was twisted in panic. Her fingers danced over the console to feed the command into the Con-Web once more.

This time not even a warning alarm answered her efforts.

A woman screamed.

Donalt's head jerked around. The man who had moments ago given the readings on the Erna's star lay on the deck. He twisted and writhed convulsively. Saliva came foaming from his mouth. His legs, arms, and fingers twitched spasmodically as though trying to tie themselves in knots.

Then he was still. His chest rose and fell in an almost imperceptible rhythm.

"The Kendler-Erna!" Donalt looked at Moven. "Jenica looked just like that."

"Samo, Taler, get him to the med-bay." Moven waved an

arm at two crew members seated to either side of the fallen
man. She swiveled her command couch to the right. "Jen-
nings, put the ship on full alert. Defense systems manual."

"Engineering reports three team members are experiencing
some type of seizure. . . . Outer Level reports . . ." The man
paused, tapped the console before him several times. "I've
lost the shuttle bay. Clements was reporting similar seizures
among his crew when he suddenly groaned and was gone. The
channel is still open, but no one's there."

"Defense systems, Webber?" Moven shouted, the pressure
straining her face.

"No response," Webber answered. "I can't unlock the
Con-Web controls."

"Captain, reports of seizures coming in from all over the
ship," someone called out. At least half the crew must be incapacitated."

Moven didn't hear the last two shouted reports. She lay on
the deck, writhing, saliva bubbling from her lips. Her eyes
were open, but they no longer saw the command deck.

Then she was still.

Donalt knelt to touch her carotid artery to assure himself it
still pulsed. She was alive, if the insanity raging in her mind
could be described as living.

First Mate Thorin Barndike motioned for two of the command deck crew to take Moven to the med-bay. It was a useless effort, Donalt realized. One by one, the Kendler-Erna was
destroying the minds of the *Seeker*'s crew. How long before
every member of the crew lay unconscious on the decks?

He turned to the holoscreen. The glowing arm of the com-
munal Erna snaked closer, reaching for the spherical starship.
Communal body, communal mind. The Erna knew what the
Kendler-Erna was doing. Why weren't they stopping it?

A thousand possibilities flashed through his mind. Humankind had been used, but for what? He could only speculate.

A grotesque moan came from beside him. He pivoted, his
arms shooting out just in time to catch the First Mate before
he collapsed to the deck. Donalt lowered the man, then started
to stand and call for help.

He never rose.

Pain! It lanced into his brain.

Psi force like the unrelenting blows of a sledgehammer

slammed against his skull. Raw power! He staggered back,
tumbling to the deck beneath the mental impact. He pressed
his hands to his temples in an attempt to push the agony from
his head. He cried out, and was echoed by others on the command deck.

An image of a young boy, a young Radman Donalt, ran
across the merger's mind's eye. His mother . . . the *Crispus
Attucks* rushed head-on toward . . . Evora . . . his father . . .

Donalt recognized the flickering rush. He had seen the same
within the minds of the woman he loved and two enemy
soldiers. He struggled upward above the torrent.

The pain! Like an ever-tightening vise, it squeezed inward
until it threatened to squash his skull as though it were no
more than an overripe melon.

No!

He screamed into the face of the insanity that sucked him
toward oblivion. No sound escaped his lips.

Around him, twenty bodies lay motionless on the command
deck. Was he the last? The holoscreen displayed a shimmering
white light that completely enveloped the *Seeker*. Was he
alone . . . with them?

Light, white and pulsing, seeped from the bulkheads about
him. Like a sparkling mist it danced over the Con-Web consoles. Evora stood before him. She ran a finger down the static
release of her jumpsuit. . . . Michaela smiled at him. . . .

Donalt gathered his identity deep within his mind. A single
seed of reality planted in the soil of madness. He clung to
himself. He nurtured that lone seed, let it germinate, take
root, grow outward.

Reality returned to his eyes. The light of the communal
body of the Erna filled the command deck. It gathered to
hover above each fallen crew member, then lowered itself. The
men, the women . . . vanished.

With the Erna.

The words of the Kate Dunbar mode of the Con-Web railed
through his head. The energy beings had absorbed the first
crew of the *Seeker*. Now they took the ship's second crew into
their communal body.

Struggling to stand, Donalt pushed to his elbows. He had to
flee, to run.

Where?

Was there anywhere he could hide from the Erna? It did not matter, he had to try!

The fist descended again, slamming against the side of his head. He reeled to the side, face down on the deck.

Something warm and wet gurgled from his lips. Saliva! His body twisted and writhed, muscles attempting to knot themselves.

The Erna, it, they, were inside his mind, merged with him. They controlled his body—moved him like a marionette.

The subtle irony of the realization was not lost amid the constant barrage of pain. He—the mind-merger—the man who dominated the minds of others—would spend his last seconds of consciousness in the power of an alien merge.

Had Nils Kendler felt what he felt now? Two centuries ago, had Kendler struggled as Donalt now struggled to retain a minute seed of his identity against the onslaught of insanity? Donalt felt a kinship with the man he had never met. Surely Kendler had realized the futility of fighting the Erna as Donalt did now.

Futility.

That, too, was ironic and appropriate. How else should a man, who had spent twenty-five years nursing the illusion he could somehow end a war, die?

Not dead . . . absorbed!

The bathing warmth of love filled him . . . hate spat forth . . . he cowered, ashamed of . . . anxiety drenched him . . . the Erna now seized his emotions and played with them, testing how each was evoked, manipulating.

Beneath him the deck shimmered. No longer opaque metal but a translucent crystal. It dissolved, leaving him floating in space. Yet his lungs still drew in fresh, cool air—his body did not explode.

The *Seeker* was no longer. It and its human crew had been absorbed in the body of the Erna.

They protect me, he thought. *They protect me as they protected the* Seeker.

Why?

Was it because he struggled? Did he present the final challenge, a victory to be won, the last barrier to be shattered, a will to be overcome as a testimony to the Erna's indomitable power?

In the end, Radman Donalt would lose. A brief challenge that had been successfully overcome.

Only one defiant act remained to Donalt. He could cheat them. Rob the Erna of its challenge.

As he had done countless times during his forty years, Donalt opened himself. He surrendered to the psi force that consumed him.

◀TWENTY-TWO▶

A solitary rose . . .

It hovered, swarmed, covered the surface of a planet it called Gress, which revolved about a star named Karal. Karal shrank instant by instant, drawing in upon itself beneath the force of gravity.

The gradual mounting of that force bred a devourer of the very fabric of time and space—a collapsar—a black hole.

. . . a white kitten . . .

It was the Erna. The Erna was one; the Erna was multitude. Individual entities composed the Erna's communal body and mind, entities that dwelled separately, but without separate existence. To human philosophers, the energy beings were an enigma. To the Erna, it was the Erna, and it existed.

. . . a woman . . .

The Erna, one yet a multitude, separate but undivided, was a single entity. The light of its bodies glowed brighter than the star Karal. For one Erna to become cognizant was for the Erna to become cognizant. For one to forget was for all to forget, though the Erna did not forget. The experience of an individual was the experience of the whole. A sensation for one became the sensation of the multitude.

. . . a seed . . .

Within the one that was all, existed that-which-had-not-been-Erna-but-was-now-Erna.

That-which-was-now-Erna once had been named Radman Donalt. Now it was Erna—a name shaped for the human tongue. It identified itself by sensations that felt and tasted wholeness, completeness. It recognized the human Radman Donalt as an alien intelligence that had been absorbed into the

Erna's communal mind and body, though it did not associate
itself with that non-Erna entity.

   ... a solitary rose ...

Time held no significance for the Erna that once had been
Radman Donalt. To the Erna, which could transform itself
into matter or energy on a whim—even into tachyons to race
through the tapestry of space/time, the concept of time was a
dim glimmer in its past.

   ... a white kitten ...

The Erna-Donalt remembered the *Seeker,* the crew, as it
recalled the first *Seeker* and its human crew. It did not conceive of itself as having been a member of either crew. The
human ships were an amusement, alien sensations to be
savored and relished, momentary reprises from boredom. For
above all things, the Erna, one and multitude, was bored.

   ... a woman ...

The Erna, who had been created at the moment the universe
exploded into the void, had been bored for longer than the star
system that gave birth to humankind had existed. It had absorbed the identities of those who came aboard the *Seeker* in
an effort to relieve its boredom. Instantaneously, the individual, the whole, could link itself to one human or all,
vicariously live a material existence, or dance lightly over the
warped mental images now contained in each human consciousness. For a nanosecond, the combinations of alien sensations diminished the eternal boredom.

   ... a seed ...

As an entity, as the total entity, the Erna-Donalt hungered
for new sensations, new experiences to amuse a consciousness
dulled and jaded by eternity.

There was no true satisfaction, no fulfilling reprise. The
Erna that was no longer Radman Donalt watched as the others
of itself observed the slow collapse of Karal. When the star's
degenerate neutron pressure reached the critical limit, when it
could no longer support the mass of burned-out stellar material ...

   ... a solitary rose ...

The Erna-Donalt did not contemplate the collapse, but accepted the communal death the Erna devised to end its
monotonous existence. That death—to be drawn into the collapsar's eternal gravity well—would be one last new sensation
to savor before being crushed into nonexistence. Even the

prospect of death offered no tantalizing anticipation for the Erna. It was bored.

. . . a white kitten . . .

Instead of limiting itself to Karal's slow death, the Erna-Donalt touched the human entities contained within the fabric of the Erna. It played among the images contained within the twisted awareness of one who called himself Howin Bickle. Leisurely it shifted to one named Michaela Gosheven. These two shared the sensation of love, a sensation it recalled from a time before the boredom. A human creature who identified itself as Vedis Moven sheltered images of power within its awareness. The images were amusing when viewed with the perception of true power held by the Erna.

. . . a woman . . .

Of all the human minds, this one drew the Erna-Donalt to it as it had a thousand times before. This entity was a duplicate of one who had lived before it, something it shared with the Erna. This one who called herself Jenica Stoy clung to the belief she was to mate with the Erna.

Delusion, wonderful, delicious delusion locked within the energy patterns that had once been a human brain. It had been the struggle, the fight, the human's refusal to be dominated that froze the human mind, locked their experience into set patterns of insanity. Had the human creatures but accepted, they would now be one with the Erna.

. . . a seed . . .

The image of another human flashed within the mind of Jenica Stoy. The Erna looped the vision so that it was continuously displayed within the woman's awareness. A male, familiar, yet unfamiliar. Donalt—the memory of Jenica Stoy identified the mental vision. For this man, the woman radiated love, cherished love.

The Erna-Donalt, which did not associate the man with the not-Erna it had once been, compared the Stoy image of Donalt with the sensations associated with her imagined Erna-mate. They were unequal.

. . . the solitary rose . . . the white kitten . . . the images that had repeated themselves in the Erna-Donalt's consciousness were here within the awareness of . . . a woman . . . called Jenica Stoy.

. . . a seed . . .

The individual Erna sought an entity that was Radman

Donalt. The multitude followed the search, amused by a part
of itself that experienced mild curiosity. The one felt the all
seeking a brief break in the monotony. Within the mind and
body, it found the Donalt identity; it found it within itself . . .
a seed.

. . . a seed . . .

The Erna remembered the last human, how the lone
man had ceased to resist the union with the Erna. How he had
stopped the struggle to preserve identity, and allowed himself
to be absorbed.

. . . a seed . . .

The seed germinated. The Erna-Donalt remembered. He,
for the Erna accepted the sex of the human it now recognized
as once being its self, opened the identity of Radman Donalt
to the Erna. The seed accepted, it matured and flowered. Radman Donalt was at once a human consciousness and Erna
awareness.

He saw the creation of the Erna, the intelligence forged in
the hearth that birthed the universe—energy that coalesced
and bred as though it were a matter entity.

Millennia swept past him; he watched the Erna explore the
galaxy humankind labeled REV90732P in search of another
lifeform to share the wonders surrounding it. No sentient
beings dwelled within REV90732P. The Erna searched other
galaxies, but found them, too, void of intelligence.

They did find life on a myriad of planets. On those that they
perceived would evolve a sentient lifeform, they constructed a
great pyramid, a generator of the Kirlian energy on which the
Erna subsisted. Within these constructs, one Erna, separated
from the whole, awaited the rise of intelligence and the development of psi ability by which to communicate with the Erna.

One such planet was Earth; one such pyramid was Giza.

While the emissary waited on Earth for developing man, the
Erna grew bored. The universe no longer contained secrets to
be probed. The Erna shared—was—the universe's greatest
secret: energy that was matter, matter that was energy. It
degenerated; the Erna became a single mind and body that existed for sensation only, any sensation, no matter how great or
small, that would relieve the tedium of its existence.

Godlike.

The Donalt-Erna recalled the voice of Kate Dunbar as it
came from the Con-Web on Lanatia. To the human within the

Erna, his alien consciousness was just that, godlike. In awe he viewed the Erna's communal memory. He saw the creations of suns and planets at the mere extension of the Erna's will, and saw these star systems destroyed on whim.

Time passed and the emissaries stationed throughout the universe reaped the harvest of their vigils. Sentient life rose and hungered for the vast knowledge that awaited within the union of the Erna.

A god of death came in answer to promises of knowledge and wonder. The Erna descended upon each of these races to gobble them into the communal consciousness in a never-ending decadent search for new sensation. The emissaries who could not share what the Erna had become were willed into nonexistence.

Within the Erna's power was the ability to recreate the races they destroyed—had it wished to do so. That was not the Erna's desire. The intelligence they discovered bored them; no race they encountered contained the consciousness held within the Erna's own awareness. All were inferior and deemed unworthy of life.

It was a gentle Erna that greeted Nils Kendler and Caltha Renenet on Earth and the planet Morasha, one of the original emissaries. It was a different Erna who awaited the arrival of the *Seeker* within REV90732P.

The original *Seeker* crew had been driven mad and then absorbed by the Erna in its search for new sensation. The communal entity sustained the insane identities for the same reason.

In its hunger for sensation the Erna recreated the *Seeker* and a duplicate of Nils Kendler to lead more human minds to them. The Erna, the whole, was too bored to traverse the universe to absorb the race that seeded the stars of a galaxy humans called the Milky Way.

Only he, Radman Donalt, had cheated the Erna's purpose. He had accepted their unlimited power, reached out and merged with the alien consciousness. He had survived, had harbored that seed of the awareness that was Radman Donalt.

It was the human portion of the Donalt-Erna merge that now wept. The weeping transformed to rage, a denial of what had happened to himself and the humans that had once been his companions.

The Erna, that had been one, that had been the multitude,

was now Radman Donalt. It shielded its identity from the communal mind and body. Simultaneously it felt, tasted, probed, and grasped. It fed these sensations to the human awareness within itself and delighted in the varied emotions created.

Donalt learned the Erna's power to shape raw energy to matter, to transform matter to energy. The Erna portion of his consciousness provided him with the method and ability to restore what the Erna had taken from the human beings that had come to the Erna. He could recreate the *Seeker,* transform energy to flesh-and-blood bodies, and place minds in those bodies with their sanity restored.

Defiant of the whole, he, the Donalt-Erna, dissipated the shield that protected the human portion of its awareness. There was no resistance to his presence, no challenge from the communal Erna.

Assured of his power, of his ability, of success, Radman Donalt reached out to begin his task.

That was his only mistake.

The Erna would not permit that. In an instant it rose against him. Before he was aware of what occurred, Donalt felt a single, intense thrust from the Erna.

The individual entity that was the Donalt-Erna was transformed into tachyon particles and hurled into the faster-than-light universe.

‹TWENTY-THREE›

The Donalt-Erna willed itself back to normal space. The Erna portion of the merged entity made no distinction between tachyon and normal space. Energy was energy whether it was faster-than-light or sublight particles.

It took a mere nanosecond for the transformation. In that same instant, Donalt knew the planet Gress lay ten light-years from his present position. He could return to the dying star Karal and its lone planet as quickly as he had been sent to this nowhere, simply by willing it.

The return would be meaningless. From the Erna portion of the dual consciousness, he recognized that duality was the reason for his-its explusion from the communal body and the mind of the Erna. His desire to reclaim the lives of the two crews of the *Seeker* were of no consequence to the Erna. If the act provided diversion for one, it would provide diversion for the whole.

Jenica. His awareness still felt the woman, every physical and mental detail, locked within the Erna. He sensed the love that had flowed from her for Radman Donalt. The starman remained in her mind, no more than a clairvoyant vision unfulfilled, but she loved Radman Donalt as he loved her. When he completed his task, they would once again share that love. Not as energy beings, but as man and woman.

To achieve that, Radman Donalt had to be truly absorbed into the Erna, and the Erna absorbed into Radman Donalt. Then and only then, when the human instincts no longer dominated his actions, could he return to the multitude of one and reclaim the twenty-one hundred men and women frozen in madness within the Erna.

Donalt's awareness stretched across space and flowed into the Erna's consciousness while his energy form remained ten light-years from Karal. He blended himself to the texture of its mind and body. In turn, he allowed it to weave into him. They became one, a single entity, two consciousnesses molded together. They thought and they acted as one.

The Donalt-Erna felt the surge of its newfound awareness. To the Erna, Donalt gave purpose for existence. To Donalt, the Erna gave power. The discovery of that magnificent molding coursed through the Erna, one and multitude. Power and awareness expanded to crest in a tidal wave of childlike exhilaration that engulfed Radman Donalt. The power and he were one; he was the child and the universe was his. Like a child he played—and learned.

He-it opened arms of glowing energy to the great chasm that yawned about him-it and drew the void inward. Random atoms of hydrogen coalesced in the Erna's embrace. He hugged them to him in joyous delight. A child who now molded the very stuff of life, he squeezed.

Atoms compressed, tighter, tighter, until their simple structure could bear no more. They ignited—a star was born!

Within that fiery core, the Donalt-Erna sat and reveled in the inferno it had brought to life. *So simple!* the human consciousness realized. *A mere thought and a new star blazes in the heavens. If a star then why not . . .*

. . . planets!

The Donalt-Erna reached out and scooped a handful of the flaming starstuff. It shaped a ball and slung it outward into the blackness. Two stars now filled this small piece of the void, but another star was not what he-it wanted. The solution was simplicity itself; he sucked away the fury of the smaller star, drawing energy back into himself. The ball cooled and stabilized, and a planet now orbited the Donalt-Erna sun.

Delighted, childlike laughter reverberated from the Erna, one and multitude. The voice of that mirth was the consciousness of Radman Donalt as he playfully scooped another handful of the star and hurled it into space—and another. These he cooled as easily as he had the first. And three planets circled his sun.

The power that was his at the merest thought was intoxicating. In the span of a few seconds, he had brought a star to life and molded three planets to orbit the red giant.

Godlike.

Kate Dunbar's words echoed in his awareness. The Erna was exactly that—godlike! He could create, he could destroy. He could . . .

Again mirth rolled through the Erna. There were planets, but of what use were barren balls of rock and clay?

He reached out once more. From the stuff of the second planet, he shaped a man, an image of himself, Radman Donalt.

The energy tendrils he manipulated paused, quivering hesitantly. *Godlike* was the word, not God.

The Erna *could not* create—only *recreate*! Only reform that which it had absorbed within itself. It was *not* a god—just an entity.

The realization shuddered through the Erna-human. With its sentient consciousness, with its unlimited control of matter and energy, the Erna could not create. Creation—Donalt found no such concept within the Erna's communal memory. The being whose mind and body he shared only recognized something lacking within itself, something that left it incomplete, less than whole. Yet, the Erna, one and multitude, could not define that missing portion of itself.

The Donalt-Erna reabsorbed the hollow shell of a man. Later, when the two crews of the *Seeker* had been reclaimed, Donalt the human would live again. And although he would once more be a lone man, his mind locked within a bony shell, his power limited to the grasp of four fingers and an opposing thumb, he would possess something more precious than all the power contained in the communal body and mind of the Erna. The Creator of the universes had instilled within humankind its greatest gift—the want, the ability, to aspire to be a creator itself.

Leaving three new planets circling an equally young and peaceful sun, the Donalt-Erna willed itself back to the sterile mind of the multitude of one.

Change.

The Donalt-Erna sensed it immediately. Half the Erna's individual entities were gone. They had willed themselves into nonexistence rather than await Karal's collapse. The remaining beings, in their boredom, simply bided time waiting for the creation of the black hole that would suck them into oblivion.

Karal . . .

The Donalt-Erna felt the star's core movement. The collapse lay but four standard hours away.

Suppressing the human panic that surged, Donalt delved within himself and found memories of the *Seeker*. As easily as the Erna had transformed the behemoth of metal into energy, the Donalt-Erna reversed the transformation. The starship floated within space again, protected from Karal's unmerciful pull by a force shield formed by the Erna's will.

In the ship's Con-Web memory, Donalt programmed a full account of all that had occurred since the arrival of the *Seeker* in REV90732P. He then drifted through each level of the craft, providing the supplies and tools the crew would need for the journey back to Lanatia.

The Erna shared his task, for the one was with the whole again. The communal mind and body offered no resistance, nor did it question the actions of the Donalt-Erna. It simply did not care; the majority of its attention focused on Karal and the star's approaching death.

Once more delving the shared memory of the Erna, Donalt found the awareness of Nils Kendler, the human, not the Erna imitation. From the very atoms that had been absorbed into the Erna, he recreated the man, placed him aboard the *Seeker*, then touched his mind to remove all traces of the Erna-induced insanity. He left only a message to Kendler that a full explanation lay within the Con-Web.

This was Donalt's pattern as he moved on to Caltha Renenet, Kendler's wife—recreation, erasure of insanity, and restoration aboard the *Seeker*. One after another, he recalled to life the two thousand members of the craft's first crew.

Then he gathered the patterns and atoms of the ship's second crew. Michaela, Moven, Howin, Tegner, Watters—ninety-eight in all—he willed to human form, cleansed the insanity from their brains, and placed them aboard the *Seeker*.

His penultimate task was Jenica Stoy. Tenderly, he gathered the energy patterns that were the woman he loved and shaped them into their original form. He then placed Jenica aboard the *Seeker*.

Softly, he touched her mind to remove the twisted images molded by the Erna. For the briefest instant, he considered erasing the image of the starman. Instead he left it intact. The vision, whatever it foretold for Jenica or for him, was part of the woman. He had no desire to reshape that which he loved.

A solitary rose . . . a white kitten.

Within Jenica's mind, he found the images that had led him back to human awareness. He used the Erna's ability to imitate and placed a single rose in Jenica's hand. The fluffy kitten, which she had called Wumpus, he laid beside her on her bed. Then he woke Jenica and withdrew.

Before he assumed his human form, Donalt had one task left. He reached into the Con-Web and programmed it for a return to Lanatia and launched the gigantic ship toward its destination. While he watched, the craft winked from normal space into tachyon transformation, carrying its precious human cargo toward their distant home.

A single conscious thought would will the Donalt-Erna aboard the ship for Donalt's own transformation. Pleased with his labors, Donalt allowed himself to probe the wholeness of the Erna. The communal mind and body held no judgment of what he had done. They quietly awaited Karal's collapse and that final sensation before disappearing into nonexistence.

The Donalt-Erna felt only pity. The greatness that had almost belonged to this race, the power they held, was meaningless without that spark of creation to guide it. The universe was theirs, but it was a hollow possession.

Here and there within the communal mind he felt individual entities will themselves into nonexistence, too bored with life to await Karal's collapse. Donalt sensed a similar urge within the Erna whose body he shared. He had given it a momentary purpose. When that passed, it wished to die.

Donalt could not allow that, not until he was safely aboard the *Seeker* and in human form, a man, totally a man again. Then and only then could the Erna find the oblivion it desired.

Donalt reached out to locate the *Seeker*. Then he heard cries—cries wailing from within the consciousness of the Erna.

‹TWENTY-FOUR›

Cries!

They came from the Donalt-Erna's memory, from within his-its consciousness—three separate and distinct cries, desperate with the awareness that Karal would collapse in upon itself in a matter of minutes.

Donalt probed and found the source. His human consciousness reeled. These were the remnants of three alien races, all absorbed into the Erna as had been the crews of the *Seeker*. His own desire to rescue his human companions had caused him to ignore the cries. Now . . .

The Seeker . . . *Karal* . . . each second took one further away, while the other grew closer. Panic swept through Donalt, while the Erna portion of the merged entity relished the sensation, real sensation.

There was no choice. Donalt delved his Erna memory and found them.

First was the Uzoma: a gigantic sluglike race that had been accidentally absorbed two million standard years ago when the Erna found them within a galaxy humans labeled AJ070012J. The race consisted of five hundred beings—they had no apparent means of reproduction. Their planet, Canor, had been a hot, swampy world circling a Sol-type sun.

A Sol-type sun had also warmed the home of the Liluye, a billion of which had once inhabited the planet Gaee. Now only a million of the bird-descended creatures remained with the Erna. But their will to survive, to live again, equalled Donalt's.

Third was the Brodny, who Donalt's human consciousness could only describe as bearlike. The Brodny, a half million in

146

all, were doomed to a slow death when the Erna discovered them on the planet Orji. A race on the edge of space flight, the Brodny had been caught amid an ice age that threatened their planet. The glacial disaster had destroyed all of the race except for the few thousand who had been absorbed by the Erna. Like the humans, these, too, the Erna had driven insane. Theirs also had been a yellow sun.

Three races . . . three planets.

Donalt realized what could be done . . . had to be done. His childlike exercise of the Erna's power would provide a home for these remnants of three alien races. He willed himself into tachyon space and winked back within the star system he had brought to life.

First, he aged the new sun, stealing away the fury of its youth, yellowing its glow. Then he moved to the first planet, shifted its orbit, and transformed energy stolen from the star into matter to mold a planet twice the size of Chenoa, like the world the Uzoma had called Canor—a global swamp with an average surface temperature of twenty-six point sixty-six centigrade.

The second planet, orbiting one astronomical unit from the sun, became a recreation of the Liluye's forested Gaee.

Last, he moved to the third planet and shifted it outward. Here he shaped the small Brodny world of Orji, a planet of ice and snow, where summer temperatures barely crept above the freezing point of water.

Three environments, each complete, each taken from the memories held within the Erna—the Donalt-Erna was pleased. He willed himself back to Gress and the three alien races who awaited.

Donalt, his Erna body a glowing globe in the skies above the three newly inhabited planets, smiled. Even the Erna portion of his existence savored the sensations of self-satisfaction that came with the completion of the task. Now it was . . .

Pain. Loneliness. Isolation.

The Erna merged with Donalt writhed. Donalt knew, without having to return, that Karal and Gress no longer existed. Nor did the multitude of one.

The Erna was an Erna, singular in its consciousness. Save for the merged consciousness of human and Erna, the Erna were no more.

Weak, strength abruptly drained from its body, Donalt felt the Erna attempting to orient itself to the loss of communal mind and body. Its own energy body felt as though it would disincorporate. Its life and consciousness had been one, but had been a part of the whole. Remove the whole . . . it died.

No! Donalt sensed he was wrong. It did not die. It dwindled.

The Erna would live, but it would be powerless, an ever-diminishing consciousness adrift in the universe. And with it, the absorbed mind and body of Radman Donalt. He had to reach the *Seeker,* had to reform himself on its decks. Even prosthetic arms and legs were better than the existence waiting to claim this last survivor of the Erna.

Donalt willed himself into tachyon space.

Nothing happened.

The energy for the transformation was no longer at the Erna's control: There was no communal body from which to draw energy.

He could draw from the star and planets he had recreated!

He refused to consider the possibility. To do so would rob him of the victory he had won over the now-dead Erna. He was but one, and the planets below harbored the remnants of three sentient, alien lifeforms. He could not balance the scales in favor of himself. The energy to obtain tachyon transformation was no longer the Erna's to control.

Desperately, he probed space. He could find a barren star from which to drink. He could gather the random atoms floating about this sector of space and use their energy for the tachyon transformation. He lied to himself: the Erna no longer held the ability to gather atoms. All that remained was the very stuff of Radman Donalt. He had the ability to transform himself back into human form . . . nothing more.

Reaching out, Donalt sensed the three races below him. They would survive, each possessing the knowledge that sentient creatures shared the same star system. Theirs would not be the lonely existence of humankind. He had planted that within their minds . . . the incentive to reach into space.

The Brodny!

The Brodny held the knowledge of space flight. Were there a facility to shelter his human form until they could recapture its use, he could return home, return to Jenica.

The Donalt-Erna reached out and touched the minds of the bearlike aliens. They felt him, recognized him as the human-Erna who had saved them from Karal's collapse. They responded. Within an hour, they began construction of a facility to shelter his body from the harsh Orji cold.

Donalt gently thanked them, then closed his consciousness. He rested to conserve the energy remaining to him.

The Donalt-Erna awoke. Eight Orji days had passed. The Erna's body weakened rapidly, sustained only by the energy it drew from the star's radiation. It was not the Kirlian energy the entity required for life.

Again, Donalt touched the Brodny. The facility they prepared was complete, but untested. Could he possibly wait a day, an hour?

Donalt could not wait.

Slowly, to save the energy held within the Erna, he drifted downward. He focused on the Brodny's single city, Ranithun. Across the low-rising buildings he floated while he announced his approach. The Brodny begged him to wait, to give them time . . .

There was no time.

Donalt located the compartment constructed for him and sank through its ceiling. Ten of the Brodny awaited within, their coal-black eyes peering from pink-skinned faces. Their bodies were covered with short, silky white fur.

The Donalt-Erna willed himself into the form of Radman Donalt—the final, total transformation. The Erna, the one, the multitude, was no more.

Donalt stood facing the Brodny, human meeting alien. He smiled, bathed in the warmth of the compartments. "Thank—"

His lungs gasped for air.

Wrong.

Something was terribly wrong within him. Orji atmosphere was suitable for human beings. Yet, he could not breathe. He stumbled forward a half step. It was as though . . . he did not know. He was human once again, no longer Erna, the total awareness of himself no longer existed. But something was wrong.

Perplexed, he stared at the Brodny greeting party. Their

pink faces wrinkled in incomprehensible expressions. They rushed toward him, arms extended as though to catch his fall. It was too late. Radman Donalt, who had twice been human, collapsed. Darkness rushed in to blot out his consciousness in one swelling wave. *Death,* he realized in that last moment. *I'm dying!*

Then there was nothing. Radman Donalt died.

‹TWENTY-FIVE›

Pain.

It rushed at him out of an eternity of darkness. Mechanized muscles constricted to thrust him from an artifical uterus, beyond a stainless steel cervix and through a plasticized vaginal channel. He cried out as cool air filled stinging lungs. He screamed in outrage that his rest was disturbed. He wailed —for such had been the way of birth since humankind's primitive beginnings.

He, Radman Donalt, who had tumbled headlong into the arms of eternal Morpheus, was recalled to life, resurrected. The how, the why, was beyond him, but he remembered himself, all he had been and the death that had claimed him.

The Erna?

He searched his mind; only wispy memories of his nonhuman existence remained. He was human, totally.

And he lived.

Sounds, patterns of rumbling utterances, snarled snaps and growls, floated about him. Hands, large, warm, and gentle, moved over his nakedness, lifting and shifting him from one side to another. He sensed motion, a rolling movement beneath him.

There was too much at once. A thousand sensory inputs to assimilate in an instant. He was not prepared for the bombardment. That he somehow lived and breathed was enough for the moment.

He relaxed and ignored the world about him. And he slept a real sleep, not the nonexistence of death.

Donalt awoke in a bed. It was a very human-appearing bed,

except that it was two and half times too big. The room in which he lay had the sterility of a hospital—which it was.

Two Brodny stood beside the bed. Each was at least two meters tall. Their eyes were jet. Their square-shaped faces were pink and quite human in appearance but for the fact that beginning behind the cheeks, under the chin, and atop a narrow forehead, they were covered in a silky, sleek, downlike white fur, as were the rest of their massive bodies.

At least what Donalt could see of these two were.

Although both wore white neck-to-floor caftans, he remembered the naked creatures the Donalt-Erna had restored to independent life.

He also admitted that the aliens were impressive. In spite of the neatly lying fur, there was a beauty to them that was very pleasing to the merger.

"*Huhhh-nnalttt,*" the larger of the two spoke as it stepped closer to touch the back of Donalt's hand. "*Huhhh-nnalttt.*"

The psiotic heard the deep growling as "*Huhhh-nnalttt,*" but "Donalt" formed in his mind. The same conflicting sensory-mental interpretation occurred when the smaller female spoke his name in a growl half an octave higher.

Female? Did the breastlike protuberances beneath her robe signify female in the alien? Or did his human prejudice color his perspective? *No.* The Brodny was female. That, too, he remembered.

She also touched the back of his right hand.

"Yes, Radman Donalt." He pushed to his elbows. Suddenly and sharply, he swallowed. His throat felt as though a rasp raked up and down it.

The words his tongue formed-growled had not been Radman Donalt, but something that sounded like "rrrraammunn huhhh-nnaltt." The "yes" syllable was completely alien to his ears, although his mind informed him he had spoken correctly.

"The strangeness of the semantic enhancer injection will pass," the larger of the two Brodny said. "In all likelihood you will accustom yourself to our tongue just in time for the injections that will allow you to 'tweet' with the Liluye and 'glub-a-glub' to the Uzoma."

"Semantic enhancer?" Donalt stared at the Brodny.

"I thought the first question for a man who had died three hundred of your years ago would be 'How did I get here?' "

The corners of the alien's mouth rose in an expression that was definitely a smile, though the teeth that were exposed were longer, sharper, than Donalt's own counterparts.

"The injection basically is cloned cells from the language center of your brain imprinted with the knowledge of our language," the Brodny male said.

The Brodny explained how the cells were absorbed by the brain, thus providing the ability to speak an alien language.

Donalt half listened to the detailed technical description of the process. He understood that whatever had been done worked.

His mind kept repeating, *three hundred years*.

The Seeker . . . *Jenica* . . . his life lay three hundred years in the past. The war, the Kavinite Empire, the Lofgrin Alliance—did they continue or were they faded glimmerings from humankind's past? Did *Homo sapiens* exist or had the human race succeeded in eradicating all trace of its brief stay within the universe?

Three hundred years!

". . . Tohom," the Brodny's voice caught Donalt's attention. The male alien introduced himself. "A simple *mezeritt* who attends your medical needs. And this is Niquela . . ."

Mezeritt translated slowly in Donalt's brain to physician. The Brodny turned and touched the shoulder of the female beside him.

". . . who will attend all your needs, no matter what they may be," the Brodny Tohom said. "As with the generations of her family since you gave us life on this planet we call Orji, she is the Donalt-Watcher."

Donalt-*hyggant* was the word Tohom actually spoke, but the emphasis the Brodny placed on "all your needs" contained a nuance Donalt was uncertain he interpreted correctly.

"It is my honored duty to serve and teach you," Niquela said, once more touching the back of the mind-merger's right hand. "I, too, shall prepare you for the audience the *Zelimir* had requested."

Zelimir. The meaning was vague in Donalt's mind. The word held honor in it, a council of . . . government . . . peace.

He studied Niquela. There was a human femininity about the female Brodny. She glanced away under his probing gaze, a gesture that seemed almost shy.

"Later today, I must give you a complete examination,"

Tohom said. "Until then, I will leave you with Niquela. It will provide the Donalt-Watcher time to perform her duties . . . and answer the myriad of questions that surely fill your head."

Lightly touching the back of Donalt's hand with his fingers, Tohom walked from the room.

Donalt looked back at Niquela. There were a thousand questions, though those he wanted answered the most, the Brodny would be unable to ever answer.

The *Seeker*? Humankind? And above all, Jenica? Had she found her starman? Had her prescient fairy tale of a man come from the stars with all-encompassing love ended in a "they lived happily forever after"? With all his being, he hoped that happiness had come.

Niquela raised a hand—four fingers and an opposable thumb, though half again as large as Donalt's hand—and touched the throat of her robe. An invisible seam opened from neck to floor.

Before Donalt could comprehend what happened, she tossed her shoulders back. The caftan fell to the floor about square-constructed feet with toes that were equal in length and size. Her feet were surprisingly small.

Everything about Niquela was surprising. Except for the pawlike size of her hands, she was built slim, sleek, and tall with all the curves of a female human.

Her breasts, firm-looking cones, tilted upward to end in aureoleless, fur-bare, coral-pink nipples. The softness of the downlike whiteness covering the rest of her body was more than mildly erotic and exotic.

"Niquela?" The alien pronunciation and his surprise raked painfully up his throat.

The Brodny reached down and edged back the bed covers.

Uncertain why this was happening, or what to do to stop it, Donalt gasped for words while Niquela slid beside him. Her warmth pressed along his side. A hand, cool and gentle, cupped his genitals.

Donalt's own hand reached down and removed her intimately caressing fingers. Gently, but firmly, he said, "No. There is no need for this. I . . ."

"The *Zelimir* and Tohom suggested *drisan*." Her hand moved to his bare thigh, but he removed it once more. There was no doubt as to the translation of *drisan*. "For us to share *drisan,* they said, would assure you that you are indeed alive. For me, the Donalt-Watcher, it would be the highest of honors. It is my duty.''

Niquela's voice no longer sounded like a growl, but was soft and hesitant. Her eyes questioningly searched his. "Am I repulsive to you? Is it the strangeness of our different bodies?''

Donalt slowly sucked a long breath through his teeth. Jenica was gone; centuries separated them. He intellectually recognized the passage of years.

Emotionally, however, only moments had passed since he had sent the *Seeker* and the woman he loved on their return journey to Lanatia. The reality of his situation had yet to fully penetrate.

"The honor of *drisan* would be mine. In time, perhaps I will be worthy of what you offer. But now . . . there is a woman . . . *was* a woman . . .''

He stumbled for the right words, the correct way to, in effect, reject the Brodny without insulting her. He explained his love for Jenica, the immediacy of the situation although three hundred years had passed.

Niquela's hand touched the back of his hand, and she eased from the bed without comment. Taking her robe from the floor, she dressed while he watched. Her fingers pressed the fabric together at the neck and the caftan sealed, its seam invisible once again.

"We Brodny understand what it is to mourn the death of a loved one. It is our way to seclude ourselves for two of our weeks and completely shed the grief that wounds us. When the time has passed, we return to the world of the living," Niquela said. "Do you wish to be secluded? Only the Uzoma would not understand, though they would accept whatever you requested.''

"I will mourn, but in my own way." Donalt explained that human beings could not shed their grief within two weeks, that it was a slow, painful process.

"With too much time, grief becomes self-pity. Mourning should be short-lived and deep. It should honor the one who has died. Never should it be a weeping for one's own loss," Niquela said. "But I shall not question the ways of Donalt. When your time of *yannis* is passed, we shall share *drisan*.''

Donalt nodded, unable to tell her that he had mourned Evora for ten years before Jenica entered his life. Only then did he realize the mourning *had* been a long-enduring expression of self-pity.

"Shall I leave you to consider *yannis* now?" Niquela asked.

"No, there is too much I don't know about the past three hundred years, about the Brodny, about myself." Donalt's gaze moved about the room with its light pink-painted walls.

A window opposite his bed opened onto a city—Ranithun, he recalled—of low-slung buildings. White-topped mountains rose in the distance. He vaguely remembered recreating this world of ice and snow where the average temperature was minus one point one one degrees centigrade. "There is so much I must know."

"Then I shall begin at your death," Niquela said. "My ancestor Anane Qat constructed this compartment for your arrival from the Erna. Though untested, it would have provided for your survival. However, when you took human form, your body lacked electrolytes . . ."

Electrolytes!

The Erna's energy had been so depleted that the transformation had been incomplete.

Donalt tried to recall his merged consciousness with the energy entity. There was an awareness of his dual existence, but beyond that his mind was blank. The abilities held by the Erna were incomprehensible to the human mind. The power to mold energy and matter was lost.

He listened while Niquela told how the Brodny had cryogenically preserved his corpse, in the hope that their seminal cloning experiments would eventually provide a method to restore life to the being who had resurrected three races. Niquela said Anane Qat had been the first Donalt-Watcher, a position of honor that had been passed from one generation of her family to the next.

"Cloning was perfected. But it was not enough to repay what you had given the races of Brodny, Liluye, and Uzoma. It was not sufficient to return the body of Radman Donalt. The original consciousness had to be restored to that body," Niquela said. "Though all three of our races accept you for what you are—a single, mortal being, we also view Radman Donalt as a demigod, our savior."

Radman Donalt, demigod, the irony was inescapable—a man three centuries out of sync with the universe, mourning a woman he would never see again. He half listened as Niquela told how the Brodny had used their space technology to reach out to the Liluye and the Uzoma.

"The moment you drew us from the Erna, you implanted a part of yourself in our awareness, Donalt." Niquela's gaze was locked to his. "That was the overwhelming desire for peace—the peace you wished for your own people. But for us, it was between the three races of this system."

Donalt tried to smile to show his pleasure. The pleasure was real. If only he might have used the Erna's power to instill that within the mind of humankind.

He caught himself: such wishes were futile. He had no guarantee his race existed or that they had not found a peace among themselves during three hundred years.

Niquela explained that the Liluye pioneered the research in "consciousness preservation." The personality, the memory, the emotions were transcribed into a series of chemo-electrical impulses.

"It was crude, but it was a beginning." Niquela smiled. "For two hundred years, your original brain was analyzed, disassembled, reassembled again and again, each time we moved closer to perfecting our techniques."

She paused and glanced at the floor. "There was more than the desire to restore you motivating us. There was knowledge in your memories which the three planets did not possess. The things you gave us in death were far greater than you will ever realize."

"Such as?" Donalt's brow wrinkled in puzzlement.

"In all areas . . . the sciences . . . the arts . . . psi ability . . . We perhaps know more of what is your mind than you do, Donalt," Niquela said.

Easing back in his bed, Donalt closed his eyes and listened while the Brodny told him how his personality was eventually transferred to a cloned body. A hollow ache spread through his chest.

Jenica. He felt a new bond to the woman he had left centuries in the past.

". . . and your hand and leg are now your own," Niquela said.

Donalt's eyes opened. He examined his left hand. It *was* his! As was his leg! He grinned at Niquela. A pleased expression spread over the pink of her face.

"I'll be needing a manicure soon," he said. Niquela

frowned at him. "Nothing important. Just remembering one of the benefits of having a prosthetic hand."

Niquela's expression did not change for a long, silent moment, as though she expected more.

Donalt inwardly contained his chagrin. His small joke was lost on the Brodny. Did the bearlike creatures even know what humor was? The thought struck him as odd, although it rang true.

He was on an alien planet, a single human within an equally alien culture. The Erna, not he, had known everything about the Brodny. He knew nothing of this white-downed race, or of the Liluye and the Uzoma. He was a stranger in a strange world three hundred years in what he still considered the future.

He flexed his left hand several times. Even his body in its completeness was a stranger. How many years had he yearned to be flesh and blood again? And now his hand and leg only accentuated his alien environment.

". . . for the past five years the *Zelimir* pondered the moment of your return."

Donalt realized Niquela was once more speaking.

"The Three Planets had waited for so long to give back the life you had given us, that I believe all were afraid of completing the task."

"Afraid?" Donalt looked at the female Brodny.

"One is often afraid of concluding a dream," she said. "Especially a dream that had helped unite three separate peoples."

"But I'm here, and I'm alive." Donalt could see the logic.

"The populace of the Three Planets could not be ignored forever," Niquela said. "The *Zelimir* had to consent to your rebirth sooner or later. It was my duty as Donalt-Watcher to see that they did."

"Then it is you I owe my life to," Donalt said, realizing his rejection of *drisan* might have held a deeper connotation than Niquela revealed.

On the other hand, his body might be repulsive to her.

"You owe no one on the Three Planets anything. It is we who owe you," Niquela said, her voice a reprimand. "The *Zelimir* is yours to command if you wish."

"Surely you're joking?" Donalt still was uncertain what the *Zelimir* was, although the word's connotation held power.

"You are legend among the peoples of the Three Planets. Even religions have developed about that legend—the return of Donalt . . ."

"Religions?" The concept was preposterous. But then organized religion, at least among humans, had a propensity for the preposterous.

"Small cults, to be certain," Niquela answered. "It will be interesting to observe their reaction to your rebirth."

From the Erna's would-be godhead to demigod among three alien races. The implied power of both were ironic. Neither could erase the three hundred years separating him from Jenica.

"Tell me of the Three Planets," Donalt requested. His throat rasped when he spoke the implanted alien tongue.

Niquela began with the giant sluglike Uzoma. She was still describing the world of what she labeled the "philosophers" of the three races when Tohom entered for the promised examination.

When the Brodny physician completed his task, he pronounced that Donalt would require at least two weeks standard under his observation before the merger would be allowed the freedom of his new life. He then ordered Niquela from the room until the next morning and told Donalt to rest.

Donalt complied; at least, he closed his eyes and relaxed his body. Hours passed before true sleep came and temporarily erased the image of Jenica from his mind.

◄TWENTY-SIX►

Demi-godhood was not without its drawbacks. To begin with, it meant complete isolation from anyone outside Tohom's staff.

The one exception was Niquela.

The Three Planets knew of Donalt's resurrection. They waited patiently for his full recovery and his audience with the *Zelimir*. Niquela assured him that this was the way of the three races he had saved from the Erna.

Donalt suspected the real reason was that no one, Uzoma, Liluye, or Brodny, wanted a demi-god who could barely walk. A tarnished deity would be a major disappointment after a three-hundred standard year wait.

Niquela was the perfect taskmaster. The woman—Donalt thought of her as a woman—was constantly there to see that he achieved what was required of his new body. She nursed him. She browbeat him. She cajoled. She reprimanded.

Donalt learned, or relearned, to crawl, walk, and run in Orji's one point one gee. He mastered the Brodny language. Or at least, he could converse with the medical staff without the sensation that his throat was being methodically shredded.

With the help of two additional sematic enhancing injections, the mind-merger learned to *tweet* Liluye and *glub-a-glub* Uzoma. Niquela was there for the alien language lessons also. She demanded perfection. That was what she got—the best he could provide.

Physically, he became Radman Donalt again—perhaps a new and improved version of the original. Twice-daily physical therapy sessions left him feeling as though he could match

Howin kilo for kilo in a weight-lifting match. A delusion, he realized, but a nice one.

Daily, too, were the cultural and history lessons Niquela provided. He learned of the virtually immortal Uzoma who dwelled on the swamp world of Canor. The Uzoma were without social structure. They existed, and they pondered life and the universe.

The Liluye Niquela described as beautiful, but flighty creatures, capable of the profound, yet preferring hedonistic pursuits.

The Brodny, Donalt learned from Niquela and personal observation, were private creatures. Closely confined in a world of ice for too many generations, the race existed under the rule of rigid social structures and a philosophy of *farik*.

Farik was the belief that physically an individual entity belonged to society. Privacy, prized among the Brodny, was achieved only through inner harmony. The concept eluded Donalt, although he accepted the social structure and its rituals.

He learned; he assimilated. And still he met no one— Brodny, Liluye, or Uzoma—beyond those assigned to his recovery.

"For three races so different to exist peacefully with each other, personal privacy is a priority . . . even among we Brodny," Niquela explained. "This belief has been extended to you. Your seclusion will continue until you meet with the *Zelimir*. And after that, if you wish. Although the Three Planets desire to meet you, it is not required."

"The *Zelimir*," Donalt asked, "when will they meet with me?"

"They have been waiting for an audience since the day of your revival." Niquela's two very round eyes blinked.

"Why wasn't I told before?"

She stared at him a long moment as though uncertain. "I thought you understood. The *Zelimir* awaits you. You do not await them."

Donalt did a classic double take. He shook his head, realizing that communication channels had been crossed somewhere between nursemaid and demigod. "I *want* to meet with them. As soon as possible!"

"It can be arranged. Will tomorrow be soon enough?" Niquela asked.

Donalt nodded. A wide grin beamed on his face, and an electric excitement tingled through him. Tomorrow he would meet the representatives of three—not one—alien races! Humankind's millennia-old dream come true.

"A telecast has also been requested." Niquela glanced at him, her eyes shyly avoiding contact with his.

"Telecast?" Donalt eyed the Brodny woman.

"The Three Planets are connected via a communications network similar to the holo-network of your galaxy," Niquela explained, her gaze fluttering away from sustained contact with his. "The *Zelimir* has requested that you appear so that the people of the Three Planets may see you."

Donalt laughed. Niquela had just offered to make him a media star on three worlds. "Of course. What will it be like? An interview?"

"That too."

"Too?" An uneasy sensation squirmed through Donalt.

"Our races have known you—your body—for three hundred years. Even the youngest child knows you," Niquela continued in a soft tone that only increased Donalt's suspicion. "They wish to be certain that we have completed our task to perfection."

The woman's emphasis on "know" worried him. "Why do I sense you haven't said all there is to say? That you're leaving out a small detail . . . or two?"

"They expect to see all of you, Donalt."

"All of me?" Donalt repeated. Her meaning penetrated. "*All* of me!"

"All of you." Niquela nodded.

Donalt laughed. He was to be a media star with a twist of xeno-porno.

"Nude, buck-ass, baby naked?"

Niquela nodded once more. "Fully disrobed."

"I'll be the voyeur's delight on three worlds." Donalt could not refrain from laughing. The thought of him standing nude before cameras was ludicrous. "Who would have thought that I would recreate three races of Peeping Toms!"

Niquela's brow knitted with puzzlement at the term "Peeping Toms." "It is the only way to assure the Three Planets that you have been totally returned to yourself."

Donalt touched the back of Niquela's hand—a gesture of affection and honor among the Brodny.

"I'll do it. It's the least I can do for those who have given me a new life."

Naked before billions of alien eyes. The fact that they were alien eyes did not make Donalt an iota more comfortable with the scheduled appearance.

With what could be only described as a coy batting of eyelashes, Niquela left his room to arrange the meeting with the *Zelimir* and the telecast afterward.

Donalt stared after the Brodny woman for a moment. Then he laughed.

Niquela led him into an immense circular chamber. A transparent dome overhead held back Orji's occasional flurries of powdery snow. Past the veil of falling snow was a slate-gray sky.

Panels of glow lights set in the walls were the room's only decorations. The austere surroundings were a reminder to the *Zelimir* that the council served its peoples and not vice versa, Niquela explained.

A single chair—human size—sat at the center of the room.

"Where will the *Zelimir* sit?"

"They will stand in your honor," Niquela replied.

"No!" Donalt shook his head vehemently. "I should honor them. The three races returned me to life. I'll stand and they will sit."

"They honor you, Donalt," Niquela repeated firmly, her eyes narrowing in reprimand. "To refuse that honor would be an insult."

Donalt paused and considered. "If we all stood or sat?"

"After the introductions." Niquela nodded her approval. "You may honor the *Zelimir* by requesting that seats be brought in. It will mean that you accept them as equals. Those who sit will accept the honor. Those who stand will pay you an even higher honor. . . ."

Donalt shrugged his acceptance. The rituals of the Three Planets were confusing.

". . . That is, except for the Uzoma, who do not sit," Niquela continued. "The Uzoma will be brought nestling rugs. If they move onto them, it will signify that they sit. If they do not, they show that they stand to honor you."

"You will remain with me during the meeting?" Donalt looked at the Brodny woman.

"It is not my place. However, since I am the Watcher of Donalt, none will object," Niquela replied.

"Then please order two nestling rugs for the Uzoma, two Liluye-size chairs for the representatives of Gaee, and three chairs for the Brodny," Donalt requested.

"Three for the Brodny?" Niquela stared at him, a puzzled expression on her face.

"Two for the Brodny *Zelimir* members and one for my Watcher."

Niquela's questioning look remained, but she hurried off to fill his request. Minutes later she returned to announce the arrival of the *Zelimir*.

Under Niquela's direction, Donalt took his place in the chair at the center of the room.

The *Zelimir* entered through the room's only door. First came the Brodny, male and female. Next were the Liluye, also male and female. The Uzoma, who had no sex, lumbered into the room behind the others.

Doreh and Lusal, of the bearlike Brodny, introduced themselves, then presented Donalt with a small wooden box. Inside a gowgem was strung to a chain of gold.

Uncertain of the gift's significance, the mind-merger lifted the necklace from the box. He examined it thoroughly and placed it about his neck.

From the corner of an eye, he caught Niquela's approving nod.

The Liluye representatives, Elee and Glekee, placed the bird race's equivalent of a microfiche reader in Donalt's lap. This, they explained, was a complete history of their race.

Donalt thanked them. He was unable to take his eyes from the two creatures. Niquela's description of Liluye beauty had been an understatement.

Both male and female were unclothed, displaying the iridescent plumage of their race. Niquela had assured him that the silky, soft down covering every inch of their bodies was in fact feathers—or what evolution had left of the Liluye's original feathers.

"Birdlike," too, was a misrepresentation of the Liluye. They were quite humanoid, except for the down, which caught the light and magnificently sent it rippling through the spectrum. Ethereal was the only word Donalt could find to describe their faces, the delicate grace of the Liluye.

They had arms and hands—four fingers and an opposable thumb—not wings. Nor was the beauty of their faces marred by a beak. The Liluye were merely descended from birdlike creatures. They were not birds.

The two Uzoma *were* slugs.

Mountainous gray slugs, whose bodies undulated when they approached Donalt. And their voices were "glub-a-glubs," just as the Liluye spoke in "tweets." Both Uzoma were also psiotic. Donalt sensed the emanations from the two representatives of the planet Canor.

Lunt and Uhm were their names. For Donalt, they brought a cloth sack filled with *oliry* seeds. Donalt's chemically induced memories told him the *oliry* was considered the staff of life among these giant slugs.

When the *Zelimir* lined themselves before his chair, Donalt stood.

"An orphan on your worlds, I have nothing to offer in return for your generosity. To show my gratitude, I give the only thing I have . . . myself."

He caught Niquela's disapproving frown. Whatever mistake in alien protocol he had committed, it was too late to retreat now. He took the only avenue open to him. He proceeded.

"As with the Brodny, the touching of hands is considered the offering of friendship among my race. I now extend that hand."

Without waiting for a reply, Donalt took the Brodny Doreh's hand and shook it. He walked down the line of the *Zelimir* members repeating the gesture.

The reaction to the hand-shaking was mildly startled expressions. Although he noticed the hint of smiles at the corners of the Brodny's and Liluye's mouths.

The Uzoma had no hands to shake. Donalt placed an open palm against their great necks.

Their skin texture was surprising. Not cold and slimy, but a rock hardness that was extremely warm. Equally surprising was the purr that rumbled in their massive bodies at his touch.

Donalt ordered the chairs and nestling rugs to be brought into the chamber when he returned to his seat. Only Niquela refused her offered chair, choosing to stand beside the human demigod she watched.

Seated in chairs, or lying on nestling rugs, the *Zelimir* faced the solitary human being they had come to honor. The merger returned the uncertain gaze. The resulting silence was almost tangible.

Donalt breathed a soft sigh of relief when the Uzoma Lunt spoke, asking of human religion. It could have been an easier question. But that did not matter. What was important was that it was a question, something to initiate conversation.

One human and six aliens—they talked the talk of strangers meeting for the first time. They shared their worlds and cultures.

For Donalt, who had anticipated a grilling bureaucratic cross-examination, it was an unexpected delight. The suspicion he had expected from the *Zelimir,* had expected from himself, was not there.

When the Uzoma, Liluye, and Brodny concluded the descriptions of their worlds, they offered them to him in the form of extensive tours of the Three Planets. They wished to show him all that had been achieved in the three hundred years since the Donalt-Erna's rescue.

"We offer you a home among the Three Planets," the Liluye Elee said.

Home.

The single word awoke a flood of confusion. Donalt attempted to suppress the sensations, the memories. Home lay three centuries in an irretrievable past.

"We also realize that you, Donalt, are not of the Three Planets." This from the Brodny Lusal. "That to dwell among our peoples would not be the same as to be among your own. We also offer to return you to your own galaxy . . . if that is your wish."

Donalt did a double take. He stared at the white-furred Lusal. Had he heard correctly? "You have the capability of intergalactic flight?"

"Another gift you have given us," Lusal said, explaining the knowledge of tachyon transformation had come from Donalt's brain.

Amazed, the merger listened while Liluye and Brodny described the twenty worlds that had been colonized within their galaxy. The Uzoma listened also, patiently. The sluglike race found interest in the stars only on a philosophical level. Actual travel to alien worlds held no attraction for them.

With childlike delight Donalt imagined the worlds the Three Planets reached out to claim as their own. Something, though, niggled at the back of his mind. It slowly worked itself forward. He had been offered a return ticket to the Milky Way. Surely that meant . . .

"Then . . . you have made contact with humans!" he blurted out during a description of the world Qat. "You traveled to the Milky Way!"

The *Zelimir* fell silent. Eyes darted nervously among the representatives of the Three Planets. Eventually the six looked back at the psiotic. Donalt needed no psi ability to realize something was wrong.

"Once we constructed ships to travel to your galaxy. We hoped your people could provide the knowledge of resurrection," Lusal said hesitantly. "Three ships to seek your people . . ."

The venture had taken place a century before Donalt's return to life. The three ships had been greeted by a small armada of human ships—warships.

"Two of our vessels were destroyed," Lusal concluded. "The third managed to escape and limp back to the Three Planets. No further ventures into your home galaxy have been attempted."

Donalt felt their eyes on him—expectant, waiting for an answer. There was no answer, only the heaviness in the psiotic's chest. Had so little changed? Two centuries after his death humankind still met the unknown with force rather than thought.

"And you are willing to make a return trip?" Donalt asked with realization of what they offered.

Lusal nodded. "If that is your wish."

Back to Chenoa, Lanatia—back to the worlds of humankind. Excitement rushed through Donalt. He could return! Death had claimed him twice, and he could return. Three hundred years and he could . . .

The excitement transformed to fear. What did the human realm offer him? Three hundred years had passed since last he walked with other humans.

Jenica's image floated like a phantasm in his mind. Those he had known were gone—all dead. Was there a place for a man who had not existed for three centuries? Was he even willing to attempt finding that place?

Donalt's gaze moved over the members of the *Zelimir*. They offered him an opportunity humankind had sought for millennia—three alien races with which to share the stars. No man had ever been presented such a chance.

No. That was wrong. Every human had been given the opportunity a hundred years ago. They had met it with violence.

"I have no wish to return." Donalt's head moved from side to side.

"Do not be hasty, Donalt." This from the Uzoma Uhm. "Take time to consider what we offer. You may wish to . . ."

"No," Donalt said firmly. "I will remain among the Three Planets."

"A schedule will be prepared for you then," Elee the Liluye said in high-pitched whistles. "If that is convenient."

"Each of our planets anticipates your arrival, Donalt," said the Uzoma Lunt. "Each city will hail your presence."

"All will be prepared, if you are certain it is your wish." Lusal stared intently at the man who had saved her race from the genocidal Erna.

"It is my wish," Donalt said, more certain of his choice than of anything in his life.

For a moment the *Zelimir* sat silently. Then they rose together.

Lusal spoke. "It is time for you to meet our peoples. If you are ready, Donalt?"

Donalt nodded as he stood. With Niquela at his side, he followed the council of the Three Planets from the domed chamber to stand naked before three races.

Donalt left the telecast in a ground effects vehicle—also in a deep burgundy jumpsuit. Except for a chauffeur, he was alone. Niquela had disappeared during the lengthy interview.

The merger's Brodny chauffeur, a giant among the bearlike race, who bore the name Chiah, explained that Niquela waited at their destination.

The destination was not Donalt's hospital room, but quarters that had been especially prepared for the psiotic during his stay on Orji.

Donalt settled in the seat beside Chiah and watched the monstrously large Brodny maneuver the vehicle. It was a touch of a past the merger had never known. Ground effects vehicles were the forerunners of the skimmers common to Donalt's time.

Niquela did wait at his new quarters. She quickly gave him a tour of the five rooms—all furnished with Brodny and human-size chairs. The beds, two of them in separate rooms, were both Brodny in design and size. Donalt did not complain; they were far more comfortable than the bunks aboard the *Crispus Attucks*.

The last stop on the hasty tour was a glass-enclosed balcony. The enclosure was to protect its human occupant from Orji's frigid temperatures.

Donalt stood on the balcony, watching the sky's thin blue slowly fade to the black of night. No moon moved in the heavens. The Donalt-Erna who had created this star system had overlooked moons.

Donalt remembered Chenoa's moons, the Three Sisters, and missed them. There was something special about moons, the wonderful silver of their light and the frosty touch it gave to the night.

He smiled. Orji had no need of the illusion of frost. The real article abounded on this world of ice and snow.

There were stars in the heavens. The entity that had created this solar system had nothing to do with the stars. Donalt's gaze caressed the diamond points inset in the velvet blackness. From where he stood, the Milky Way was no more than a phantomlike echo.

A sadness wove through the mind-merger. He did not know in which direction the Milky Way lay. At that moment, it seemed like the most important thing in the universe to know.

"Is there something wrong, Donalt?"

Donalt shook his head. There was, but he would learn to live with it.

"Is it me?" Niquela studied him. "Do I displease you in some manner?"

"No," he assured her, touching the back of her hand.

Did all sentient beings share insecurity, always believing themselves the source of another's discomfort?

"Is it the thing you have called nostalgia?"

"A longing for a place that never existed." Donalt smiled and shook his head again. "Once humans called it melancholy. A general state of the blues."

He had explained "blues" to Niquela; she did not approve.

"May I help in any way?" Her paw-sized hand touched his. "Perhaps to talk?"

"It will pass."

"No, it will not pass, Donalt," Niquela said sternly. "I have watched you closely. You revel in your blues. You delight in the sadness. It is not right. You should delight in the happiness of living."

"It will pass," he repeated.

He looked back at the night. His chest ached for something lost to him in time—three centuries in the past.

He heard Niquela move behind him, stepping away. He recognized the internal conflict he created within her. But he could offer no solution or comfort. He could not even comfort himself.

"Donalt," Niquela's voice was low and soft.

"Yes." His attention remained on the cold stars overhead.

"Donalt, please look at me."

He turned. His eyes widened and his mouth opened in surprise.

Niquela stood naked before him, her jumpsuit cast aside and lying in a rumpled heap on the floor. He had seen her naked before. But now . . .

His gaze slid over the soft, silky down that covered her breasts, barely hiding the pinkness beneath. The firm mounds trembled slightly.

"Niquela . . . I . . ." Donalt felt a stirring within him.

"There is no need for words." Niquela stepped forward. She took his hands and placed them on her breasts in a very human gesture.

"*Drisan,* Donalt. The time of *yannis* is over. Mourning must pass. You must learn to live again."

His palms gently slid over her breasts. His fingers sought and found the pink nipples that topped the downy mounds. He felt the buds of flesh thicken beneath his touch. He sensed anticipation quiver through the Brodny woman.

"Niquela . . . I . . ."

Ghosts drifted through Donalt's mind. Phantoms of two women who were mother-sisters. "It would be . . ."

"Wrong?" Niquela shook her head. "What we will share is never wrong, Donalt."

Her hands tauntingly drifted below his stomach. He felt himself stiffening beneath her light caresses.

"I don't want . . ." Donalt tried to protest, stubbornly clinging to visions dead for three hundred years.

"Your body says differently." Niquela refused to be

denied. "Is it that you fear conception? Tohom assured me that it would be impossible."

Donalt shook his head. "There was someone . . ."

"She is gone. If I could give her to you again, I would. That is beyond my ability, Donalt." Niquela's hand grew more persistent. "All I have is myself. That I give gladly."

Niquela's eyes met his. She was not a ghost. Anything but a ghost.

"It is what we need, Donalt. Both of us."

He nodded.

Together they walked into the closest bedroom. It *was* what he needed. He clung tightly to Niquela, holding back the need within him until her own need was sated. And when the consuming rush of desire had passed, they held each other through the remainder of the five and a half hours of the Orji night. Man, woman, male, female, human, Brodny, the differences did not matter, only the intimate contact of *drisan*.

‹TWENTY-SEVEN›

The first months were a blur in Donalt's memory. He hopped between the Three Planets on a personal appearance tour, never finding the involvement he sought. The months blurred into a year.

Even a demigod can tolerate the thin air atop a pedestal for only so long. The mind-merger protested loudly to Niquela, who in turn protested to the *Zelimir*.

Donalt was then allowed to come and go as he pleased. The interplanetary vessel *Mikpice* was placed at his beck and call, a chariot for a demigod.

Donalt's life continued at a much slower pace.

He began his own travels on Orji in its three cities, Ranithun, Kipar, and Qatir. He spent months in each. He observed, learned, and soaked in the alien culture of the Brodny.

No doors were locked to him. The *Zelimir* saw to that. The Brodny and their planet were his. On a whim he could visit laboratories where the bearlike race modified tachyon drives or live with a Brodny family. He did both.

And when a year had passed, he boarded the *Mikpice* and journeyed to the planet Gaee.

On the flight, Niquela met Ezer, captain of the vessel. Though neither of the Brodny said anything, it was obvious they had chosen each other for *karrme,* the Brodny equivalent of mates.

Donalt slept alone—his choice.

He refused to stand between the two Brodny. Niquela was uncertain, perhaps hurt by his decision, but Donalt stood firm. Ezer's bed became Niquela's. After a month, Niquela no longer protested, but accepted the unilateral decision.

Several times Donalt attempted to broach the subject of a formal ceremony with Niquela and Ezer. When Brodny took *karrme,* it was with joyous celebration and ritualistic ceremony. Neither Niquela nor Ezer would comment, nor would any other of the Brodny crew aboard the vessel.

Donalt was certain Niquela's role as Donalt-Watcher somehow inhibited the formalization of *karrme* between the two. He was unable to ascertain, however, exactly why, or how he could change the situation. Donalt accepted the present arrangement as did Niquela and Ezer. He also made a mental note to speak to the *Zelimir* again at the earliest opportunity.

The Liluye opened themselves in the same manner as the Brodny. Gaee was his. And Gaee was a world completely opposite to Orji.

The barren rock, the ice, the snow so common to the Brodny world were nonexistent on Gaee except at the polar caps. The Liluye's planet was one of forests and grass-covered plains. Donalt saw them all.

The Liluye cities, too, were unlike those of the Brodny. The bird-descended Liluye were unable to construct a single-story building. Their edifices mimicked the giant trees that covered most of their world, delicate spires that jutted like needles into the sky, spires of metal and glass.

On Gaee, Donalt met with the *Zelimir* for the second time. After an exchange of cordial greetings and pleasantries, he learned what he had suspected.

Niquela was his *karrme.*

The Donalt-Watcher was officially married to the man she was assigned to serve. The six members of the Three Planet council assured Donalt that he could sever his relationship with Niquela by the uttering of one simple public proclamation.

Unfortunately, that act was also considered the greatest of shames among the Brodny—a stigma Niquela would never be able to escape.

What appeared to be a dead end was not. The Brodny had no laws governing polygamy—just as they had no cultural taboos against homosexuality.

Donalt took his plan to Niquela and Ezer; they listened with bearlike frowns that slowly transformed into smiles and nods.

A month later a marriage of convenience took place.

Donalt now had two *karrme*—Niquela and Ezer. The latter

shared a bed; Donalt slept alone. The choice was his, not Niquela's, who offered *drisan* to both her *karrme*.

Eleven months after the *karrme* ceremony, Niquela bore a child, a male, which she named Radzer in honor of her two husbands. One of which had absolutely nothing to do with the conception.

And three years passed.

Canor was the planet of the sluglike Uzoma. There Niquela bore her second child, a daughter she called Doquela.

On Canor Donalt merged time and again with the awareness of the Uzoma. The Uzoma were philosophers. Unable to reproduce and immortal except for accidental or violent death, they were creatures devoted to thoroughness.

Both Brodny and Liluye held misconceptions about the third race of creatures sharing their star system. The Uzoma yearned for the stars. At the same time, they refused to leave their swamp world until they had total understanding of it.

"Knowledge is like the water of my *untu*," Lunt, a representative to the *Zelimir*, explained to Donalt after a lengthy merge.

Untu roughly translated in Donalt's brain as "home pool."

"It is not enough to recognize that it is water," Lunt continued. "I must recognize each molecule and the way it interacts with the others. If an entity does not possess the knowledge of that which it considers familiar, could it truly understand that which it considers unfamiliar?"

The Uzoma and their methodical probing of the small portion of the universe where they dwelled was as maddening as discussions about the number of angels who could dance on the head of a pin. At the same time, Donalt found a beauty in the Uzoma's minds he had never encountered before. The simplicity of the giant slugs was their complexity. The complexity, simplicity.

The Uzoma lived for the sake of living. They learned for the joy of learning. They moved in care of their world and the various lifeforms Canor sheltered. The Uzoma were without violence. They understood it, had seen it; it simply was not part of their existence.

After two years, Donalt, aboard the *Mikpice,* left Canor and returned to Gaee. Eight years had passed since the Brodny resurrected a three-century-old dead man, and Donalt discovered he was filled with discontent.

• • •

They placed him and his two *karrme* on top of the Liluye world. The demigod Donalt had returned. Thus they honored their human savior by quartering him in spacious apartments on the highest level of the tallest spire in the largest of Liluye cities, Pialeet.

Donalt stood on the balcony with hands planted firmly on the metal railing. Above, the Gaee night burned with a million blinking stars. The discontent the merger had first felt among the Uzoma would not leave him. The cool Gaee breeze offered no comfort.

A door hissed open behind him. Donalt turned. Niquela stepped onto the balcony and smiled.

"Stargazing?"

"Just getting a breath of fresh air." A wistful sigh unintentionally punctuated his words.

Niquela did her Brodny best to arch a nonexistent eyebrow, an expression she had adopted from her human *karrme* over the years. "Is there something wrong, Donalt?"

The psiotic shook his head. There was, but he had been unable to locate the source of his discontent.

"The melancholy has returned?" Niquela walked to his side and took his hand in hers. "Would it help to talk?"

"It would, if I could put it into words." He squeezed the paw-sized hand.

"Perhaps I could try and put it into words for you."

He glanced skeptically at her.

"I am the Donalt-Watcher. It is my duty to understand the subject of my observations." She smiled and shrugged, another gesture she had learned from him.

"A clinical way of putting it."

"A part of this Donalt-Watcher remains clinical. We are *karrme,* we are friends, we have been lovers. But I remain the Donalt-Watcher, whose duty is to serve Donalt."

"And how may Donalt be served?" He smiled, still skeptical.

Niquela glanced to the stars. Her gaze hung there for a moment before looking back at Donalt.

"Out there you can be served." There was a sadness in her voice. "The stars call to you. They have always called to you, but you have denied their call. Now you listen."

"There is nothing out there for me," he assured her.

"There are your people," Niquela said simply. "You yearn to be among your race. You have always wanted that."

Donalt shook his head. That life lay three centuries behind him, lost in time. There was no returning to it. He had accepted that years ago.

Acceptance did not remove the ache. *Jenica.* Her memory clung to his mind, a three-hundred-year-old ghost that could not be exorcised.

"I have a place here, now. A life." Donalt glanced back to the stars. He still did not know in what direction lay the Milky Way. "You're wrong, Niquela. There is nothing for me out there."

"You hear the call, but you refuse to listen," she continued persistently. "Donalt, you have not found a place among the Three Planets. The life you live is not your own. Lunt sensed it. He tried to tell you as much."

Something he did not want to admit wedged into his mind and he tried to bury it. It wiggled to the surface again.

"And you think I'll find it out there?"

"Not out there . . . but with other humans." Niquela's eyes seemed more moist than usual. "You've tried to find a life here. It hasn't worked. You want to go home."

"I love the Three Planets," Donalt protested.

"I do not doubt that love. But you are . . ."

"A *tourist*." Donalt spat the word that summed up what he had refused to admit for too many years.

He was a tourist, sight-seeing on three alien planets. He even maintained the charade of an alien marriage and family, a charade that had fooled no one. He existed, but found no purpose for that existence. He accepted the life the Three Planets paid in tribute to a demigod, but he gave nothing in return. He was not a demigod; he was a man.

In that single admission lay the source of his discontent.

"My people are gone," he said, turning from Niquela. "They are dead."

"No," she said firmly. "They are your people. You can deny them with words, but not with your spirit. You are a human being and need others of your race. It is natural. The love you have found for the peoples of the Three Planets is undiminished by that need. . . ."

She paused. Donalt looked back at Niquela. The wetness at the corners of her eyes threatened to overflow as tears. He took her into his arms and held her.

"You understood my need for Ezer. Do you think I am incapable of seeing that same need within you, my love?" She lightly kissed his cheek.

They eased from one another, hands squeezing.

"The *Zelimir*'s offer . . . a ship," he said as though just recalling the Three Planet council's offer to return him to a galaxy humans called the Milky Way. The thought was not new. The ship had always been at the back of his mind.

"All you have to do is ask for it," Niquela said. "I could arrange for a meeting with the *Zelimir* this night, if you wish."

Donalt grinned. Niquela was once more the Donalt-Watcher. "Tomorrow will be soon enough. How long do you think it will take for the ship . . ."

"To be ready," she completed his sentence, as though she had always been prepared to answer it, "six months at the most. Earlier if you request it."

"Six months." He grinned. "Six months."

He looked back to the Gaee night. The stars appeared warmer and closer.

‹TWENTY-EIGHT›

From the *Mikpice,* the starship *Kwam Giile*—the *Light Dancer*
—appeared to be a great gleaming elongated egg rather than a
spacecraft capable of slicing across the galaxies as a coalesced
stream of tachyons. No human could ever call the *Kwam Giile*
beautiful, but in space beauty was not a prerequisite for efficiency and effectiveness. The *Kwam Giile* was both efficient
and effective, Ezer reassured his human *karrme* of convenience.

"The *Kwam Giile* was Ezer's ship before the *Zelimir* honored him by appointing him captain of the *Mikpice*." Niquela
craned her neck to see out the observation bay.

"Tomorrow the craft will be mine again," Ezer said, his
chest swelling like a barrel. Donalt eyed his friend. The appointment as captain of the small interplanetary *Mikpice*
might have been an honor, but Ezer's official duty of chauf-
feuring a demigod between the Three Planets had left something to be desired.

In the past years Ezer had never displayed any hint that he
missed the life that had been his aboard the faster-than-light
ship. Now the merger recognized just how much Ezer had
missed it.

Tourist.

The word echoed in the merger's mind. He had *lived* with
this Brodny! And still he did not know him.

His eyes rolled toward Niquela. What secrets did she still
hide? What had she kept hidden from him? If he were to
spend a lifetime among the peoples of the Three Planets,
would he know them any better?

Tourist.

The rumble of maneuvering rockets vibrated through the *Mikpice* as its nose swung toward the *Kwam Giile*. A docking bay opened on the larger vessel like a yawning mouth ready to swallow the *Mikpice*.

"Two months." Niquela's voice and expression were distant as she watched the metal egg loom closer. "I never thought the *Zelimir* would move so quickly."

Nor that both your karrme *would leave when the time came,* Donalt filled in her unspoken words. He reached out and touched the back of her hand.

Niquela glanced at him and smiled weakly.

The *Mikpice* slid smoothly into the open bay of the larger ship.

First on the tour of *Kwam Giile* was Donalt's quarters. The compartments—a total of three—would have made five of Psi Corps Operations aboard the *Crispus Attucks*.

In spite of the spaciousness, Donalt was struck by the similarity between these rooms and innumerable rooms that had been his on countless LofAl ships. A spacecraft was a spacecraft whether it be Kavinite, LofAl, or Brodny. The bulkheads were bulkheads; the overheads, overheads; the decks, decks.

Donalt and entourage moved to tour the vessel's six levels.

The *Kwam Giile* was big—Brodny-sized. But it was all too familiar to the psiotic. The only major difference from LofAl ships that Donalt noticed was that the tunnel-corridors were square rather than round.

As with LofAl vessels, at least those of three centuries before, the *Kwam Giile* was fully armed. The Three Planets had journeyed to humankind's galaxy once; this time, they were prepared for the worst.

So was Donalt.

On the command deck, Donalt, Niquela, and Ezer were joined by Lunt, Doreh, and Glekee. Half the *Zelimir* would also make the voyage, official envoys from the Three Planets to the worlds of humankind.

Donalt smiled at the Uzoma. Lunt peered at the various consoles and equipment that packed the command deck. A rumble of disapproval rolled from the throat of the mountainous slug.

Lunt looked to his human friend. "It is not my *untu*,

Donalt. But I shall endure. It is my duty. It is expected of me.''

"It is said that adversity is good for the soul. It strengthens character.'' Donalt placed his palm against the creature's massive neck.

"The being who said that was a fool,'' Lunt rumbled in a boulderlike voice. His attention returned to the consoles and winking lights.

After the guided tour, Donalt returned to his quarters, where he dressed formally—in a new white jumpsuit—for what he dubbed "The Last Supper.''

The meal was a gathering of officers and crew in the *Kwam Giile*'s immense galley. Brodny officials, like their human counterparts, relished ceremony. "The Last Supper'' was seven courses of speeches and one of food, telecast to the people of Canor, Gaee, and Orji.

The merger, like the other speakers, made no mention of what might await the *Kwam Giile* when it reached its destination. There was no need; the fate of the first three ships that had ventured into the human realm was history, and known all too well.

When the telecast, ceremony, and meal were concluded, Donalt remained in the galley with Lunt at his side for an hour. He met those among the crew who wished to talk with the demigod they were to ferry across the universe.

Niquela and Ezer disappeared. Donalt approved. It would be the last night they would share for months, perhaps years.

He refused to believe that it might be their last night *ever*.

The crowd thinned, and Donalt bid good night to the Uzoma and retreated to his quarters. Alone, he gave the three rooms that would be his home for the next months a final inspection.

And then?

He carefully avoided envisioning what might await the *Kwam Giile* on the other side of the universe. What would be, would be.

Donalt undressed and slipped into a Brodny-sized bunk. He closed his eyes, but sleep would not come. He tossed to one side, then the other. Neither was comfortable.

While he silently cursed his anticipation of tomorrow's launch and the unknowns that lay ahead, he fell asleep.

•   •   •

The hiss of an opening hatch intruded on a dream more than three centuries old. Donalt's eyes half opened. He listened and heard nothing. He rolled to a side, pushed the imagined sound from his mind, and closed his eyes again.

The sound of soft footfalls came from one of the other compartments.

Donalt pushed to his elbows.

"Donalt?" Someone whispered his name. "Donalt?"

"Niquela?"

A light flashed on in the compartment next to his bedroom. He blinked against the harsh invasion of the darkness. When his eyes opened, Niquela stood in the doorway.

"I'm sorry to have disturbed your sleep." She moved to the edge of his bed.

Donalt sat up; his brow knitted. "What's the matter? Is something wrong?"

Niquela's head moved from side to side. "I needed to talk with you."

He patted the edge of the bed for her to sit. Niquela's knees bent, then she stood straight.

"It is not talk I came for, Donalt." Her dark eyes locked to his. "I came to be with my *karrme*—to share *drisan*. You have denied me your bed for too many years. Now, this last night before you leave our worlds, I will not be denied."

Donalt nodded, offering no word of protest. This night he needed the closeness of another being, the warmth of one he loved. And as Niquela had said, it had been too many years since they had shared the pleasures of *drisan*.

He watched as Niquela touched the neck of her jumpsuit and the invisible seam opened down the front. With a toss of shoulders and a wiggle, the suit fell free.

She slid into the bed beside her human *karrme*. For a moment Brodny and human gazed at each other as though uncertain. Then their hands spoke, relearning the language that is never truly forgotten.

Tenderly they touched, allowing the gentleness of their palms to transmit the love that had grown between them, that would always be with them. An aura of timelessness englobed and held them. Donalt sensed it, sensed Niquela recognized it. Almost leisurely, their hands and mouths explored, neither wishing to destroy the intimacy of the moment.

When she eventually moved beneath his weight, he entered

the liquid warmth of her body. Their bodies rocked in a slow, sleepy duet. The lulling rhythm spoke not of desire and lust, but of a need for the intimate contact of two beings who loved —who faced the possible end to all they had shared.

Donalt woke to the persistent nudging of his shoulder. He grunted and opened his eyes. Niquela lay beside him, dark eyes studying his face.

"It is morning," she said.

Donalt glanced at the overhead, squinting. The lights were on—the artifical sunrise aboard a spacecraft. He groaned. The night had been long with little sleep.

"They will be calling for the *Mikpice*'s passengers soon." She tossed back the covers and slid from the bed. "I must get ready."

Sitting in the bed, Donalt watched the Brodny woman who had been his *karrme,* companion, lover, and friend for more than eight years. For the first time in longer than he wished to admit, he realized how truly beautiful Niquela was—how much she had become a part of him during his years among the Three Planets. The heaviness in her voice settled on his heart.

"There is still time for you to change your mind and come with us," Donalt said as he stood and took a fresh green jumpsuit from a closet inset in a bulkhead.

Niquela stared at him a moment, then shook her head.

"There is no need for a Donalt-Watcher when Donalt is among his own people. Ezer will watch over you until then."

"Niquela . . ." he began.

"And there are Radzer and Doquela," she said before he could complete his sentence. "The decision was mine to remain with them. They, too, need watching."

Donalt nodded, acquiescing. The three of them, Niquela, Ezer, and he, had discussed Niquela's coming on the journey a month before. She had been adamant about not wanting to participate in the *Kwam Giile*'s flight. She never offered an explanation.

The mind-merger was uncertain why she refused a place aboard the ship. He did not press. Too many unknowns awaited the flight to unnecessarily risk her life.

A buzzer sounded. A Liluye voice came over the intercom to announce the departure of the *Mikpice* in thirty minutes.

Donalt dressed and with Niquela in arm walked to the Brodny equivalent of a dropshaft, a null-grav tube with a steady stream of air that moved its occupants downward. Ezer waited in the bay area. The big Brodny grinned widely when he saw them. He gave both of them a very bearlike hug.

"The night was good. *Karrme* should share *drisan*. It is right." He beamed, then his face turned solemn. "It is the way it should be at times of parting."

Donalt looked at Niquela, who returned her Brodny *karrme*'s hug, then kissed him. She turned to Donalt, giving the merger a long hug and kiss. There were tears in her eyes when they parted. The same wetness blurred Donalt's vision.

"Come back to me, Donalt . . . if only to visit the one who was your Watcher," she said.

"I will be back," Donalt tried to reassure her, less than certain of his words. "I'll be back."

With two quick hugs and kisses for her *karrme,* Niquela pivoted sharply and boarded the *Mikpice*. She did not glance back.

"We will both return, Donalt." Ezer's hand reached out to squeeze the psiotic's shoulder. "I am now the Donalt-Watcher, and I will see to that."

Donalt looked up at the big Brodny male and smiled. "That's a promise I intend to hold you to, Ezer."

Again Ezer nodded solemnly. The heavy clang of metal on metal jerked his head around.

The bay doors closed behind the *Mikpice*. The sound of pumps filled the bay area as they sucked the air from the airlock in preparation for the smaller craft's launch to Orji.

Ezer turned to the mind-merger. "We can watch from the command deck, Donalt, if you wish."

Donalt nodded, then followed Ezer to a liftshaft that led to command level. There they watched the *Mikpice* reenter Orji's atmosphere and safely descend on-planet.

An hour later only the grays of tachyon space filled the optical sensors. And Donalt found that the transition to faster-than-light speed aboard a Brodny vessel was just as hard on his system as it was in a LofAl cruiser.

‹TWENTY-NINE›

The *Kwam Giile* entered the Milky Way near the planetless star Lasser. It remained there ten minutes to verify and reverify trajectory. Course modifications complete, the Brodny spacecraft punched back into tachyon space to continue its journey to Lanatia.

A week later the process was repeated in the Molimo system. The third and final trajectory check came seven standard days later in the Jacinta system.

A greeting party awaited the *Kwam Giile*'s arrival—fifteen human-designed destroyers. Afloat around the battleships was a small armada of Swarmer-class attack vehicles. They englobed the alien ship.

Donalt stood beside Ezer on the *Kwam Giile*'s command level, studying the optical sensor images displayed on the array of monitors. The ships englobing the Brodny craft hung five kilometers from the hull. Donalt had no doubt that they waited for the slightest display of aggression—or what the destroyers' captains interpreted as aggression—to bring them into action.

"Defensive shields?" Ezer looked at his human companion, obviously seeking any advice he could get.

"I think it would be suicide." Donalt shook his head. Although the human ships were protected by their own shields, the merger feared even normal defensive procedures would be interpreted as offensive moves by the human vessels. "Right now," he said, "I believe it would be wise to just sit here until contact is made."

Ezer tilted his bearlike head in affirmation, then called out for communications to attempt contact with the vessels on full frequency range. At Donalt's suggestion, the captain of the *Kwam Giile* ordered the optics telescoped.

The psiotic slowly moved his head from side to side while he examined the close-up views of the englobing spacecraft. "I've never seen the markings before. They're neither LofAl nor Kavinite ships."

He glanced back at the white-bordered octagon painted on the naked metal of each ship. The design contained a yellow triangle within its red field. Again Donalt shook his head. The marking was totally unknown to him.

"Captain," a Liluye called to Ezer, "no response from the alien vessels on normal frequency range."

Alien vessels. It sounded strange to Donalt, but what else were humans to the inhabitants of the Three Planets? He had been among them long enough that he no longer considered the three races alien.

Ezer's mouth opened; his reply was left unspoken. A Brodny called out to him.

"Captain, sensor readings indicate a photon beam has been focused at *Kwam Giile* since tachyon shift. The computing unit is unable to identify the beam beyond locating its source —a ship at point three-seven off the port."

"Communications?" Ezer frowned at his human *karrme*.

"Could be." Donalt sucked at his cheeks and shrugged. "Three hundred years can bring a hell of a lot of technological changes."

"Which does not offer us many options." Ezer turned to communications and ordered the attempt to contact the ships to continue.

"There is another way we might be able to contact the destroyers," Donalt said as he studied the englobing ships on the monitors.

"How?"

"Me," Donalt said simply. "And perhaps Lunt. We're both psiotic."

Ezer nodded his approval.

Linked with the Uzoma, Donalt floated on the mental streams of alpha level. Unlike a human psiotic, Lunt remained able to move and speak. The giant slug gave Ezer a running account of what Donalt was doing.

If . . . *if* . . . the attempt to merge was misinterpreted, Ezer would at least have the opportunity to throw up the *Kwam Giile* defensive shield and punch back into tachyon space before the destroyers reduced the vessel to molten slag.

A slim chance, Donalt admitted, *but a chance just the same.*

The merger reached out. Across space, beyond the sphere of englobing Swarmers, he wove the harnassed psi energy. He worked toward the destroyer transmitting the photon beam.

He touched a mind—a human mind.

It recoiled.

Then it was there again.

If Donalt had been able to smile while in alpha state, he would have smiled. He recognized the mental gymnastics, the probes, the subtle delving of the mind he encountered. He recognized them because they were the same intricate maneuvers he had performed a thousand times during his Psi Corps service.

They were the delicate threads of a mind-merger attempting to wiggle his way beyond the mental barriers Donalt had erected to protect his own mind from invasion. The delving probes came quicker, a barrage that exceeded Donalt's own abilities. But they were the same.

Gradually, Donalt lowered his mental defenses. For the first time in his life, he allowed another human mind to control him.

Ezer loomed over him when Donalt edged away the fuzziness of alpha state. Worry tautened the Brodny's face.

"What happened? Lunt said your mind was blocked from his contact."

"Contact made." Donalt smiled up weakly. "A fellow merger aboard the destroyer . . . the *Excel* of the Tripartite Confederation."

"Tripartite Confederation?"

Donalt recounted the thumbnail history of the human race's past three hundred years that he had gleaned from memories implanted during the merge with the psiotic Dagaim Kesin onboard the *Excel*. The Tripartite government had been formed two centuries ago from the remains of the LofAl, Kavinite Empire, and a federation of one hundred independent planets. It now governed the five hundred worlds of humankind.

"Then they accept our mission as a peaceful one?" Ezer asked when his friend concluded.

"With reservations," Donalt said. "We have been given a choice. To surrender the ship and ourselves into the custody of the Tripartite Confederation . . . or to be destroyed."

Donalt saw anger tense every muscle in Ezer's bearlike body. The ultimatum was an insult to the peaceful envoy sent by the Three Planets.

Body rigid, Ezer nodded. "Tell them we place ourselves in their protective custody, Donalt. Emphasize *protective!*"

Donalt once more entered alpha level to convey Ezer's decision.

Interrogation atop interrogation followed the Tripartite Confederation's boarding and occupation of the *Kwam Giile*. Donalt was confined to his quarters. Teams of two to four persons questioned him for forty-eight standard hours before allowing six hours sleep. The questioning continued for a week.

During that time he saw no one but his interrogators and the psi team that delved his mind twice daily. And questions he asked were ignored. Only by an instant of nausea and disorientation did he realize the Brodny vessel was once more in tachyon space. Its destination, however, remained unknown.

On the eighth morning after the boarding, the guards and interrogators left his quarters. Lieutenant Jon Marit entered. The young officer waited while Donalt ate, showered, and dressed, then led the merger to Ezer's quarters.

Inside the Brodny sat talking with a man wearing gold braid on his shoulders and sleeves. The man rose and introduced himself as Captain Tymon Wald of the *Excel*.

While Donalt seated himself beside Ezer, Wald touched two fingers to his left wrist as though taking his own pulse. It was a gesture Donalt had seen often during the past seven days. The merger questioned the gesture when Wald took his fingers from his wrist.

"My Com-Net link," the captain said with a smile the psiotic could only describe as condescending. "Every individual is fitted with one at birth. It places us in direct interface with Com-Net's computing and memory banks."

Com-Net was a three-century-updated version of the now outmoded Con-Web, Wald explained. Genetically engineered nerves transmitted mental commands to a micro-micro-interface-interpretor surgically implanted in the wrist.

"Com-Net has informed me the transmission will be ready in ten minutes," Wald concluded.

"Transmission?"

The Tripartite Confederation captain glanced at his Brodny counterpart. "I see no reason for going through this explanation a hundred different times. Your crew will be briefed as I brief you. Everything we say and do will be transmitted to the other ships as well as to Lanatia."

Wald touched a buttonlike medallion strung about his neck. "Full holo and audio capabilities."

"Lanatia?" Donalt looked questioningly at the man.

"The same planet that once headquartered the Lofgrin Alliance," Wald assured him. "It's the closest Tripartite governmental seat. The top brass want to meet with the *Zelimir* representatives as soon as possible. The existence of three alien cultures is big news, Mister Donalt. You'll probably earn a place in the history files for what you've done." Wald smiled. "Me, too, if Com-Net deems my command of the fleet worthy of memory storage."

"My crew . . . why can't you speak directly to them? The galley was designed for such briefings."

Wald glanced at Ezer, his expression one of chagrin. "Eighty per cent of your crew is no longer onboard your vessel, Captain."

He paused as though searching for the correct words. "I deemed it prudent to divide the members of your crew among the various ships in the fleet. It made debriefing easier for all and assured the security of those in our protection."

From the frown on Ezer's face, Donalt realized his companion understood that debriefing meant interrogation and protection meant confinement under armed guard.

"Now I realize such measures were unnecessary. But I am certain you can appreciate my caution and concern. You would have acted similarly had our positions been reversed." Wald smiled politely.

"You have much to learn of the peoples of the Three Planets, Captain Wald." Donalt's throat and vocal cords tingled strangely, unaccustomed to his own language. When he noticed it, his head jerked around to Ezer, eyebrow raised. "You spoke . . ."

"An injection similar to those you received when Tohom resurrected you," Ezer smiled. "Compliments of Captain

Wald. Under protest! I was not told what the injection was."

"Injections have been given to all members of the crew," Wald said. "Orders from Lanatia. Communication is far easier this way."

There was something about the man that Donalt did not like—an air of superiority. When he spoke, it was as though he were conversing with children.

Wald's head bobbed a bit. He appeared to be listening to a distant sound; it was his link with Com-Net.

"Captain, Mister Donalt, we will begin transmission in . . . ten seconds."

Wald seated himself across from Donalt and smiled another condescending smile. His head once more did a little jerk.

"On behalf of the Tripartite Confederation, I extend a welcome to the officers and crew of the *Kwam Giile* and the three representatives of the Three Planet *Zelimir*," Wald began. "And, of course, we extend our appreciation for returning a lost son to his home. . . ."

Wald's words were official, long, and ninety percent crap. *Lost son*. What speechwriter had labored a week to come up with that phrase, Donalt wondered.

"From your lengthy debriefings we have concluded that a grievous error was unknowingly perpetuated on the peoples of the Three Planets by our ancestors," Wald continued. "It is my hope that the circumstances surrounding that first tragic meeting of our races will not overshadow the mission of this peaceful envoy."

Diplomatic crap now. Still, Donalt listened while Wald offered an official quasi-apology for the destruction of the original Three Planet ships that had entered the Milky Way.

"You must consider the events that embroiled the human worlds at that time . . ."

Wald then gave a sketchy history of the LofAl–Kavinite conflict, carefully avoiding the word *war*, followed by a full history of the *Seeker* and its two voyages. Donalt smiled to himself. According to Wald, Donalt's participation in the second *Seeker* journey was stored in a sub-sub-memory filed with Com-Net, which was why the "debriefing" had taken a full week.

"Mass paranoia, mass hysteria, best describe the state of the human worlds when it was revealed *what* the *Seeker* had encountered in REV-nine-oh-seven-three-two-P," Wald said.

"Xenophobia was more than just a word to our ancestors. It was a reality. The Erna existed and they were capable of destroying our worlds.

"The war between Kavinite and Lofgrinist never reached a formal conclusion. It simply faded to the background, forgotten while humankind rallied to face a possible invasion by the Erna . . .

". . . or unknown alien threats that awaited beyond the limits of our own galaxy," Wald said, his eyes on Ezer. "This unreasoning fear still ruled our race when the first envoy from the Three Planets entered the Milky Way."

Wald paused and looked at Ezer for understanding. The massive Brodny said nothing.

Wald began again apologizing for the attack on the original ships from the Three Planets without ever truly apologizing. Nor did he say humankind accepted responsibility for the tragic mistake that it had made. Instead it was blamed on stupidity, paranoia, ignorance, and fear.

Donalt listened. Time had changed technology, but diplomacy remained the same. So much easier to place the burden of the butchery on intangible concepts and long-dead ancestors.

Cynic.

Donalt chided himself as his attention returned to Wald and the offer he extended from the Tripartite Confederation. In two weeks, on Lanatia, the new government of humankind was willing to officially begin negotiations to open diplomatic and commerical relations with the Three Planets.

The proposal, which Ezer accepted in the name of the *Zelimir,* seemed anticlimactic and mundane. Humankind had made contact with three alien races—and bureaucracy reigned!

Again, Donalt recognized his cynicism.

His worst fears about the fate of his own race had not been realized. *Homo sapiens* still existed—still lived. And they had learned to live together in peace.

And that, Radman Donalt, is reason to celebrate. It just might mean there's hope for the human animal after all. He smiled. *There is hope!*

His smile grew. In his own way, he had played a part—now relegated to a sub-sub-memory file—in bringing about that peace.

There is hope!

‹THIRTY›

Donalt slidewalked from the Lanatia Museum of the Arts. He had wanted to plug a few of the myriad holes in the three hundred years of human history that had passed while he had been dead.

The museum only served to stretch three centuries into what now seemed like millennia. He remembered the art portfolio he had given Michaela Gosheven prior to the *Crispus Attucks* flight to Lanatia several lifetimes ago. Even if the prints had not been to his taste, he *had* recognized *Polymorphic Flesh Dreams* as an art form.

He could not say the same for what he had just viewed for six hours. The definition of "art" changed with each generation. His definition lay in a sub-sub-memory file of Com-Net.

A couple slid toward him on the walk. The woman—young, perhaps twenty—tugged at her companion's sleeve and pointed toward the mind-merger. The man glanced in Donalt's direction. He shook his head.

"It can't be him. He's . . ."

The man's words were sucked away in doppler effect as the two moved past the psiotic. A bittersweet smile uplifted the corners of Donalt's mouth. Thus passed the glory of a man.

Six months ago, he had been unable to walk alone on Lanatia without gathering a crowd. The media had found an instant hero in Radman Donalt—**MAN FROM PAST UNITES THE GALAXIES**—so proclaimed the news commentators.

He had united nothing. The *Zelimir* representatives were still in negotiations with the Tripartite Confederation. Apparently the Three Planets relished the legal intricacies of diplomacy as much as their human counterparts did.

Donalt searched the city passing on each side of him. Its architecture reminded him of the museum's contents—unrecognizable. Each edifice bulged upward without angle. There was an organic appearance to the structures. They gave the illusion—a claustrophobic illusion—of melting into one another. Great oozing lumps of stone and glass.

He recalled a restaurant that had once provided a "real" beefsteak for Jenica and him one noon three hundred years in the past. The restaurant and the street that had held it no longer existed. He knew; he had spent a day looking for it.

Beefsteak was also a thing that belonged to history.

Protein—meat—was now human protein produced by recombinant DNA. It had taken Donalt a month before he could take his first bite of the synthesized meat, despite the claims that it was more readily usable by the human system than any other meat.

He had eaten it once, then became a vegetarian. He did not enjoy feeling like a cannibal while he dined. An archaic attitude, he realized. But then Radman Donalt was archaic—a living fossil that dwelled in a universe of culture shock.

He stepped from the slidewalk in front of a monstrous bubble of seamless glass. *Home.* The thought brought an inner cringe. The building, or at least a three-room apartment within, was home.

The apartment, and a monthly tax-free one thousand standard credits, were his for life—a gift from a grateful Tripartite Confederation for escorting the Uzoma, Liluye, and Brodny to the human worlds. Enough for three men to live on comfortably, he had been assured. He did not doubt that. The standard credit had doubled in value each century since his death.

The apartment and monthly allotment had been given in good faith, but they made Donalt feel like a man living on charity. He had nothing to offer in return for the gifts, not even his psi ability. Genetic engineering had produced ambulatory psiotics. Team that with Com-Net–boosted minds, and he was as obsolete as skimmers on a world with matter transmission . . . which the human worlds also possessed.

Inside the gigantic blister of glass he liftshafted to his floor, exited, and walked to his apartment.

"Good afternoon, Radman." The voice of Kate Dunbar greeted him.

He nodded toward the Com-Net terminal to one side of a circular room.

The terminal, Brodny-designed, was the Tripartite Confederation's answer to the merger's lack of a biological interface with Com-Net. Kate Dunbar had been Donalt's idea when he discovered the former Psi Corps Director's brain was still a functioning part of the system. Dunbar and he shared a certain sense of immortality that was out of step with the rest of the universe.

"I triple-checked the files as you requested, Radman," Kate continued. "Would you care to view the results?"

"Only if you've got something new."

Donalt plopped down on a form-fitting lump that served as a sofa. Probing Com-Net's memory files had become an obsession during the past month. He searched for any and all records that pertained to his psi team; he searched for Jenica.

"I have located two more of Michaela Gosheven and Howin Bickle's descendants," the voice of Kate Dunbar said from the terminal. "One is a woman named Gressa Shen. She is a government employee on the planet Seker. The other is a Asela Pokii. She is a holodrama star on the planet Nissim."

Donalt smiled. "Do you have a holo of Asela . . . whatever her name was?"

"Pokii," Kate supplied. "I have stored one of her holodramas if you wish to view it."

"Later," Donalt answered. It would help pass the evening. "And Jenica Stoy's descendants?"

"Radman, Com-Net contains no records of any descendants of the woman Jenica Stoy."

Donalt edged forward. The lump contoured itself to his new position. "Nothing whatsoever?"

"There is a problem with Jenica Stoy," Kate said.

Donalt thought he detected hesitancy in her voice.

"The memory files pertaining to Jenica Stoy were destroyed during the last days of the war between the Kavinite Empire and the Lofgrin Alliance."

Donalt pushed forward again. "Destroyed? How?"

Kate's most recent report on Jenica traced her activities in the Psi Corps for five years after the return of the *Seeker*. At that time, she had resigned from the Corps.

"A Kavinite attack on the planet Roi-Tamu destroyed fifty percent of the Con-Web facilities there."

"Roi-Tamu? Where in hell is that? How did Jenica get there?"

A holographic display formed in front of the terminal to provide a three-dimensional star map showing the planet's relative position to Lanatia. Roi-Tamu lay within a spiral arm of the galaxy.

"Jenica Stoy was among a group of two hundred colonists to the planet Roi-Tamu. She left Chenoa a year after her resignation from the Psi Corps."

The hologram dissolved. Donalt stared at the terminal again.

"For two years, she worked as a psiotic for a mining interest on Roi-Tamu. That's when the Kavinite attack came."

"Then there is no more to be found about Jenica. . . ." Donalt sank back in/on the lump. *Had she died in the attack?*

"One last bit of information. Being a colonial planet, Roi-Tamu did nothing to replace the destroyed memory files. However, an accurate record of births and deaths were maintained. The records contain a single entry pertaining to a Jenica Stoy. It records her death at age one hundred eight years," Kate replied.

She had not been killed in the Kavinite attack!

"Nothing else? No mention of marriage, contract-mates, children?"

"Nothing, Radman. As I said, I triple-checked the files at your request."

"Nothing else!" He spoke his frustration aloud.

Jenica lived out the remainder of her life on a LofAl colonial planet named Roi-Tamu. And she died. That was all he knew. All that he would ever know.

If the years were an indication, Jenica had lived a full life. He tried to imagine what those years had been like for her. He attempted to envision the eighteen-year-old girl he had known as an elderly woman. Had there been someone there to grow old beside her? He hoped so. How he hoped so.

Memories flooded Donalt's mind. Bittersweet reminiscences of the one night he had shared with Jenica. One single night . . . and her ghost still haunted him after three centuries.

The starman, he wondered. Had Jenica ever found the fire-winged image of her prescient visions? Had she found anyone to love? To return that love?

The door to the apartment hissed open behind Donalt. He

turned to see Ezer enter. The big Brodny gave a very bearlike growl, a sign of his own frustration.

"No progress at the negotiations," Donalt greeted his friend.

Ezer's large head moved from side to side. "They have lost any semblance of sanity, Donalt. Brodny, Liluye, Uzoma, and human argue over the punctuation of a document they have been working on for six months. Adult beings should have more common sense. Either ships travel between our galaxies, or they do not. It is that simple."

"Lunt must be—" Donalt began.

"Excuse me, Radman," Kate interrupted. "Before you and Ezer become engrossed in today's lack of progress at the negotiations, I would like to know if you wish me to continue searching for information on Jenica Stoy."

"No . . . yes!" Donalt answered. "There might be something more tucked away within one of Com-Net's sub-sub-memory files."

Donalt turned back to Ezer. The Brodny frowned.

"You're still attempting to find information on Jenica Stoy?"

"Nothing better to do." Donalt shrugged. "It keeps me busy."

"My *karrme,* there is much to be said for your own lack of sanity." Ezer joined Donalt on the lump-sofa. "We have discovered a galaxy filled with technological wonders and you spend your time probing memory files of the past."

Donalt ignored him. They had talked the subject to death on a hundred occasions—to no avail. The Tripartite Confederation viewed the psiotic as a ward of the state. He had no useful function in their universe. They had given him a niche and he was expected to remain within it.

"Well, I maintain my sanity, Donalt." Ezer intently studied his friend. "And I still am able to use my mind."

Again the mind-merger ignored him.

"There may be a way for you to obtain the life you desire."

Donalt shook his head. "Three hundred years is a long way for even a sane and *thinking* Brodny to reach back."

It was Ezer's turn to ignore the sarcasm. "But it is only a moment for the Tripartite Confederation."

Donalt raised an eyebrow. "The Confederation doesn't employ a team of magicians, do they?"

"No, but they *do* have a research program called Retrieve."

"Retrieve!"

Nils Kendler—Caltha Renenet!

Donalt remembered numerous references to the time-travel program that he had found while he researched the history of the *Seeker*. The short-lived project had died from lack of LofAl funding.

"I didn't know the program had been revived." Donalt grinned at the Brodny. "How do I get in touch with them?"

"You've got an appointment with a Doba Pilar tomorrow at ten." Ezer grinned wider; his chest expanded with pride to twice its normal barrel-size.

"Ten," Donalt repeated numbly. "Ten in the morning?"

"Ten."

A week after his first meeting with Doba Pilar, Donalt returned to the woman's office. Her desk stood devoid of the files and paperwork the mind-merger was accustomed to seeing on the desks of bureaucrats. The common biological interface with Com-Net had eliminated the need for ream upon ream of forms in triplicate.

Doba Pilar's fingers slipped from her left wrist and she looked up at Donalt and took a deep breath.

"I'm sorry . . ."

A chasm opened beneath Donalt and swallowed him.

". . . but my researchers say your proposal just isn't feasible," Doba Pilar continued. "It's a two fold problem. To begin with, individuals down-jumped by Retrieve may only remain in the past for short periods. Time travel is not a permanent transition. An energy source is required to keep a traveler within a time frame. When that energy is depleted, the traveler is returned to his own time."

"But I was told you keep teams in various time periods?" Donalt sensed the futility of his words as he uttered them. But he had to try. Had to!

"You're correct. To do so, a base must be established," she replied. "That base generates the energy required to maintain the team down-time. There is no base in the era to which you wish to journey."

She paused. Her gaze darted nervously about the office before it returned to Donalt.

"There is another problem, Mr. Donalt. Retrieve has no

record of your ever arriving in the past. What is past is past. There are no paradoxes to time travel. No record of your travel exists, thus you have never jumped down."

Donalt sat, staring at the woman. Two brief statements and it was over. Gone. Jenica remained forever in his past. He, forever in her future.

"Will there be anything else?"

Donalt shook his head. "It was just a possibility. Thank you for checking."

Doba Pilar nodded. Donalt rose and walked to the door. He saw the relief on the woman's face when he stepped from her office. Another minor bureaucratic problem had been successfully sidestepped.

"There is another possibility, Donalt," Ezer said when Donalt concluded his report on the meeting. "It was Lunt's idea. It involves risk . . . danger to yourself."

Ezer paused, studying his *karrme*.

"Well," Donalt urged him, "what is it?"

Ezer explained in detail.

It *was* dangerous. But if it worked!

When the Brodny finished, Donalt nodded his acceptance of the proposal.

"I was afraid that would be your answer, my friend." Ezer sighed. "I will communicate with the Three Planets to begin constructing a ship. When we return depends on the negotiations."

Donalt nodded again. He would be returning to Niquela as he had promised. Though if Lunt's plan worked he could never again return to this time—these worlds of his own future.

If it failed—he would never return to any time.

‹THIRTY-ONE›

A year after its departure the *Kwam Giile* returned to the Three Planets. The merger had returned to the alien worlds to find his way home.

Alongside the *Kwam Giile* moved the Tripartite Confederation diplomatic cruiser *Venture*. After nine months the *Zelimir* and the confederation had worked the kinks from their negotiations.

Those aboard the *Kwam Giile* felt that the demigod Donalt had been slighted when the Tripartite Confederation had not appointed him ambassador to the Three Planets. After all, what human understood the way of Brodny, Liluye, and Uzoma better than the man who had saved the three races from the Erna's suicidal plunge into their collapsar Karal?

Only Ezer and Donalt understood the merger's lack of disappointment in being overlooked by the Tripartite Confederation. And for Ezer that understanding was reason for ever-mounting sorrow.

For Donalt it meant a reason for hope—a future that lay three centuries in the past.

Planetfall on Orji brought a celebration. Publicly the Three Planets honored the representatives of humankind.

Donalt participated in the ceremonies. He would have preferred privacy with Niquela, but both the *Zelimir* and the confederation suggested that his presence during the formal ceremonies and an endorsement of the diplomatic and trade agreements would help pave the way for a smoother transition to the Three Planets' new relations with humankind.

The official introduction of the human envoy was time-consuming: six months for a tour of the three alien worlds.

But time was the one thing Donalt had to give.

Once again, Niquela was the Donalt-Watcher. It was a role she gave herself to fully. During the journeys to Canor and Gaee she remained at the merger's side. Ezer and the two children were left on Orji. There Ezer oversaw the final construction and testing of a prototype of the vessel that would carry Donalt back to his time.

Back to Jenica?

Donalt tried not to anticipate. The time that remained to him here in a future in which he did not belong was reserved for his ceremonial duties, and for the Brodny woman who had been his protector, mentor, companion, friend, lover, and *karrme*.

Although Niquela never mentioned what awaited her human mate at the end of the six months, it was obvious that Donalt's inevitable departure was on her mind. Should the psiotic attempt to discuss the venture with her, she artfully dodged the subject. When Ezer and Donalt discussed the development of the prototype via tachyon communications, she quietly left the room.

In their most intimate of moments, Niquela displayed a hunger Donalt had never seen from her before. Her lovemaking was fierce and desperate. Each union was consummated as though it were their last, as though she struggled to physically hold back the passage of time.

She could not. Three months passed.

The Tripartite Confederation envoy's return to Orji was brief, for attendance at the opening of Winter Festival on a planet that knew nothing but winter. The time of the festival corresponded to the first—the only—test of the prototype craft.

Donalt watched the launch via a communications link; Ezer sat at his side. Niquela and the children had left the apartment for the afternoon.

"Two months, Donalt, and we will know if the field can withstand the gravity." Ezer stared at the screen. The craft was no more than a spot of light.

The Brodny's head turned to the mind-merger. "Are you certain you wish to go through with this?"

Donalt nodded. He had made the decision the moment Ezer had first mentioned the possibility.

"Then we are both insane, my *karrme*." Ezer sadly shook his head. "Me for suggesting the journey—you for even considering it."

"It will work," Donalt said firmly. "It will work. I know it will."

Donalt sensed the resolve within Niquela. The ferocity was gone from her body—from her spirit. She enfolded him in her arms and held him deep within her while they rocked gently.

When their bodies' needs had been sated, she clung to him, unwilling to break the intimate contact they shared. He offered no protest, but returned the embrace.

"There is still time to reconsider, Donalt," she whispered when he rolled from her.

Donalt looked at the night-darkened ceiling. He had dreaded this moment, knowing it would come, knowing he would have to face it—and Niquela.

"Has life here been bad?"

"No." He lifted to a side and stared into her dark eyes. "It has been good. But it hasn't been mine. I'm adrift, floating on the currents around me."

Niquela did not reply.

"I have no control of my life here . . . in this time. On the Three Planets I remain a demigod, a being held in awe. I am to be served, never allowed to serve. My participation in life is never permitted to extend beyond the role of an observer."

Donalt cradled Niquela's cheek with a palm. He bent and gently kissed her.

"Among humankind, I'm three centuries out of step—an obsolete model human being. On Lanatia, I was neatly set aside in a safe and secure niche. I would have remained there until I died."

He kissed her again, a kiss she returned.

"And here is but another niche," she said.

Donalt did not answer. There was no need to.

"Donalt, know this, that I love you." Niquela drew him to her. "When you reach the world you desire, remember that somewhere in the future, I will still be loving you."

He came to her again.

When they slept that night, they did so with bodies entwined.

●   ●   ●

Niquela stood at the door, waiting for her two *karrme*. She hugged and kissed Ezer, then took Donalt in her arms to hold him long and close.

When she released him it was with a finality. Both gazed at each other; neither spoke. The farewells had been said last night. The moment lingered, neither wishing to make that final move that would separate them forever.

Niquela's dark eyes rolled downward with resignation. Donalt saw a shuddering tremble through her before she turned away and walked to her children.

Donalt watched her. She was no longer the Donalt-Watcher, nor would she ever be again. He ignored the twisting knot in his gut, telling himself it was only preflight anticipation.

He lied to himself. The ache would be a long time fading—if it ever did.

By hover-van, Brodny and human made their way to the shuttle field, and by shuttle to the *Kwam Giile*. Two hours later, Donalt watched the screens on the command deck blur with the gray of tachyon space, erasing his last view of Orji.

Two mechanics, one Brodny, one Liluye, sat hunched over a tool table when Donalt entered the *Kwam Giile*'s bay area. Both looked up and nodded, then returned to their conversation.

The mind-merger felt relief that neither rose to greet him. He needed a few moments to himself, time to reflect on tomorrow and his flight into the past.

He scanned the immense bay. Two ships sat within the *Kwam Giile*'s metallic belly. The larger was the *Mikpice,* which served as a shuttlecraft for the faster-than-light vessel. The smaller . . .

An ironic smile touched the corners of Donalt's mouth. The smaller vessel had never been given a name. The oversight would have to be remedied before its launch in the morning. A name for his vehicle seemed unreasonably important to the mind-merger, as though it would make the craft complete. Someone had to paint a name on the hull.

He glanced back at the two mechanics, then turned away. He had no name for the stubby-bodied ship. Nothing that came to mind seemed appropriate. His immediate choices seemed artificial.

His footsteps echoed from the bay's bulkheads as he walked closer to the ship. For all practical purposes it looked like a gigantic silver egg with delta wings running from nose to stern. A rounded tail, like a misplaced dorsal fin, jutted from the aft.

The tail and wings would have no purpose for ninety-nine percent of the journey. In all honesty, he admitted that they might not be around after the first step of the voyage.

Donalt slowly circled the vessel. The winged egg had no portholes. When and if he reached his final destination, the landing would be on instruments and optical sensors. When and if . . .

He ducked beneath one of the wide-fanning wings. The craft was the size of the ten-man scout that had been found aboard the *Seeker*, but the majority of the ship's interior space was occupied by the tachyon propulsion system and the field generator needed to protect the ship and its single-man crew during the first leg of the journey.

A razor-thin seam ran in a tight circle on the ship's underbelly—the single hatch.

Donalt had entered the ship daily since leaving Orji. Now the closed portal appeared alien—too small to ever accommodate his body. The lone control couch that lay beyond the hatch loomed like a claustrophobic canister in his mind.

The ship was not designed for comfort, merely function. The control module was a self-contained sphere, electronically interfaced with the rest of the ship. Should the situation warrant, the module could be jettisoned from the craft. It would then serve as a lifeboat—for a week.

After that—his coffin.

Donalt ran his fingers along the smooth underside of the ship. It felt strangely warm. Or were his hands abnormally cold?

Donalt shook his head. Now was not the time to doubt the ship or himself. This winged egg was the only avenue left to him.

Donalt turned and found Ezer standing by the rounded snout of the ship, staring at him. The distant expression on the Brodny's face vanished when he realized Donalt saw him.

"I looked for you in your cabin," Ezer said. "When I couldn't find you, I thought you might be here."

Donalt ducked from beneath the wing. His gaze roved over

the ship again. "She looks sturdy enough."

"Sturdy has nothing to do with where you're going. The field generators are everything." Ezer looked at his friend. "And those have been tested a hundred times over. They will not fail you."

The reassurance in Ezer's tone could not erase the doubts in Donalt's mind. Nor the ones he saw furrowed across Ezer's brow.

"She has no name." Donalt glanced back at the ship.

Ezer shrugged.

"It seems right that she should bear a name for her one and only voyage."

"Tell the mechanics and they will paint whatever you wish on its hull," Ezer said.

"That's the problem." Donalt puckered his lips. "I can't think of anything that's suitable. I thought of *Niquela* . . . but I don't believe our *karrme* would appreciate that."

"She would be honored, Donalt."

Ezer's was a typical Brodny response. Niquela *would* be honored. However, it was not the type of honor she would like to be saddled with.

Every time that she looked up to the night sky, the *Niquela* would only serve to remind her that her human *karrme* was still alive—still falling into uncertain nothingness. Would continue to fall until her children's children reared children of their own. He refused to give her that as his parting gift.

"Donalt, the crew is gathered in the galley," Ezer's voice intruded his thoughts. "They wish to share this last eve with you."

"A bon voyage party?" He looked up and grinned at the questioning expression on his friend's face. "A final celebration before the big send-off."

A wake for the living edged into Donalt's mind.

Ezer's befuddled expression did not lessen. "They simply want to wish you fortune on your journey."

Donalt nodded. He would not refuse the Three Planets one last ceremony. The psiotic started toward the bay's exit hatch with Ezer. Abruptly, he stopped and turned back to the ship.

"The *Donalt-Watcher*!"

"What?" Ezer stared at him uncomprehendingly.

"The ship . . . have them paint *Donalt-Watcher* on its hull."

Ezer nodded and walked to the mechanics. Donalt smiled. It was a good name. A name Niquela would understand. With it, he removed the hereditary obligations from her shoulders and placed them on the craft.

Donalt buckled himself into the contour couch. While the *Kwam Giile* checked and rechecked the *Donalt-Watcher*'s various systems, he did the same from within the smaller craft.

"Donalt." Ezer's voice came from a grille inset in the control console before the merger. He sounded formal and official, the captain of a faster-than-light starship rather than *karrme*.

"Donalt here." His own voice echoed as though rolling up from a deep well.

"Systems check complete. Ejection in two minutes," Ezer continued.

Outside the small, winged egg, Donalt heard the air being pumped from the bay. The bay hatch opened with a metallic rumble. A digital display on the console read thirty seconds to ejection.

"May fortune be with you, Radman Donalt," Ezer's final well-wishing came from the grille.

Before Donalt could answer, the *Donalt-Watcher* was thrust into the infinite chasm of space. The small craft and its one-man cargo fell.

Fell—fell toward the never-ending, yawning mouth of total oblivion.

Donalt flipped on optical sensors. For an instant the image of the *Kwam Giile* filled a mini-display screen on the console. The next moment it was gone—punched back into tachyon space. In an hour, it would return to normal space to monitor his descent into nothingness.

The optics scanned the space stretched before the *Donalt-Watcher* and revealed nothing. Karal had not been seen in the heavens for over three centuries. What remained was a material nothingness—and the infinite gravity well of a collapsar.

Karal, the black hole remnants of the Erna's long-dead sun, was his first step home.

Donalt punched a glowing green button on the console. The ship's field generator whined to life.

The plan was simple—in theory. The collapsar was to be his time machine. Gravity was the weakest force in the universe.

The generator's field would prevent Karal's gravity well from ripping asunder the molecular structure and then the atoms of the *Donalt-Watcher* and its single passenger.

Once the craft pierced the singularity's event horizon, the dimensions of time and space would reverse themselves. The *Donalt-Watcher* would maneuver through time itself, carrying its lone passenger three centuries into the past.

When the temporal destination was reached, the tachyon drive would transform the craft to faster-than-light particles —thus escaping the collapsar's eternity of nothingness.

Once in tachyon space, the *Donalt-Watcher* was programmed for its spacial destination—Roi-Tamu—and Jenica. During the flight, Donalt would be in cryogenic sleep. The *Donalt-Watcher*'s life support system was only capable of providing life for an awake and active man for one week.

Upon reaching Roi-Tamu, Donalt would be brought from his cold sleep for planetfall.

Simple—in theory.

The facts were that no one knew exactly what occurred beyond a black hole's event horizon—a *Schwarzchild* such as Karal, which carried no charge nor did it rotate.

The generated field would protect him and the ship. At least to the event horizon. The prototype had proven that. Beyond that point . . .?

Donalt tried not to ponder the final result should theory be proved wrong. He told himself he had died before.

There was little comfort in the thought.

‹THIRTY-TWO›

The event horizon—in the geometry of time and space, it was the horizon beyond which nothing can be seen. Normal space did not exist beneath it. It was disjointed, disconnected, no longer a part of the "normal" universe. It was nothingness.

For Radman Donalt, aboard the winged, egg-shaped craft called the *Donalt-Watcher,* the plunge to the event horizon surrounding Karal took two hours. For those outside the black hole's gravity well, the fall took an eternity.

At the event horizon, time stopped—for the outside observer.

While the *Donalt-Watcher* descended, those the merger knew and loved on the Three Planets lived and died—except the Uzoma, who were immortal in their own way. Niquela and Ezer's children lived and died, as did their descendants, and theirs.

Had Donalt aborted the flight, the worlds he returned to would have been totally alien to him once again.

Donalt did not abort.

The *Donalt-Watcher* penetrated the event horizon.

The generator whined, continuously adjusting to the ever-increasing force that sucked the ship into the mouth of oblivion. From outside, the optical sensors displayed a spectrum shifted, inversed.

Psiotic and craft plunged toward the singularity. Both were robbed of spacial motion. Both now moved through the dimension of time.

Donalt attempted to watch the digital readout of the chronometer, but averted his eyes. The backward rush was a blur of phosphorescent green.

The theory held! He no longer rode inside a spacecraft, but within the eggshell of a time machine. He rushed head-on toward his own ancient past.

Now, if . . .

Donalt did not have time to complete the thought. The tachyon drive jolted to life. A bone-jarring shudder ran through the ship. Then . . .

Elation!

Donalt soared. Like a man whose consciousness had been expanded to encompass the universe, he flew. Every cell of his body was alive—and he felt them!

He grinned. *Tachyon transformation!*

Beyond the event horizon, the transition into faster-than-light speed was reversed. The mental and physical elation was unbelievable. He laughed aloud in joyous revelry of the moment.

A buzzer sounded.

Donalt glanced at the console. A display blinked:

TRANSITION COMPLETE
TO BEGIN CRYOGENIC SYSTEM ENTER
CRYSLEEP. COMM

Donalt typed the code into the console. A hiss came from behind his head, and he twisted to locate its source.

Pinpricks of pain jabbed his forearms. His head jerked around. Two syringes withdrew from his arms and disappeared into the arms of the couch.

He blinked, eyelids heavy. *Cold.* The hiss grew louder and with it the cold deepened. He tried to blink again. His eyes refused to open.

A sensation of total well-being suffused the psiotic. He drifted with it, letting it lull him into cold sleep.

A rose floated in the star-speckled vastness of space, untouched by the vacuum surrounding it. Three drops of dew, glinting like crystal jewels, lazily rolled down the deep red of the flower's opened petals.

Contact?
Memory?

Donalt slept cryogenic sleep, the cold sleep. He did not

dream, though his mind moved. He rode the streams of alpha level, reaching out toward the planet Roi-Tamu, seeking a single mind—a beacon to guide his mental flight across the galaxies.

The total darkness of alpha level engulfed him. He sensed a prescient's mind. He saw and felt through her. Jenica and he were linked—merged, two minds now one.

A single point of light appeared in the distance. It raced toward her. A gem! A spining diamond against the velvet blackness. Closer it came.

The jewel shattered. A shower of careening fragments rained in glittering disarray.

Flames leaped behind the slivers of crystal. Atop both superimposed the silhouette of a man.

Donalt felt the love that rushed out from the figure. Love that radiated outward from Jenica.

The fiery tongues coalesced behind the man—like wings of fire. Closer. Closer. Light played across his features. Flickering hints of . . .

Darkness.

The prescient vision dissolved and the mental link shattered.

Donalt pulled back into himself, into the cold sleep that embraced his body.

Contact?

Memory?

Long, cool fingers moved through fur. White fur. The fur of a kitten.

No.

It was not a kitten. It was a cat!

And its name was Wumpus, the kitten the Donalt-Erna had reconstructed from Jenica's memories. The kitten was now a mature cat.

Donalt sensed the deep-throated purr that rose from the sleek animal. He felt its warmth through hands that were not his.

Jenica!

It could not be memory. He touched a mind, felt the sensory input.

Jenica!

Nothing.

Jenica!

Gone! The contact dissipated, leaving only blackness. Donalt eased back into his cold sleep-caressed body. But . . . there had been contact! The mature Wumpus could be interpreted as nothing else. He had touched—merged with— Jenica's mind!

"Rad?"

He felt the doubt that suffused her, the disbelief. She trembled with incomprehension. Radman Donalt was dead, destroyed when the Erna suicidally plunged into their collapsing star.

Jenica, it's Rad—Grandpa Donalt.

"Don't call yourself that. . . ."

She caught herself. Doubt clouded her thoughts. "It can't be. It can't be!"

It is. It is.

Donalt opened his mind to her, hiding nothing. His death, the Three Planets, Niquela, Ezer, Lunt . . . he wove his life since their parting into her memories.

"Rad! Oh, Rad!"

Too much, too soon. Jenica could not maintain alpha level in the rush of excitement. The link crumbled into blackness.

Closer. Donalt smiled within his frozen body. *Contact.*

With ease, he threaded himself into her consciousness, her fully awake and cognizant consciousness. For a week they had prepared for the merge, readied themselves for his entry without the benefit of Jenica being in alpha level.

Donalt opened himself to her awareness and sensory input. He saw with Jenica's eyes, felt with Jenica's fingertips, thought with her thoughts.

"I want you to see something."

She sat alone within her bedroom. She glanced at a full-length mirror on the door of a closet. Immediately, her head jerked away, as though afraid.

They had not discussed this. Yet, he knew what she intended. But he did not understand her hesitancy.

"I wanted you to see me. . . ." Her thought came with the same uncertainty. "Fifteen years is a long time, Rad. It has brought changes."

Fifteen years?

Something had gone wrong. He was supposed to have punched into tachyon space simultaneously with Jenica's flight to Roi-Tamu.

She rose and walked before the mirror. She wore a robe, a white robe. But Donalt saw only a flickering glimpse of her total length. Jenica's eyes focused on the face reflected in the silvered glass.

Time had brought changes. He saw the emerald-green eyes, their sparkle a bit dimmer. The hints of fine lines were beginning to show at the corners of those eyes. Other lines ran across her forehead.

The auburn hair was still there: longer now, falling about her shoulders. Here and there were hints of what would become streaks of gray.

"It's not been easy, Rad. Roi-Tamu is a hard world. It hasn't been kind to . . ."

Donalt swelled within her mind. Love. It was all he felt. He allowed that love to permeate her mind. For a man who had died twice, who had lived three centuries in his own future, fifteen years meant nothing. She was the reason he returned, and she waited for him.

Tears welled in Jenica's eyes as his overwhelming love filled her. The uncertainty, the hesitancy faded. Her love flowed outward, attempting to cross the light-years that separated them and enfold him. It did.

Donalt extended his love toward her. Jenica offered no resistance, giving him total control of her mind and body.

Her hands now his, Donalt reached for the loosely tied knot in her robe's belt. He slowly pulled. The knot slipped free and the front of Jenica's robe fell open.

Donalt gave her shoulders a little toss. The robe slid off shoulders and arms, dropping to the floor behind her. His love swelled anew. Through her eyes, he gazed upon the reflection of her unashamed nakedness. He drank in the image.

He lifted her right hand and used its fingertips to lovingly brush that light brown mole beneath the nipple of her left breast. He felt the shivery tremble that ran through her when she realized what he intended. A shiver of anticipation—of complete acceptance.

His mind merged with hers, Donalt led her to the bed. And there, her hands now his, he made love to her.

• • •

The frozen eternity ended with an annoying buzz announcing that the *Donalt-Watcher* prepared to enter Roi-Tamu's atmosphere. Planetfall—the final step of Donalt's journey back in time and across the universe.

Despite the slowly receding numbness of his body, the cottony clouds fogging his brain, elation coursed through him. It had worked. Total insanity had worked. If he had been able, he would have kissed that gigantic Uzoma slug Lunt! He had made it! Made it back to Jenica!

Joints popping with stiffness, Donalt reached out and silenced the buzzer. A mini-display came to life:

FOR AUTO DESCENT
ENCODE FILE
<LLBP.STW>

Donalt did as instructed. He was a mind-merger, not a pilot. Immediately he felt the ship change altitude.

Closing his eyes, he drifted into alpha state. He reached out and touched Jenica's mind, a last long-distance message, an assurance he had safely arrived and within an hour they would—

A buzzer blared, intruding into their merge. Donalt withdrew. The control console was wild with flickering lights. The mini-display blinked red:

CRYOGENIC MALFUNCTION
FILE <LLBP.STW> NOT FOUND

"Not found?" Donalt's stiff fingers stabbed at the console seeking an answer for the missing file—the preprogrammed autopilot for planetfall!

The only answer he received was:

CRYOGENIC MALFUNCTION

He tapped the optical sensors to life. Only one responded, a lens inset in the tail of the ship. It provided a topside overview of the *Donalt-Watcher,* or what had been the *Donalt-Watcher.*

The psiotic rode within a crystalline iceberg. He now understood the console's message. The cryogenic unit had not limited itself to his module during the long flight. It had frozen the entire ship, and in the process erased the autopilot program.

To come this far. To . . .

He shoved thoughts of defeat aside. There wasn't time. Not if he was going to live.

Punching a series of commands into the console, he took manual control of the winged egg. It did no good. Ice locked the craft's guidance mechanisms. The mini-display assured him that the *Donalt-Watcher* was shedding its iceberg outer skin and that he would have full control—after the ship had entered Roi-Tamu's atmosphere.

Again Donalt's fingers flew over the console. Trajectory, course modifications, and remaining fuel supply listed on the display. There was a chance. If control came when promised.

For now, all he could do was wait and hope.

He flicked on the only functioning optical sensor and watched himself fall toward the planet. He repressed the desire to reach out to Jenica for . . .

He shuddered as the words *one last time* formed in his mind. If he died, it would be alone. Jenica would be spared living those last moments with him—dying those last moments with him.

Droplets of water were torn from the icy sheath covering the *Donalt-Watcher*. They burst into fiery tongues as the friction of atmospheric entry burned them away.

Donalt heard-felt the ice encasing the ship crack. At the same time, he saw the ice shatter. A thousand crystal fragments were torn from the hull as the heat of planetfall melted the remains of the cryogenic malfunction. The ice was instantaneously transformed into fire.

The display blinked. Control of the *Donalt-Watcher* was now in his inexperienced hands. Eyes locked on the console's readouts, he adjusted the craft's attitude.

Overadjusted. The *Donalt-Watcher* went into a spin.

Panicked, his finger jabbed and punched. The ship shuddered as though being ripped apart at the seams. It was not. The winged egg was as sturdy as it had appeared aboard the *Kwam Giile*. It righted itself. Corrected its trajectory. Donalt released his breath.

The sigh of relief came too soon. The console blinked the bottom line of his ill-fated attempt to leap across time and space—his awkward attempt at piloting the vessel had depleted the fuel supply. Donalt now rode inside a meteor of alien metal destined to plow itself into the planet below.

Sturdy or not, the *Donalt-Watcher* was not designed to survive that kind of impact. Nor was he!

For the last time, he punched the ship's console.

The *Donalt-Watcher* rolled. Belly to the sky, a hatch exploded. A spherical module was ejected, and with it Radman Donalt.

Exactly five seconds later, there was another explosion.

The module around Donalt split into halves: cold air tore at his face. Strapped to the contour couch, he fell, tumbling helplessly, toward the world below.

There was a cracking pop, then the fluttering sound of opening fabric. In the next instant, Donalt's plummeting descent stopped with a bone-jarring shudder.

He looked overhead. A white mushroom cap floated above him. *A parachute!* He dropped gently now, downward, toward the surface of a colonial world called Roi-Tamu, and to Jenica.

The contour couch struck the ground, bounced once, twice, then rolled to its side on the third bounce. Donalt lay waiting for the fourth. It did not come. He was down, and, as best he could tell, in one living piece.

He released the straps holding him to the couch and rolled to the ground. The earthy effluvium that filled his nostrils was like perfume. He stood and stared about, his eyes soaking in the world he had fallen to.

An engine rumbled to his left. Donalt turned to see an approaching skimmer swing in a wide circle about him, then gently float to the ground. The vehicle's door rose. Jenica stepped out.

In the next instant she was running to him. Then she was in his arms and her mouth was on his—his cheeks, his neck.

When the flurry of kisses and hugs subsided, they clung tightly to each other. She whispered softly, "My starman has come."

Donalt edged her back slightly and stared into her face, questioning. Was the starman still real to her—after all this time?

"You . . ." She gazed up at him with a wide grin. "You are the starman. The ice, it was the diamond. The fiery wings . . .

it was all there . . . I saw it all as you entered the atmosphere.''

"The ice? How did you know?'' Donalt saw it now.

"When our last link was broken, I had a prescient vision.'' She hugged him close and kissed him passionately. "I saw it all before it happened. I saw my starman come to me . . . coming home. How else could I have been here waiting for you when you landed?''

Donalt returned the kiss. Then he laughed aloud and squeezed her tightly to him. The starman had come home.

BEST-SELLING
Science Fiction
and
Fantasy

☐ 47809-3	**THE LEFT HAND OF DARKNESS,** Ursula K. LeGuin	$2.95
☐ 16012-3	**DORSAI!,** Gordon R. Dickson	$2.75
☐ 80581-7	**THIEVES' WORLD,** Robert Lynn Asprin, editor	$2.95
☐ 11577-2	**CONAN #1,** Robert E.Howard, L. Sprague de Camp, Lin Carter	$2.50
☐ 49142-1	**LORD DARCY INVESTIGATES,** Randell Garrett	$2.75
☐ 21889-X	**EXPANDED UNIVERSE,** Robert A. Heinlein	$3.95
☐ 87328-6	**THE WARLOCK UNLOCKED,** Christopher Stasheff	$2.95
☐ 26187-6	**FUZZY SAPIENS,** H. Beam Piper	$2.75
☐ 05469-2	**BERSERKER,** Fred Saberhagen	$2.75
☐ 10253-0	**CHANGELING,** Roger Zelazny	$2.95
☐ 51552-5	**THE MAGIC GOES AWAY,** Larry Niven	$2.75

MORE SCIENCE FICTION!
ADVENTURE